where you are

(between the lines #2)

by
tammara webber

Where You Are Copyright © 2011 by Tammara Webber

Cover image used under license from Shutterstock.com
Copyright © Yuri Arcurs, 2011
Cover design by Stephanie Mooney

Interior design elements copyright © Aleks Melnik, 2012
Used under license from Shutterstock.com

ISBN: 978-0-9835931-7-1

Dedicated to Georgia and Leslie:
one for giving me life
and the other for teaching me to live it

Prologue

GRAHAM

"How's this for clear?" I said, tracing her beautiful mouth with my fingers, unable to keep from touching her lips. *I just wanted to kiss her, but that's all I'd done the first time, and my intent wasn't, apparently, as obvious as I'd thought. Emma needed words. Declarations. We were more similar than I'd given us credit for, and I trusted in that knowledge and gave them to her.* "I haven't wanted anyone but you since the night we met. And as much as I value our friendship... being friends with you is not what I have in mind."

Her eyes widened and her breath caught as I slid my knuckles across the soft skin of her jaw, curled my fingers and cupped her chin in my hand. When I leaned my face to hers, her eyelids fluttered closed, and in that seemingly trivial movement I felt her surrender and acceptance. That was the turning point, the precise split second when I knew.

I forced myself to go slow, inhaling the emotion behind her response as decidedly as I inhaled her sweet breath. My tongue skimmed her lower lip, tasting her gently while I reminded myself repeatedly that I could not press her to the corner of the booth, that I could not pull her beneath me and unleash every pent-up desire I'd held in check for months.

Very little of my restraint had to do with the fact that we were in a public place. I'd never been so uncaring of that fact, to tell the truth.

1

The kiss in her room the night before had almost broken me, but I'm practiced in denying myself what I know I can't have. She was having none of my caution this morning. Her hands twisting in my T-shirt, she opened her mouth, cracking my control like a hammer against glass. I kissed her deeply, my mind going fuzzy and refusing to allow my logical side any say whatsoever. She curled into me—I don't even know how—just that we were suddenly a knot of torsos and limbs, her knees pulled up and folded against my side, my arms around her, one hand at her nape and the other pressing her lower back as though it was possible for us to be closer.

It wasn't.

My only thought was more of a feeling than a conscious deliberation: Mine. Mine. Mine.

We broke the kiss to breathe, and I hated that I needed air at all. Exploring her mouth was so much better than breathing. I rested my forehead against hers, both of us panting like we used to at the end of an uphill sprint. Our daily runs in Austin were a lifetime ago—those weeks I thought she belonged to Reid Alexander, or soon would. My fears and insecurities pressed into the space between us as I watched her eyes open and focus slowly. I wondered then, if she pulled away, if I could take it. If I could survive losing her again.

"Huh," she said, blinking her gray-green eyes, and I almost laughed with relief. That non-word of hers was a code I knew by heart, and when she uttered it in that moment it was an unguarded secret set of instructions I knew how to follow. And follow it I did.

"You know, I think I'd prefer you keep that particular habit after all," I told her before I pulled her closer and kissed her again.

Chapter 1

GRAHAM

I was sure I would never love anyone as much as I loved Zoe.

Something about first love defies duplication. Before it, your heart is blank. Unwritten. After, the walls are left inscribed and graffitied. When it ends, no amount of scrubbing will purge the scrawled oaths and sketched images, but sooner or later, you find that there's space for someone else, between the words and in the margins.

I accepted some time ago that for me, that someone else was my daughter, Cara. The conclusion seemed reasonable at the time. She was the only tangible thing that survived that tumultuous relationship, and the only piece of Zoe I was allowed to keep in the end.

I called Zoe the day after she told me it was over to ask her why, and what I'd done, and if I could do something, anything to win her back. I thought we were in love—that whatever it was that made her end it, I could fix. Neither of us knew yet that she was pregnant.

"Why are you trying to make me feel bad?" she asked. "This is hard for me, too."

I took a controlled breath. "Doesn't seem that way." Earlier that day I'd passed her in the hall as she leaned against her locker, flirting with a couple of our classmates, guys whom summer had turned into men. The same couldn't be said for me. Though Zoe and I were both seniors, she was more than a year older. My summer birthday and the skipped grade in elementary school meant I'd only been sixteen for four months. I wouldn't turn seventeen until a couple of weeks after graduation.

She huffed an exaggerated sigh. "Jeez, Graham—I'm in fourth-year theatre, you know. I can *act* like I'm fine when I'm not."

No way was she *acting* when Ross Stewart, varsity wrestling team hero, made some teasing comment and she giggled up at him, batting her lashes, her small hand on his ham of a forearm. It had been less than twenty-four hours since our breakup. I was hoarse from crying for half the night, and she was smiling and flirting, her eyes as bright blue as always.

"What can I do, Zoe? Did I do something wrong? If you'll just talk to me, tell me what you need me to do—"

"Graham, there's nothing you can do. I'm just not, you know, *attracted* to you anymore. This decision is about me and *my* feelings. Not you."

I'm not attracted to you anymore sure sounded like it was about *me*. I felt as if she'd kicked me through the phone. Zoe had been my first everything, though I hadn't been hers—a fact that had never bothered me. I'd been a willing enough pupil, and despite our arguments and a multitude of misunderstandings, I thought we were good together. Right up until she broke my heart.

"Is there someone else?" I don't know what I expected when I asked. Maybe that she'd deny it immediately. She was silent for too long on the other end. I could feel her deliberating. "Shit, Zoe," I whispered, my voice breaking due to the overnight crying bender.

"I'm sorry, Graham. But I don't want to talk about this with you anymore. I can't help how I feel… or don't feel. I never meant to hurt you, but you and me are over now. You're gonna have to accept it."

I didn't talk to her for a couple of weeks after that, though I saw her around at school. While our breakup was out-of-left-field and excruciating for me, it was liberating but awkward for her. I only knew the *awkward* part because her friends Mia and Taylor told me that the reason she changed her routes between classes and started going off campus for lunch every day was because watching me mope was such a downer.

"I'm not *moping*. I mean sure, I'm kind of depressed—I wasn't

4

expecting this. I can't just become resigned to it overnight."

Mia rolled her eyes. "It's been like two *weeks*."

Taylor shrugged one bony shoulder, screwing her mouth up in the no-big-deal smirk she was fond of making. "You *really* need to move past it already, Graham. *Zoe* has."

I stared at them, bewildered. "*She* did the breaking up. She was probably moving past it when she *did* it. I haven't had time to acclimate to being so expendable. I can't just snap out of it like the past year meant nothing."

Even though that's exactly what Zoe had done.

"Graham and his *I'm-a-genius* vocab," Mia mumbled, just loud enough for me to hear as they walked away.

"Seriously," Taylor agreed.

When Emma kissed me last night, right before I bolted from her hotel room, I recognized a resurgence of the yearning I'd felt for her the whole time we were in Austin. I thought I'd conquered it, because she wasn't possible—for so many reasons.

For one, she's young—eighteen now, seventeen when I met her. She carries herself with a maturity that belies her age, though, and once I knew her better, I knew why that was. With a deceased mother and an emotionally absent father, she'd been parenting herself for years. But I couldn't forget that behind that mask of maturity was a girl who'd fallen for Reid Alexander, king of the Hollywood douchebags. I had pushed her into the friend box in my head and held her there forcibly. I couldn't fall for a girl who'd fall for Reid—reason number two.

Reason number three—she lives on the opposite coast, though my subconscious mind (okay, fine, my completely conscious mind) did everything imaginable to change that fact. Once we started talking about college and her desire to act on the stage instead of in front of a camera, it made sense to suggest universities and conservatories in New York. That's what I told myself, while thoughts of her being that near, all the time, buzzed feverishly through my head.

Finally, reason number four—I don't share Cara with anyone but family and a couple of very close friends. Her existence is unknown to the world at large, though that won't be true for long. When Emma ran into us at the coffee shop yesterday and interacted with Cara, that part of my wall began to fall.

Our kiss last night all but detonated the rest of it.

"Let's get out of here," I say now, glancing at my watch before tossing bills onto the table and taking her hand. "What time is your flight?"

Her eyes don't waver from mine as I pull her from the booth. "Noon." Holding her hand as tightly as she's holding mine, I lead her through the café to the exit, a riot of thoughts whirlpooling in my brain. Soon, she and her dad have to leave for the airport, where they'll board a plane for Sacramento. Suddenly, the end of August is intolerably far away.

The first time I saw Emma was almost eight months ago. Leaving my hotel room to talk Brooke down from a freak-out over seeing Reid for the first time in years, I noticed Emma, slipping a key card into her hotel room door. Small and slim, surrounded by luggage, she glanced up as my gaze scanned over her, blinking her beautiful green eyes. I smiled, instantly curious who she was. I was on a Brooke-support mission, though, with no time to stop and chat with beautiful strangers.

"Hey," I said, feeling like a dork. What kind of guy comes out of his hotel room wearing pajamas and says *hey* to some random girl in the hall right before entering another girl's room?

Two nights later, we finally met after the first cast outing. I recognized her in the club, talking with MiShaun and dancing with some of our costars, but Brooke kept me close until it became clear that Reid intended to ignore her completely. On a smoking break outside, I spotted Emma waiting for a taxi back to the hotel, and on a whim, I asked to share her cab. Brooke was ticked that I just left her there, but I couldn't be sorry.

I lay in my bed that night tasting the sound of her name on my tongue—*Emma*.

We began running in the mornings and we hung out alone a couple of times, talking, while I weighed her involvement with Reid. I was patient and cautious until the morning I sat next to her on a covered picnic table, soaking wet, waiting for the rain to lighten up so we could finish our run. As we sat there small-talking, another conversation was taking place under the surface.

Her ponytail dripped down her back, her thin T-shirt clinging like a second skin, and she smelled incredible. One loose strand of hair snaked across her cheek and clung to the corner of her lip, and I think I almost stopped breathing, staring at it. I reached to move it behind her ear, thinking *don't, don't, don't kiss her.* Followed by *kiss her, kiss her, you idiot.*

I congratulated myself on following the former and ignoring the latter.

Until I walked out of Brooke's room that night (another Reid-related panic attack) to see Emma leaving my door and sprinting to her room like she didn't want me to see her. I had two choices: go to my room and beat my head on the wall, or knock on her door and try to mitigate the damages of her having witnessed me leaving Brooke's room late at night.

I knew the best case scenario for keeping Emma at arm's length was to let her assume Brooke and I were involved. She was already halfway there; all I had to do was *nothing.* Then the image of her upturned face that morning flashed across my mind's eye, and my memory conjured the smell of the rain on her skin and in her hair. I considered the easy rapport we'd established, and the comfort I felt when she was near. In a fit of unprecedented impulsiveness, I was at her door inviting myself in, and before I left her room I'd held her and kissed her and fallen so hard that I was happy to be broken into bits.

24 hours later: Emma and Reid's kiss-seen-around-the-world. The kiss that occurred the night after my daughter was rushed to the hospital, unable to breathe. The night I'd stoically accepted a blistering lecture from Mom about my smoking and Cara's asthma, incredulous at the timing of Emma's big plan to help me quit. That night, shot through the concern for my daughter, was the anticipation of returning to the first girl I'd fallen for since Zoe.

And then Brooke texted me the photo from the concert—the same photo that ended up on multiple gossip sites the next day, though she swore she only sent it to "a couple of trusted friends." I didn't chastise her, not really, though I was disappointed that she'd been so careless. Her defense was that Reid and Emma had kissed in public, and anyone could have taken a photo of them.

"*Anyone* didn't, though—*you* did," I said.

She shrugged. "The point isn't the *picture.* The point is the *kiss.*"

She was right. For me, the point was the kiss.

Now, we have less than three hours together, and we're on the street and I'm remembering belatedly how freaking cold it is, along with the fact that I was in such a fog this morning that I forgot to grab a jacket when I left the house. I glance down at her, hunched and shivering in her thin sweater. Nestling her against my side, I point to a subway entrance. "It's warmer underground, I think." We head for the descending stairs and hop on the R. The view from the bridge into Brooklyn can make you fall in love with New York, if you haven't already.

Once we're seated in the sparsely occupied car, Emma leans her head on my shoulder, our arms entwined and hands tightly clasped on my knee. I don't think we even let go for the turnstile. "Let's play Truth or Dare," I say, "but without the Dare."

Her brows elevate. "I thought you weren't a games sort of guy."

I smile down at her. "I did say that, didn't I?" She nods. "All right, then. Let's not call it a game. Let's just call it getting the hard questions out of the way, because I know we both have them. You can go first. Ask me anything."

She chews her lip, staring into my eyes. "Okay… Why did you kiss me in Austin?"

I laugh softly and she frowns. "Sorry. That one's too easy." My gaze flicks to her mouth and back. "I'd wanted to kiss you ever since Quinton suggested playing spin the bottle, and by that night in your room, I'd run out of the willpower to fight it."

"Why were you—"

I place my fingers over her lips and shake my head. "Nuh-uh. My turn." When I slide my fingers across her mouth, she parts her lips. I want to kiss her again, but if I start, I suspect I'm not going to stop, and we need this talk. I'd rather spend the next month dreaming about kissing her than worrying over questions never asked or answered.

"Why did you kiss Reid the day after you kissed me?" I've pulled no punches. This is the sorest point I've got, and I want it behind us.

She takes a deep breath, staring at our intertwined hands. It's a full minute before she speaks. "When I went to Austin, I thought he was what I wanted." She checks my reaction, and I urge her to go on with a slight nod. "I was wrong. I just… didn't know it yet."

Her eyes fill and her voice is uneven. "I know that's not good enough."

Fingers below her chin, I tip her face up so I can look into her eyes. "It's the truth, so it's good enough. Did you... love him?"

Sniffling, she shakes her head, setting a finger over my lips. "Nuh-uh," she says. "It's *my* turn." When I frown, she laughs, and a tear escapes the corner of her eye. She dashes it away with the back of her hand. "But no, I didn't."

Squashing the urge to beat my chest like a Neanderthal, I pull her closer and inhale her scent, so familiar, even these months later. My voice drops. "Can I kiss you now?"

Her expression turns coy. "Graham, that's three questions in a row. I'm starting to think you don't understand the concept of taking turns."

To hell with questions. We can talk on the phone. I can't kiss her long-distance. "Oh, I'll give you your turn, Emma." Closing the small space between us, I slide my hand behind her neck and touch my lips to hers. She presses closer—warm lips, sweet breath, soft fingertips drifting down the side of my face as we kiss.

Up to this point, we've been ignoring the small number of fellow passengers entering and exiting as we move down the line, stopping every few minutes. And then the train squeals to a stop, and three dozen loud, matching-T-shirt-wearing middle schoolers and their harried chaperones crowd into our car. A small pack of girls stare at Emma and me unabashedly, like we're on a screen and not real people. Whispering behind their hands, their eyes wide, their attention swings between us and the group of boys who plop onto the adjacent seat and proceed to make fart noises with a weirdly impressive array of body parts.

So much for that kiss.

Emma

I thought of Graham a dozen times since we arrived in New York, chiding myself when my focus lingered on some tall, dark-haired guy standing hands-in-pockets at a deli counter, or crossing quickly at an intersection, or smoking in a courtyard.

Graham quit smoking months ago, of course.

More to the point, though—what was the likelihood I'd just happen upon Graham in a city this enormous? I felt silly for even considering it a possibility. And then—there he was, sitting in a coffee shop on MacDougal. With his daughter.

"So, Cara is four?" I ask, taking my turn.

"She'll actually be four in a couple of months," he says, leaning close, his breath warm in my ear. "Right after my birthday."

"Landon is *so immature*," one of the girls across the aisle declares to the others. They all nod and level disdainful looks on the boy responsible for the majority of rude noises.

"What'd *I* do?" he says, palms up. "*What?*"

One of the other boys offers, "Bitches, man," and a fist bump in consolation, and they all howl with laughter while the girls huff and refuse to look openly at them again.

Graham and I stare at each other, our eyes tearing and lips compressed in an effort to remain outwardly indifferent. "I would be willing to *swear* I was never a preteen boy," he says, rolling his eyes.

"That sounds like denial."

"Yeah, well, that's my story." His eyes dance. "Next question: Are you seeing anyone now?"

Emily set me up with several guys during the past few months—dinner, movies, ballet, bowling. Each one was perfectly nice, but I didn't feel a connection with any of them. Then, during the community theatre production of *It's a Wonderful Life* over the holidays, I met Marcus. He'd already been accepted early-decision to Pace, and was elated at the possibility of us both starting college in New York in the fall. Since December, we've been out multiple times. I saw him last weekend. We're supposed to hang out tonight when I get home. And... I agreed to go to his small private school's prom next weekend.

"Hmm. Not the quick refusal I was hoping for," Graham says, his thumb moving hypnotically over the back of my hand. "Should I plan to follow you home and challenge some guy to a duel?" In his eyes, I see the teasing and the sincerity behind his words. "I've never been a horribly possessive guy, Emma, and I know this is all sudden and unforeseen for both of us. But watching you with Reid was almost more than I could take. I don't think my heart can tolerate sharing you again. You're free to make your own decision, of course. But I have to be allowed to make mine, too."

I hate the thought of hurting Marcus. He's been patient, never grilling me about my well-known failed liaison with Reid Alexander. When I came back home after the *School Pride* photo shoot last month, Marcus maintained his cheerful disposition while I pulled myself through a delayed depression over the whole Reid debacle and came to grips with the fact that I still cared for Graham and felt his absence, though whatever was between us in Austin was long gone.

Except now, suddenly, it's not gone. And Graham is sitting here next to me, waiting for me to tell him I want him.

"I *have* been seeing someone, but it's not... *this*." I swallow, hard, hoping he'll give me the time to be compassionate. "I'll end it when I get back home." When he exhales, I realize he was holding his breath. "But... I did promise to go to his prom next weekend."

His lips quirk and he watches me closely. "Should I be worried?"

I shake my head slightly. "No."

His forearm flexes as he brings our interlaced hands up, rotating his arm and kissing the back of my hand. "Then I guess there's no reason to begrudge some poor guy his prom date."

The knot of girls across the car sighs audibly, and I think one of them just took our picture with her phone. It's possible that they know who we are. *School Pride* doesn't come out until next month, though the media blitz has begun. Or maybe they're just starry-eyed girls, and the two of us tangled up in each other on the subway is classic NYC romantic—which makes me think of Emily. I'm going to have a *lot* to tell her when I get home.

"Are *you*, you know, seeing anyone?"

He shakes his head, his dark eyes intense despite the half-smile on his lips. "I passed the point of being willing to settle a long time ago. If I'm not fiercely inclined, I don't bother."

I press my lips together, but they kick up on one side. It isn't really fair, that I'm happy to have no competition for his attention while he trusts me to go home, go to prom with some faceless boy and then kick him to the curb.

The preteens reach their stop, and the noise escalates to something resembling the running of the bulls as the chaperones attempt to make sure every single one of them makes it off the subway before it pulls away. It's so quiet once they exit that I can hear my own breathing.

Graham leans closer. "How is it that I've survived seeing you only once in the past five months, and now the thought of being separated from you for four months seems insane?"

I lean my cheek onto his shoulder, caught up in his penetrating gaze. "The premiere is next month. My agent says there'll be TV and radio talk show appearances before then, probably starting next week."

He grimaces. "Emma, I'm not the star of *School Pride*—you and Reid are. I'll be at the premiere, of course, but most of those other appearances will just be the two of you."

For some reason, I'd not considered this possibility. "Huh," I say, and Graham chuckles.

Chapter 2

GRAHAM

Telling her I'm not possessive isn't technically a lie... but it's not completely true, either, particularly where Reid Alexander is concerned. After watching how he managed to win Emma's trust last fall—even if he blew it shortly thereafter—I have a grudging respect for his ability to play charming. The truth is, he *is* charming. That part of his persona isn't faked. He's just too selfish and immature to care about the bodies he leaves in his wake. Literally.

I'm ninety-nine percent certain Emma won't fall for his façade again, but that one percent of insecurity nags at the back of my mind. Raised by a feminist, I learned early to resist the urge to go all alpha-male. But after years of disliking Reid on Brooke's behalf, followed by a desire to pound the shit out of him for hurting Emma, an uncharacteristic longing to claim and protect her surges through me, telling me I may have to man up.

"Graham?"

I glance down at her worried face, gathering from her expression that I'm scowling. "I hate the thought of you spending time with him." *God.* If my mother or sisters heard me say this, I'd never hear the end of it.

Emma looks surprised, her head angling as she reveals a slow smile. "You don't need to be jealous of Reid, you know."

I grimace in return. "I guess I sort of *don't* know."

She stares at our clasped hands, dragging the tips of her fingers over my forearm, and I'm immediately wishing we were somewhere more private. "Last month, he talked to me after the photo shoot wrapped up. He told me wanted another chance. I don't know how sincere he was, really—I mean, he's *Reid*, so who knows—but he seemed more earnest than he's ever been."

They spoke privately that last night at the hotel, in his room. He caught her hand and held her back as the rest of us poured into the hallway, and I watched from my slightly-ajar door as she left his room minutes later. She was in tears as she pushed open the door to her room, and my feelings were torn. I didn't want her unhappy, but I was relieved that whatever was said between them hadn't resulted in a reunion of any sort.

Reid Alexander has never, that I know of, been good for anyone.

"What he had to say didn't matter, though," she continues, peering up at me, "because I knew what kind of guy I wanted, even if I was sure I couldn't have *him*, per se."

I kiss the tip of her nose and laugh softly, shaking my head. "I had no idea. You could clean up as a poker player, Emma. You've got no tell."

Just then, the train emerges from the ground at the edge of the East River, heading for the Manhattan Bridge, one of several leading into Brooklyn. The sun in our eyes renders the scene semi-blinding, at first. And then, individual beams thread through the buildings lining the opposite bank, reflecting like waves off the skyscrapers behind us and sparkling across the short expanse of water. It's a magical view, one to which few people are immune. "Oh," Emma says, blinking. I've officially begun my plan to dissuade her from ever wanting to leave New York once she moves here.

My oldest sister, Cassie, is an early riser. If we get off at DeKalb, we can be at her loft in minutes. I pull out my phone and turn Emma's hand palm down on my leg. I like the sight of it there way too much.

Me: You up? I want you to meet someone.
Cas: Now? Are you high? It's not even 7 am! WHO is this someone???
Me: Yes and yes and i know and emma

14

Cas: THE emma?
Me: Yeah
Cas: But I'm not presentable!
Me: No worries, she's not like that
Cas: If you say so. Doug is still asleep. The baby is up. The baby is always up. I'm looking forward to sleeping again someday. I vaguely remember sleep...
Me: Haha, sorry cas. See you in a few minutes.

"Let's go see my sister."

Alarm flashes across Emma's face, her eyes widening. "What—*now*?"

I have to laugh, since Cassie had the same response. "She lives just over the bridge. I want her to meet you. You'll love her." I shove the phone back into the pocket of my jeans and pull the hand she's pressing against her chest into my lap. I haven't felt this impulsive in years, which is pretty damned tragic considering the fact that I'm not even twenty-one yet. Feeling older than my age is a common enough sensation for me, but early fatherhood will do that.

We're both quiet the remainder of the way, each lost in our own thoughts. I know it's ageist to assume that Emma will have a difficult time handling the fact that I have a child. But fatherhood is the reason I don't date, the reason I hesitate to form romantic relationships. I didn't mean to imply that I've been celibate, though I may have given Emma precisely that impression. I'm not sure how to clear *that* up without an awkward conversation—one that can definitely wait.

My sisters have been supportive about pushing me to get out and lead as close to a normal life as possible, especially Cassie. Brynn is nearer to me in age—four years older, but I'm closer to Cassie—six years my senior. She's the one I always turned to when interactions with my peers went sour, as they often did. The combination of being more academically driven *and* younger than all of my classmates was bad enough. Add being something of a smartass, and that equaled very few friends. Cassie's artistic nature gave her more of an understanding of my sensitivity than our professor-parents could comprehend.

In their early twenties when their barely seventeen-year-old brother became a parent, neither of my sisters envied me the title. But Cassie volunteered to take Cara home overnight once a week, leaving me free to go out like a normal teenager, and she and our parents began taking turns watching her once I was getting film roles regularly.

University life at Columbia was immediately less intimate than my small preparatory high school, and I could easily lose myself amongst the undergrad population. Living uptown with my parents rather than on campus negated anyone's expectation to go home with me for the night. Whenever Cassie had Cara, I stayed over in dorms or apartments of friends who knew little about me, or girls who never knew more than my name and major, and sometimes not even that much.

"What are you thinking about?" Emma asks, probably anxious over meeting my sister while I'm worrying too soon over whether or not she can deal with my parental status.

"Hmm? Oh. Nothing important." I untangle my hand from hers and slide my arm behind her, pulling her to my side. "FYI, Cassie already likes you." Her expression becomes more alarmed rather than less. Uh-oh. "Er, I talked to her about you while we were filming." Better not to disclose that it was more than once, I think.

"What was there for her to *like* about me? Wouldn't she have been outraged on your behalf?"

I laugh. She'll understand when she meets Cassie. "No, she blamed ninety percent of the end result on me and the other ten percent on him."

"Huh," Emma says, and I can't make any answer to that other than to lean down and kiss her.

"Here's our stop," I say once I break regretfully from her lips, having managed to distract her for a few minutes. There are reasons I'm usually not impetuous, and one of them has to do with sucking at it. The only thing I had in mind when we got on the subway was warmth and that amazing view—one that can only be topped by the view on the way back. Visiting Cassie was full-fledged spontaneity.

Now that I'm thinking more clearly, dragging Emma to meet my sister less than two hours after declaring ourselves might be well past spontaneous and well on the way to unreasonable. *Shit.*

Emma

I can't believe Graham is taking me to meet his sister this early on a Saturday morning. Within minutes of emerging onto the street, we're standing in front of her building, and I reason that at least the anxiety didn't have time to mount high enough to knock me flat.

Graham pushes a button on the speaker, and right away a woman's teasing voice says, "Who the hell's buzzing me at seven o'clock in the morning?"

"Hey, Cas," Graham says, smiling.

"Graham, you've always been a pain in the butt. You know that, right?" The speaker buzzes as the lock clicks on the door.

"So you've been saying for twenty years or so," he answers, pulling open the heavy metal door and ushering me inside a tiny lobby—one wall lined with mailboxes and the other housing a single elevator. When Graham pushes the button, the doors part sluggishly, as though someone is cranking them open by hand. "She's on the third floor."

His dark eyes tell me he has ideas in mind for the ascent, but when the doors close behind us, he merely takes my hand, his focus alternating between the ancient checkered floor and the *very* slowly shifting numbers above the door. As the claustrophobic car finally comes to a stop, he squeezes my hand and gives me one quick kiss.

We step into a five-by-five foot vestibule, and he knocks lightly on one of two doors. Multiple bolts slide, and my stomach drops to my knees just before the door opens to a smiling, female version of Graham, wearing sweats and holding a tiny baby. "Take this," she says to Graham, handing the baby off in an effortless transfer. She sticks out her hand. "I'm Cassie. You must be Emma." When I take her hand, she smoothly pulls me into the apartment behind Graham, who heads towards the living space in the center of the roomy loft, talking to the baby in his natural voice, as though it's a very small man and not an infant.

"Yes," I manage.

"Graham, I *know* you want coffee," Cassie says, heading through the room to the open kitchen on the opposite end. "Emma? Coffee?"

17

"Sure," I say, following her after a brief look back at Graham, who flashes me a smile. His dark eyes drink me in while I do the same to him. The sensation is surreal, that no part of him is off-limits to my imagination now—from his full lips to his wide shoulders to the hands cradling the baby in the crook of one arm.

Suddenly this is all moving too quickly, but before I can work up a good panic, my phone vibrates in my front pocket. At my twitch and yelp, Cassie glances back, one brow arched on her pretty, makeup-free face. When I pull the phone from my pocket, my father's picture smiles up from the display.

"Hi Dad." I left a note telling him I was meeting Graham in the café.

"Emma, where are you?" He's not quite frantic, but not calm, either.

"Didn't you find my note? Under your glasses?"

"Yes. And I'm in the café—where you, by the way, are *not*."

Oh. "Um, Graham and I decided to take a walk, and then we got on the subway because it's a little chilly out… and now we're in Brooklyn."

"*Brooklyn?*" he yells, his voice piercing, and Graham and Cassie both glance at my phone and then at each other from opposite ends of the huge space.

"We're at his sister's loft," I smile at her in what I hope is a reassuring manner, "having coffee."

He tries for a mildly concerned tone. "Emma, our flight is at noon—"

"I know, Dad."

"But…" he sighs, and I imagine him rubbing his hand over his face in that way he does when he's frustrated. We've grown closer over the past six months, but he missed his chance to be the monitoring parent years ago and he knows it. "When will you be back?"

"When do you want to leave for the airport?" I hedge.

"Nine-thirty?"

Last night and last month and last fall I wanted nothing more than to hear Graham tell me he wanted me, and now, he has. Suddenly aware that we will say goodbye in less than two hours, the whole thing feels hopelessly muddled and complicated.

"Emma?"

"Yeah, Dad, sorry. I'll be back in time to pack up." My throat tightens with the realization that it could be more than a month before I see Graham again.

"Is everything okay?"

"Mmm-hmm."

He sighs again. "We'll talk later, sweetheart. I can tell you can't talk now."

"Thanks, Dad. I'll be back soon."

Cassie is a cellist with the New York Symphony, on a short leave of absence at the moment to be a full-time mother. "I couldn't let my little brother show me up on the parenting front," she smirks, watching as Graham makes faces at the baby, whose name is Caleb.

Gesturing to a barstool, she moves to the opposite side of the granite-slabbed counter while I examine the loft. Wood cut-outs, iron sculptures, paintings, prints and mixed media arrangements hang on the rough brick walls, along with two bicycles. An upright bass and a cello flank the undivided windows and floor-to-ceiling shelves house tons of books and photos. The loft is casual and cozy.

My stepmother, Chloe, would hate this place. I love it.

"What brings you to New York, Emma?" Cassie asks, pouring coffee into three mugs.

"I'm here with my dad, choosing a college."

Her eyes flick across the room and back and she smiles. "Are you? So you'll be moving to New York in the fall?" I nod and her smile widens. "I'm sure my brother is happy about *that*."

I wonder what, exactly, Graham has told her about me. As though I'd posed this question aloud, she leans onto her elbows and lowers her voice. "He likes you a *lot*, you know." My face warms, but she doesn't seem to notice. "I wouldn't butt in, but he's too damned reserved, and if *one* of you doesn't exhibit some daring, this whole thing will be one big missed opportunity."

I clear my throat. "We've already, um, talked about things this morning..." I say, and she slaps a hand on the counter.

"Well thank *God*. It's about time."

"What's about time?" Graham's voice is right behind me. He takes a seat on the stool next to me.

Cassie's brows rise and she gives him a haughty stare. "If we wanted you to be part of this conversation, we'd have been talking louder."

He laughs, and Caleb coos up at him. "Fine. I'll just wheedle it out of Emma later."

Chapter 3

GRAHAM

She's quiet on the return trip. We both are. For all of our earlier give-and-take, there's only one issue on my mind now: the 2500 miles between us for the next four months. I have three more weeks of class before graduation. The premiere of *School Pride* is in LA the following week, with the associated whirlwind of red carpets and cast parties and Hollywood in its usual circus atmosphere. Mid-summer, I'll begin filming my next movie here in New York. It's a low-budget indie, which means fast and cheap and long hours with no time to fly to LA for a weekend.

Cassie loaned us hoodies, so we don't have to huddle together for warmth, but I hold Emma's hand, fingers laced, and she presses her thigh against mine and leans her head against my shoulder. Sighing, she stares out at the Manhattan Bridge view that keeps me from ever wanting to live anywhere but New York. The high-rise windows are thousands of tiny mirrors from this distance, the skyline lit in waves like a sun-drenched waterfall as rays strike each building. I wish I could hit replay on this five-minute span of time; it might be enough to tide me over for a while. But we reach the other side of the river and plunge underground, the fluorescent lighting casting everything with a sickly green tint.

Between the later hour and the hoodies, we won't freeze now, walking around. There's plenty to see in SoHo, even this early in the morning. Peering into wide-windowed galleries and tiny shops, we maneuver our way around street vendors setting up for the day—crowding onto the edges of sidewalks that will be jammed with people in an hour or two. Emma and I hunch together as though we live here and we're just out getting breakfast, and I realize that this is what scares the hell out of me—I already want that with her. I want to be with her, absorb her into my life and have her absorb me into hers.

A conversation I had with Cassie years ago, soon after Zoe and I broke up, pushes into my consciousness. "I don't understand what girls want," I told her. From what I could tell, girls acted like they wanted declarations of undying love, but once they got them, those confessions were taken for granted. That, or you were rejected for being too clingy, dependent, or insecure—all words Zoe tossed out during the week leading up to the breakup.

"Girls expect you to love them forever, and they say they feel the same, but they really mean *until I get bored with you.*" I was well on my way to becoming a very bitter sixteen-year-old boy.

Cassie was twenty-two, and had been through her share of relationships by that point. She'd not yet met Doug, and wouldn't for another three years and one more failed relationship. Sitting at her kitchen table in the tiny walkup she shared with two other girls, we faced a window overlooking a courtyard of dead grass and gravel. The remainder of the view consisted of an adjacent, equally dilapidated building and no sky at all.

"Graham, not all girls will be like that."

Torn between despair and hope, I said, "Hmph," and gulped from the soda can she handed me when I sat down. She grabbed my hand, wanting to fix everything for me, I know, but she was as powerless to remedy what had happened as I was. The combination of her commiseration and another wave of Zoe thoughts made my throat ache. Yanking my hand from beneath hers, I stared out the viewless window. I didn't want to cry over Zoe anymore. I wanted to be angry. Anger was so much easier to work with.

Cassie sighed. "Someday, you'll find a girl who can handle the intense way you love. Who isn't intimidated by it—because that's what this is. Zoe can't feel this profoundly about anything or anyone. She's shallow and self-centered. And she's blown the chance at a wonderful guy."

I hadn't believed her, of course—that I'd find a girl like that, someone other than Zoe.

I still didn't quite believe it last night, when Emma kissed me, and everything I'd dreamed of with her flashed before my eyes. Now, I'm visualizing us walking these streets together, alone or with Cara between us. I picture her sleeping in my bed. I imagine her accompanying me on location during breaks from school. Then everything speeds up and I watch her walk across a stage to accept her diploma. I see myself sliding a ring on her finger and promising her eternity and lifting a veil and kissing her.

If she hadn't sent that text at 2 a.m. last night, I might have let her go. I might have never confessed how I felt about her. I was so afraid of wanting too much that I couldn't trust her handing me a shot at *getting* it. I don't want to be that senselessly fearful ever again.

Our outer hands shoved into our respective hoodie pockets, I hold Emma's left hand in my right, deep inside my pocket. We end up on a bench in front of her hotel, the minutes ticking away, nothing to be done but let them fall until she's gone.

"What happens now?" she says, just as I was going to ask if taking her to meet Cassie was too uncomfortable for her. Too much, too soon.

I swallow my question and answer hers. "Now, we run up the minutes on our cell phones and we text, and Skype, and in less than five weeks, I'll be in LA and so will you." Then I realize that I'm not sure if she means *now*, this second, or *now*, this point in our newly established relationship. She chews her lip, and I say, "If all you meant was *what are we doing for the next half hour*, please don't tell me, because I'll feel like an idiot."

She laughs. "No, I'm good with the five week plan."

What about a five year plan? I think. But instead of voicing that, I take her face in my hands and kiss her.

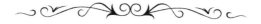

Emma

Dad sleeps during the flight. I try to read but can't concentrate, so I end up reading and rereading the same passages until it's just ridiculous and I give up and stare out at the blue sky. The cottony clouds below us come in transient batches, alternatively showing and obscuring the miles and miles of nothing, towns and cities popping up occasionally and disappearing before I can begin to guess where we are.

Every mile takes me farther from Graham.

And every mile makes me less sure that what happened between us actually happened. It's like a dream. All of it. I tried to explain to Dad what had taken place—the share-with-your-parent version, of course. I didn't tell him Graham came to the hotel last night. Or that I texted him at 2 a.m. But he knows something's up—more than just meeting a friend for breakfast. He's given me a couple of sidelong glances I'm probably not supposed to have noticed. He knows that Graham has all of a sudden become significant. I don't know how to explain myself. I know what I feel; I'm just not sure how to make it sound as sensible as it seems to me.

I turn it all over in my head. Neither of us said the words, but they hung over our heads like a shared thought bubble: *I love you*. I can't reconcile the fact that the words seem both too soon and past due.

Emily will help me sort it out. Before I left for New York, she asked me if I was falling for Marcus. We've gone out together several times, the four of us. Emily's boyfriend, Derek, is one of those guys who gets along with anyone; so is Marcus, usually. Which makes it all the more odd that they don't seem to relate to each other. Emily and I have watched the two of them talk, and we decided they're like polite coworkers, or neighbors who've never seen the inside of each other's houses, and don't really need to, thanks.

We shrugged and said, "Boys," though it annoyed us both.

I text her right before takeoff.

Me: I have news
Em: You changed your mind and aren't going to move THOUSANDS of miles away from me?
Me: Um. No. That's still happening. I thought you were okay with it? :(
Em: Of course I'm not ok with you leaving Cali! I'm going to miss the shit out of you! What is this news of which you speak?

Me: We ran into Graham
Em: Get OUT. MILLIONS of people in nyc... and you run into the hunky, mysterious costar with whom you shared a steamy hotel room moment?
Me: You're reading those trashy romance novels again, aren't you
Em: I dunno what you're talking about
Me: ANYWAY. So graham has a daughter.
Em: WHAT?!?!?!?
Me: And also, we're sort of seeing each other now.
Em: WHAT?!?!?!?
Me: Gotta go. Getting the evil eye from flight attendant. Meet me at home at like 3.
Em: I'm just... WHAT?!?!?!?

Two minutes after we land and right after I power it up, my cell is ringing. I'm surprised to see Dan's name in the display, but he did warn me he'd have *School Pride* promos set up and we'd discuss them when I returned from my "little college tour." I didn't know he meant we'd talk about them *the very minute* I got back. My energetic agent is probably on high alert, though I suppose he doesn't really have any other setting.

"Hi, Dan."

"Emma, glad you're back. I have a tentative schedule of interviews, appearances, etcetera for you—*Ellen*, by the way—woot!—we can go over that in a moment, though, because first I *really* have to ask—are you absolutely certain about this whole college slash career-killing slash no-more-movies decision? Because I'm getting tons of calls about parts you'd be *perfect* for—"

"No, Dan. I'm sure."

"Now hear me out just a moment—the call that came in this morning was actually an *action* flick and you'd need some personal training to get all badass of course, but hey if Linda Hamilton can do it for *The Terminator* sequel—oh, I guess that's before your time, though—" he chuckles and I take that opportunity to try to stop him again.

"Dan, seriously, I'm *sure* that I'm not interested. But thank you. Really."

He sighs in his long-suffering agent manner. "You're killing me, Emma. Killing. Me."

This is not an appropriate time to laugh. Not even if I can

picture the exact sad-puppy expression on Dan's face, which is made funnier by the fact that he's known in industry circles for being more of a piranha and less of a Bassett hound. "I'm sorry, Dan."
Dad, removing our luggage from the overhead bins, smiles and shakes his head. He knows Dan as well as I do.
"Yadda yadda," Dan says, which is Dan-speak for *you are saying words I don't like*.
The first interview is in a couple of days, and Graham was right—it's just Reid and me. This doesn't really bother me until Dan says, "You probably know there's still widespread speculation about the nature of the relationship between you and Reid Alexander—"
"But we don't really have any re—"
"Now, don't feel as though you have to share anything with me—"
"*Dan*. There's nothing to share. We're barely speaking. I mean, I don't even know if we *are* speaking..."
Dad mouths *What?* and I shrug one shoulder and roll my eyes as we stand in the clogged aisle with our carry-on luggage in hand.
"Let's just keep that to ourselves, shall we? Here's the deal. The studio wants you two to make nice. You can tell interviewers that there's nothing going on between you, or leave it open by saying *no comment*, but you should *look as though* something could be going on. It'll be good publicity for the film release if people already love you as a couple."
My mouth hangs slightly ajar and I snap it closed as Dad gives me an arch look. I'm acutely aware of the people crammed into the aisle in front of and behind me, waiting to deplane, so I keep my voice low. "Are you—are you saying we should *pretend* to be together?" I ask, teeth clenched. Oh, *hell* no. That is *not* going to work.
"Of course not! Just don't pretend *not* to be together."
"That's no different from pretending we *are*, and we *aren't*—"
"What I mean to say is, just don't make that an *obvious* thing."
I pinch the bridge of my nose, eyes closed. This is a nightmare. "As in, *the studio wants us to pretend we're together*."
"Well, okay, if you need to put it that way." At my silence, he adds, "Just give enough of the *illusion* of the *possibility* that you

could be in love or involved in some delicious little clandestine liaison." It's easy to visualize Dan leaning back in his huge leather chair behind his massive desk (which I've always suspected had been carved from illegally-obtained rainforest lumber). Headset in place, his elbows resting on the arms of the chair with fingers steepled, he's swiveled to face the giant plate-glass window overlooking LA. Too many times, I've been on the opposite side of his desk, listening in on these short conversations with other actors. "Oh and BT-dubs, they just let me know that there's a photo shoot for *People* in a week and a half. Whole cast. So clear time for that."

My brain skids to a stop. Whole cast. *Graham.* "Where?"

"Here in LA. They're flying everyone in."

The upcoming sham relationship with Reid forgotten for the moment, I focus on the fact that I'll see Graham next week. As soon as I hang up with Dan, I'm texting him to see if his agent has already given him the news.

Chapter 4

Brooke

I haven't talked to Graham in a week. Maybe two. His graduation is in three or four weeks. I wonder if I should offer to attend. If he'd want me to. We've been friends for four years, and I've only interacted with his family a couple of times, when I was in New York. His sisters were kind of snotty. One works on Wall Street, and the other is a classical musician of some sort—a violinist or something else with strings... She plays in the Philharmonic. Or is it the New York Symphony? Same difference.

I just got word from my manager that there's going to be a photo shoot for *People* next week, here in LA. Graham *has* to come for that. He's the best-looking guy in the cast, which people might not know if they only see the movie—his character is a flaming nerd. Nothing like the real Graham. Well, I take that back. Graham *can* be nerdy, but it's endearing, in that he-still-seems-innocent sort of way. Until you get a load of those gorgeous brown eyes staring into yours and you forget what you were just thinking. Because those eyes are *not* innocent.

Shit. Shake it off, Brooke.

Me: Hey handsome. Heard about the photo shoot next week?
Graham: Yeah, just heard from emma, and then my agent called and told me.
Me: I didn't know you were still in contact with emma.

28

Son. Of. A. *Bitch*. He's talking to Emma? When the hell did *that* happen? I'd hoped he'd gotten that little thing he had for her out of his system months ago. He hasn't mentioned a damned thing about her lately. Plus, there have been intermittent rumors about Emma and Reid hooking up ever since we quit filming, though I suspect that's all crap—none of them included any new photos.

Graham: I ran into her yesterday
Me:　　Ran into her, like in nyc?
Graham: Yeah. I had cara with me.
Me:　　Oh shit. Did she suspect?
Graham: I told her. Well actually cara told her, by calling me daddy.

My brain feels like it's on speed. He ran into Emma. *In New York*. When does that *ever* happen? Okay, time to reassess. Emma finding out about Cara could be a good thing—just another wall between them—her on one side, me on the other. *With him*. I understand Graham in a way no one else can. I've been patient, waiting for him to see what could be between us, and he's been playing typical clueless guy. Time to step it up. I am *not* letting Emma back in there.

Me:　　Wow, how did that go?
Graham: Pretty well, actually.

I wait for more and of course there's nothing, because in addition to the tall, dark and hot thing Graham's got going on, he's also infuriatingly close-mouthed. About *everything*. I've had dozens of conversations with him where I feel like we really communicated. Then later, I realize that nearly everything he contributed was a question or an observation on something *I* said. That he'd not actually revealed much, if anything.

Like I said—infuriating. And *so* frustrating. In that mouth-watering sort of way.

Me:　　I guess I'll see you in less than two weeks, then <3
Graham: Cool, see you then.

Decisions, decisions. How to handle this little glitch...
Two things stood between Graham and Emma getting together

during the months on location: Reid's all-out pursuit of her, and my pretense that something was going on between Graham and me. Graham and Emma are similar in one glaring way—neither of them will stage a shit-fit throw-down territory dispute.

When Reid kissed Emma during that concert, it was like a freaking miracle. They say a picture is worth a thousand words. Hell *yes* it is. It wasn't like I set out to hurt Graham. I mean, *Emma and Reid were kissing*—that was a fact. I was just being protective, sending him that picture. So he'd know what was going on. I couldn't have asked for a better response. He didn't say another word about her. Before, he'd driven me up the wall with occasional tidbits of Emma-related nonsense.

Convincing Emma that Graham and I had a thing going was relatively easy. He and I have been friends for so long, and I was in such a state at having to work around Reid after not laying eyes on him in person for years. All I had to do was play up the *I'm so fragile* act a bit, and the whole freaking cast thought Graham and I were screwing each other.

I *wish*.

Graham made it obvious from the start of our relationship that we could be friends, but he wasn't interested in anything more. I've never been sure why that was. At first, I think he just noticed the desperate way I felt about everything. Right after Reid broke up with me, I was raw. I was needy. I was pissed as hell. I would conclude that all that stuff scared Graham, but I don't think that's true or he wouldn't have become my friend. It was like he saw my damage and knew instinctively to avoid getting tangled up in it.

But I'm better now. I know what I want. And what I want is Graham.

REID

Brooke: Hey asshole, we need to chat
Me: Aww, how could i ignore such a sweet appeal? What do you want.
Brooke: I have a proposition. Come over.
Me: Not interested. But thanks for thinking of me.
Brooke: NOT that kind of proposition, you freak. This has to do with Emma.
Me: I'm both intrigued and suspicious.

Brooke: Trust me, what i have in mind will benefit us both.
Me: No way in hell i trust you. But i'm too curious for my own good.

"You've got five minutes to convince me to listen to anything further, so spill it." When she opens the door, I walk in talking. Her apartment is stunning, second only to her. She's wearing tiny white shorts and a violet halter tank, showcasing her warm skin and sleek blonde hair. My intent is to avoid staring at her directly as much as possible. She's like Medusa—the most beautiful woman you've ever laid eyes on, and also the most personally dangerous.

I'm a little afraid that she'd kill me if she thought she could get away with it.

I walk into her monochromatic living room, with floor-to-ceiling windows and a view to die for, and drop onto her white leather sofa, letting my head fall back and staring at the ceiling. So far, so not dead. She sits across from me in a black club chair, crossing her perfectly toned legs but not speaking. If she thinks I'm dragging whatever this is out of her, she can think again.

Finally, she sighs. "I assume that if you thought you could have another shot at Emma, you'd take it?"

What the hell? "Not really your business, Brooke." I'm still staring straight up, counting the tiny lights in the track lighting while wondering what scheme has lodged itself in her head.

"Come on, Reid, it's not like it's a state secret."

I chance looking at her. Her expression is serious, almost fierce. There's definitely something she wants from me—and me only—because if she could get this from anyone else, there's no way I'd be sitting here now. Playing along is the only way I'll find out what this is about. "Okay, I'll bite. Sure, I'd take another shot if I had it. Your turn."

The only thing that betrays her is one finger, repeatedly scratching at the seam of her chair. She sits up. "I want Graham."

I laugh. "Tell me something I don't know."

Fixing me with a mocking smile, she says, "Well apparently, they want each other."

"What?" I knew it. I *knew* it.

She laughs, not humored. "He's... reserved. It's hard to tell what—or who—he wants. But they ran into each other in New York a few days ago—where *she's* looking to go to school next

31

fall and where *he* lives. Just the fact that he mentioned their little meet-up is enough to ring my alarm bells."

I sit up, too, leaning my forearms on my knees. I still don't fully comprehend what she has in mind, but I'm starting to get an idea of it. "If they decide to hook up, what are we supposed to do about it? Maybe you're forgetting that *thanks to you*, Emma dumped me. She didn't choose some other guy over me. She chose to be *alone* rather than be with me. You set that whole shit up, Brooke. I don't know what you told her—"

"I didn't tell her anything. She was in the bathroom stall."

The silence is profound after she says this. She's actually managed to shock me. Emma didn't just get a second-hand account of what went down between Brooke and me, she heard the entire sordid conversation, along with all of the hostility I obviously still felt over Brooke's betrayal years ago. I'd thought, before that night, that I was solidly recovered. *Wrong.*

Little wonder Emma disappeared that night. I slump back into the sofa. "Holy shit, Brooke. How could you *do* that? You, and you alone, are responsible for *both* of them knowing about that pregnancy. And that I bailed on you. But do they both know you were cheating on me? Do they know *that fucking part* of the story?"

She sits back, staring out the window for several minutes with her chin in her hand. "I didn't."

I stand up. This is bullshit. "I don't know what kind of fantasy land you live in, where you can get two people to just *forget* the extremely dysfunctional shit they know about both of us—again, thanks to *you*—and fall into our arms. I don't see it happening. If I'd known Emma overheard us that night—" I run a hand through my hair. I'm so pissed I want to smash my foot through her chrome and glass table or throw something across the room. "If I'd known she heard that conversation, I'd have given her the chance to calm down instead of being a complete *dickwad* and literally screwing the first girl who bumped into me."

Brooke is silent, frowning and still staring out the window. "I can change her mind." Her words are soft, spoken into her hand.

"How? Why would she listen to you—because she trusts you so much? She's not that stupid," I sneer, still standing.

Her eyes flash to me. "Wanna bet?"

I've thought about Emma several times in the past month, ever since my spontaneous apology that night in my hotel room. The one she rejected, soundly. The thing is—I don't know if I'd have been willing, or able, to actually *change* for her. The only change I had in mind was attempting a monogamous hookup, for however long it lasted. I'm standing across from the only other girl who's ever gotten *that* out of me. But Brooke and Emma are night and day, so it seemed likely that the outcome would be different with Emma. Not that she gave me the chance to find out.

I sit back down. "Let me get this straight—you're proposing that we work together to either break up, or stop from forming, a relationship between Graham and Emma. And moreover, that we manage to seduce them for ourselves."

Her chin comes up. "Yes. Are you in or not?"

We're staring at each other across the expanse of glass table, the room impossibly bright. I can see every sliver of ice blue in her eyes, every perfect highlight altering her natural honey blonde hair to a streaked blonde not found in nature. Her nose, too, is a little more perfect than it was when we were younger, her brows flawlessly shaped and raised in silent question, waiting for my answer.

I nod once. "I'm in."

33

Chapter 5

Emma

In the taxi between my hotel and the Hollywood studio where *On the Air* is recorded, I try to psyche myself up to see Reid. I have no idea what to expect. The last time I saw him, only a month ago, he'd apologized for what he put me through last fall. *Forgive me, please.*

I did forgive him, but not in the way he wanted.

He said he thought he could be different with me. That I could help him be something better. And I replied that I wanted someone who was already that, on his own, with or without me. Visions of Graham swam through my head as I said those words. I was so sure Graham belonged to Brooke. I was so sure he was impossible and unobtainable and not for me.

And now he is possible, obtainable, *mine.*

I expect Reid to be aloof. Resentful, possibly. But Reid Alexander doesn't focus on one girl for long. He could have anyone he wants. Well, almost anyone. It would be ridiculous for him to have any residual feelings for me, but that might not stop him from being vindictive over my rejection, because one thing Reid Alexander doesn't get is *rejected.*

I've exceeded my comfort level on confrontation lately. My initial conversation with Marcus went less well than I'd hoped. When he arrived Saturday night, he was in his usual upbeat mood.

When he kissed me, a quick peck on the mouth, I knew we had to have the awkward conversation first thing. I don't want to kiss anyone but Graham, even superficially.

"So what are we doing tonight? Hanging out with Em and Derek, or do I get you all to myself?"

For some inexplicable reason, it *really* bugs me when Marcus calls Emily *Em*. There's no good reason for this. It doesn't bother me when Dad does it. Or Derek, though he only calls her Em when he's parodying some *Jersey Shore* guy, like he did last week: *"Aaay, Em, babe, whaddaya mean we ain't got time to make out? Badda-bing, five minutes—I'm happy, you're happy, every-freakin-body's copacetic."* Emily punched him in the arm, earning, *"Ow, woman, whaddaya gotta do that for? I'm a sensitive guy."* And then she rolled her eyes and he dipped her backwards and kissed her so thoroughly that *I* felt it.

I ignored Marcus's "Em," as I had every other time he'd said it.

"It's just us tonight. And, um, we need to talk."

"Uh-oh, that sounds a little serious," he said, still smiling. When I pressed my lips together and didn't deny that it was, his smile wilted, and I turned and led the way to my room.

I'd never actually seen Marcus in a bad mood, except for a few times during rehearsals for *It's a Wonderful Life*, when I thought he was somewhat overly-critical of our cast mates' performances. We were doing community theatre, not Broadway. But I took him to be a typical serious, perfectionist theatre geek and let it pass. We started going out after the show wrapped, and he'd never showed any sign of irritation with anything.

We sat on my bed and he waited for me to explain. I cleared my throat and arranged the words in my head. There was no reason Marcus and I couldn't remain friends. We'd had the rare kissing marathon, but hadn't gone any further than that. Frankly, I'd had a hard time picturing myself with Marcus in any serious physical way. I'd assumed that the botched relationship attempts with Reid and Graham had stomped those desires right out of me.

The thought of Graham flooded my imagination with thoughts of him, and it took concerted effort to push those contemplations from my mind and direct my attention to the task at hand: letting Marcus down gently. "You know the, uh, movie I just filmed?"

He arched a brow and then laughed lightly. "Yeah, *School Pride*—I think everyone who knows you is familiar."

I chewed my lip. "Well, I was close friends with a guy in the cast—"

"That would be... Graham Douglas?"

"Uh, yeah. How did you—? Nevermind. Not important." I shook my head. Those tabloid stories I'd ignored *hadn't* been ignored by everyone else. And *everyone else* apparently included Marcus. "I ran into him in New York. And... it appears that we have feelings for each other." I watched the effect these words had on him—the confused frown, the tilt of his head as what I was saying started to become clear, the incredulous look when he got it.

"So wait. You go to New York and 'run into' a guy you haven't seen for a month, and didn't see for several months before that—or is there more to this that I need to know?" His anger took me by surprise, not because it was undeserved, but because it was so uncharacteristic.

"Uh, no..."

"You *run into* him, and the two of you just decide to embark on—what—a full-fledged relationship? Are you breaking up with me?"

I was stunned at his vehemence. And his assumption. "Marcus, we never agreed we were a couple—"

"Emma, we've been going out for almost four months, and neither of us—*that I know of*—has seen anyone else for the past couple of months. I'm not crazy to make assumptions." His tone was spiteful. This wasn't the Marcus I'd known for months. Not at all.

"I'm sorry." It was lame, but it was the best I could do.

He stared at the bedspread, and I almost held my breath. I didn't want to hurt him, but I gathered that his feelings had grown stronger than I'd comprehended. Wondering if I'd been blind to this, I thought back over the past few months and couldn't pinpoint a thing he'd said or done that would have let me know he was growing possessive. But then, I hadn't given him any reason to express it before. He'd felt safe in the knowledge that there was no one else.

"I guess I'm going to my prom *alone*." His voice was sullen, hostile.

"No, I'd be happy to still go with you, if you want me to…"

His eyes flashed up to mine. "So he'll *allow* you to go with me?"

I frowned. "What do you mean, *allow* me to go—this is my decision, and I told you I'd go with you, so I'm willing to go—"

"Hey, don't do me any favors, okay?" He stood, fists clenched at his sides. "I'll call you tomorrow. I don't know if I want to see you again, Emma, prom or not. This is so out of left field. I didn't think you had it in you to lead someone on like that. I guess you're more *Hollywood girl* than I thought."

My eyes filled with tears as he stomped from the room, down the stairs and out the front door.

REID

The studio valet takes the keys to my Lotus. It's over a year old now, and I'm utterly bored with it. I've been thinking about getting a Porsche. Something sleek and black. Sexy. I have no idea what the hell I was thinking buying a yellow car. Dad's "douche taxi" comments aside, it's way too happy-smiley-sunny for me now. I'm nineteen as of last month. Yellow is something a kid chooses, not a man.

I'm psyched to see Emma, though I'm going to have to play that way down. Brooke warned me to do nothing beyond being civil and warm. Absolutely no flirting. "The last time you saw her you tried to pull her back into a relationship. She's going to expect you to either be resentful or flirtatious. Be *neither*. Just be… sweet. You can fake that, right?"

I gave her a look that clearly said, *You are a grade-A bitch*, and she laughed. Brooke is a calculating genius, and I'm glad that for once I'm on her side. Sort of.

"Oh and by the way, *no screwing around*. At *all*. You nail-gunned your own coffin with that shit last fall. If you're going to convince Emma that you're a changed man, you've gotta start by keeping your dick in your pants."

"Classy, Brooke."

"Bite me, Reid—and tell me this: was *Blossom*, or whatever

the hell her name was, worth losing Emma for? Because that's what did it. Emma's too forgiving for her own good, and I'm positive she'd have given you another shot if you hadn't screwed it up for yourself—literally."

Ouch. Bullseye.

As the valet steers the Lotus away from the curb (carefully, because he knows I'm watching), a taxi pulls up. Wearing a floral sundress, her hair piled adorably at her crown and looking as though it will all tumble down any moment, Emma steps from the back seat, watching me warily. "Hey, beautiful," I smile. Oops. So much for not flirting.

"Hi, Reid." She looks equal parts reserved and relieved, so I haven't blown it yet.

Focus on sweet and friendly. No flirting. So I guess pulling her forward and seeing if she'll let me kiss her is out. As is telling her she looks good enough to eat. "So. Um. Ready to meet Ryan?" I assume Seacrest hasn't been on her list of interviewers before now.

She takes a deep breath and exhales slowly. Nervous. "I guess so."

"No worries. He's as cool as they come—he won't do anything to make you feel uncomfortable." I hook my thumbs into my front jeans pockets and offer her an elbow. "So... I suppose you got the word from the powers that be on how we're supposed to play up the Darcy-and-Lizbeth-in-love angle, huh?"

She slides her hand into the crook of my arm and we walk up to the studio doors. I glance down at her and she looks up, a small crease between her brows. "Yeah, my agent told me. I'm not really—"

"Don't worry." I lean closer and lower my voice. "This will be a piece of cake. I've had to do it once before, and I couldn't *stand* my costar. It took everything in me not to stuff a sock into her mouth any time she started talking. We managed to keep up the pretense until the initial release was over. You and I won't have the same problem... unless you find yourself wanting to stuff a sock in *my* mouth."

One corner of her mouth turns up and she smirks, and I know we're good. "I don't feel the need so far," she retorts. "But I'll let you know."

The interview goes well. When questioned, we issue polite

denials of any romantic ties between us, stating that the whole cast was cozy last fall, what with the close quarters and our similar respective ages. Ryan quirks an eyebrow when I bump Emma softly with my shoulder and smile down at her like we have a secret. We've definitely fulfilled what the studio wants from us— ambiguity in our answers about a possible relationship, coupled with seemingly minor physical displays of affection.

What the public believes or doesn't about Emma and me is irrelevant to me personally, and I know she won't be swayed into (or out of) a relationship because of fan reaction, especially considering her upcoming exit from Hollywood this fall. Whatever's going on between her and Graham Douglas can't possibly be all that significant yet. They live too far apart and have hardly seen each other in months. He's a wild card, though. I never did figure him out. Brooke seems to think she can manipulate this with my help, and both of us will end up with what we want.

I'm less sure of that, but perfectly willing to play my part. Losing Emma was a massive disappointment. One I'd like to reverse.

Chapter 6

GRAHAM

It's been four days since I've seen her. In person, anyway. I'm currently staring at a jerky graphic of her on my laptop screen—the best Emma-substitute technology has to offer. It's not enough. Not even close.

"Don't you have class tomorrow?" she asks, blinking into her webcam, staring at a correspondingly spasmodic image of me.

"I do." The time difference between us doesn't play into my favor. She's the one who can afford to sleep in; I'm the one with eight o'clock classes. 10:03 p.m. in Sacramento is 1:03 a.m. in New York. "But if you were here, I wouldn't be sleeping, either. So what's the difference?" *Aside from the fact that sitting in my bed, laptop tilted to watch your face as you speak, is so inferior to the feel of you in my hands, the taste of you on my tongue.*

The fuzzy Emma image smiles, one hand nervously pushing her hair behind her ear. She glances away, towards her bedroom door, I imagine, and back to me. Leaning closer, her face fills my screen. "Oh?" Her voice lowers. "And what would we be doing, instead of sleeping, if I was there?"

I give her a somewhat tame version. Not exactly censored, but not enough to scare her, either. The light on her end is too dark to see if she blushes, but her lips part and her eyes widen slightly and she bites her lip adorably and listens like I'm telling her the best story ever.

I don't know how far she went with Reid. Or with anyone before him, for that matter, though I surmised that there was no one before him, from how frustrated he often seemed. I know far too much about Reid Alexander and his seduction capabilities. Not wanting a full accounting of just how critically I screwed up by not taking her from him last fall, I have no plans to ask her about their involvement. It has no bearing on what I think of her. It has no bearing on us.

"I wish you were here," she says finally, her lower lip jutting out so slightly I might be imagining it. I run my finger across it on the screen, which she can't see me do.

"I will be, in a week."

She groans. "Too *long*."

I laugh softly. "I agree."

A faint scratching comes from my closed bedroom door. "Go away, Noodles," I call. Cara's cat is usually asleep at the foot of her bed at 1:00 a.m., not wandering around the house scratching on random closed doors.

Then my doorknob turns, the door opening a sliver before a small face appears. "Daddy?"

"I have a visitor," I say into the tiny camera at the top of my screen, pushing the laptop onto the bed and padding across the room. "Cara? What are you doing up?" I open the door and she latches onto me, impeded only by the stuffed rabbit clenched in one fist.

Grasping her under the arms, I lift her and settle her in my arms. She sniffles and buries her face in my neck. "Bad dream?" I ask, and she nods, sniffling a little harder.

"Can I sleep with you?" A hiccup follows this muffled request. Emma coughs lightly, the sound coming through the laptop speakers with a scratchy unevenness, and Cara's head pops up. "Who's that?"

"I'm talking to Emma," I say. "Let's get you back to bed."

She turns her head back and forth mulishly, her dark eyes intent. "I want to talk to Emma, too."

Great. Wrestling Cara back into her bed could take me half an hour. She'll want to tell me her entire nightmare, and she's quite the dramatic narrator. I fully suspect she adds details as she goes along, just to enhance the story. And then the request for water. The request for a kiss. The need to be accompanied to the bathroom. The checking for monsters in her closet, under her bed and behind her draperies. Another kiss.

I love my daughter, but *crap*, what timing.

I walk over and pick up the laptop with my free hand, turning it towards Cara and myself. "I might as well let you go," I tell Emma. "This could take a little while."

"Hi, Emma," Cara says, posing for the camera, horrible nightmare forgotten. She's used to conversing with me this way when I'm away from home and she's with Brynn or Cassie. "This is Bunny." She holds the rabbit in front of the webcam. I'm sure all Emma can see is a screen full of worn blue fur.

"Oh, well hello there, Bunny. Are you by any chance... a turtle?"

Cara giggles, snatching Bunny to her chest and replacing the stuffed toy with her own face. "Nooooo."

"A giraffe, maybe?"

"Nooooo!"

"A doggie?"

"No, no, no!"

"Well, I'm stumped. What kind of animal has a name like that?"

"A *bunny*!" Cara is dissolving into a fit of laughter, and I can't help laughing along. She turns to me and points to my bed. "Sit, Daddy."

I sit with a sigh, torn between shock and elation at Emma's ability to switch gears. Five minutes ago I was whispering rather wicked details of what I wanted to do to her, and if the look on her face was any indication, she was having no problem following along. And now she's charming my daughter.

Cara begins to get sleepy quickly, slumping into my lap a short time later, curled around Bunny. It's inching closer to 2 a.m. "I'm going to go put her back down and hope she stays down. Same time tomorrow?"

"Earlier tomorrow," she promises. "Goodnight, Graham."

"Goodnight, Emma. See you soon." She signs off and the screen goes black.

Ah, God. My life has become more complicated than I ever

imagined it could be. I had no real idea what I was doing to myself when I decided to take on parenthood. To cope, I made adjustments I thought I could manage, like forgoing close romantic entanglements. At first, nothing could have been easier, because I was still in love with Zoe.

Once I was finally over her, I realized I'd also grown up, filled out. Girls on campus watched me with shameless curiosity and signaled uncomplicated desires, and my refusals to share any shred of personal information only amplified their interest. I didn't particularly care if they liked my no-strings position or not. A few drew lines in the sand, and I simply walked away. I never lied to anyone. I never promised anything. I never wanted anything more from anyone.

Until Emma. The friendship we developed was unlike any relationship I've ever had. So easy, so companionable, but that physical pull was there, too, from the first moment I saw her. I refused to believe I was falling for a 17-year-old girl, and I fought it, hard. The first time I kissed her uncovered feelings so compelling that they tumbled over into protectiveness. The resolve came naturally: I wouldn't touch her—beyond what we'd already done—until she was a legal adult, until she specifically asked me to. For the first time since Zoe, my guard was down.

Which was exactly why that photo of Reid and Emma sliced right through me.

Emma

The prom is a nightmare. While it's not exactly *Carrie*, it's no *High School Musical III*, either.

When Marcus called to tell me he still wanted me to accompany him to his prom, I swallowed back clichéd reassurances: *It's not you, it's me. We can still be friends. I didn't mean to hurt you.*

Though I didn't vocalize any of these, I did tell him I was sorry at least half a dozen times. My apparent guilt must have given him the mental go-ahead to transform into a total dick by the next weekend.

The downward spiral began when he arrived to pick me up. I'd told Dad and Chloe that we were going as friends, so I didn't want them to make a big deal of it. Naturally, Chloe ignored that entreaty and had the camera charged and ready.

"I remember *my* prom," she said, smiling dreamily into the distance as I thought, *Oh, crap, here we go.* "I was a total princess, all the way down to the glass slippers." She put a hand to her mouth like she was about to reveal a secret. "Actually, those shoes were acrylic and uncomfortable as hell."

"Ah," I said, attempting to look sympathetic.

Chloe blinded us with multiple flashes as Marcus slid a corsage onto my wrist in the entryway. She led us out back and posed us in front of the pool landscaping that made Dad walk around for days with his jaw clenched, mute and furious, after he got the bill for all the upgrades she'd authorized.

Snapping photos like she had aspirations as a high-fashion photographer, Chloe was oblivious to the ice-cold wall between her subjects. "Marcus, put your arms around her. Like that, but with your hands meeting in the middle. Oh! Yes! Just like that!"

I let her get off a few of shots before breaking from the false embrace. "Okay, I think that's enough pictures. You know, Marcus might actually like to *go* to his prom as part of this experience…" I hoped Marcus and I would share a knowing look about Chloe—not uncommon for us—so we could begin to salvage the night somewhat before it was entirely wrecked. But he stood, one hand in the trousers of his tux, flicking a fingernail and looking bored, and my sense of foreboding mushroomed.

Marcus's arts-heavy prep school is relatively small, with a modest graduating class. Judging by the response his arrival generates, he's clearly one of the in-crowd. The venue is the tented rooftop terrace of the Citizen Hotel—the city's oldest skyscraper. Though the view is only a very familiar Sacramento, it's breathtaking from this height. Distance alters everything.

Introducing me to his group of friends by way of, "This is Emma," and a turn of his wrist in my general direction, he doesn't introduce any of them to *me*. Unbelievably, no one steps forward, either. I'm stuck knowing no one's name—except those discovered by eavesdropping on neighboring conversations—so there's nothing to do but stand next to Marcus, my dress and his tux accoutrements so perfectly matched that it leaves no doubt we're here together. Trapped at the receiving end of stares and whispers in a crowd of people where I don't know a single person beyond my asshole of a date, I consider calling a taxi, or Dad, to come pick me up.

I can't shake the conviction that I'm getting what I deserve for leading Marcus on, as convincingly as Emily objected to that conclusion. "Marcus doesn't *own* you," she said after I told her what had happened with Graham in New York, and the resulting altercation with Marcus. "I don't see a ring on your finger, not that you'd ever want one from that pompous ass."

"I thought you liked him?" I said.

"Psshh," she said, glancing at me as she made a right turn. We were on the way to get our annual almost-summer pedicures. "I tolerated him. Derek and I didn't think he was for you."

I sputtered before answering, "You and Derek discussed—?"

"Hells *yeah*." She was, as usual, unapologetic. "We hoped it would fade out before you ended up in New York with him leeching onto you. Derek thinks he just wanted you for your film and theatre connections. With the bonus of your smokin' little bod, of course."

I almost spit berry smoothie onto her dashboard. "God, Em. I feel so cheap."

"Yeah, well, I'm just glad we didn't have to resort to breaking you guys up." She parked the Sentra and yanked up the brake.

"You mean you and Derek would have—"

"How many times in this conversation must I say *hells yeah*? Wouldn't have been that hard, either. You weren't all that attached to him, thankfully. You'd just better hope we like this Graham guy."

I leveled a look at her. "*No*. Graham is off-limits. I don't care if the two of you hate him."

She smiled and pinched my arm. "Now *that's* more like it."

When I come back to earth, I'm still at Marcus's prom, being pointedly ignored by every person here. Then my focus lands on the other side of the huge indoor/outdoor space. One of the photographers snapping shots of prom-goers appears to be aiming his camera in my direction exclusively. I think *paparazzi?* before giving myself a mental shake, feeling silly.

Still, I glance around surreptitiously, looking for the other photographers, who are progressing through the crowd, setting up shots of small knots of people talking and laughing, snapping candid shots of couples dancing and teachers chaperoning. Sliding my eyes back to the first photographer, I notice two things. One, his camera is badass in comparison to what the other two are utilizing. And two, he's still aiming every single shot in my direction.

I have an uneasy feeling about this.

Emily spent ten minutes scolding me about my recent *dumbass decisions*: first, trying to placate Marcus by going to his prom, and second, breaking my own rule about checking gossip sites. She's right, of course. I can't unsee the photos of me—alternating between miserable and pissed—standing beside Marcus, being snubbed by everyone at that dance. I can't unread the stories claiming that it was my choice to isolate myself, or the bonus rumors that I'm cheating on Reid Alexander.

My best friend stomps back and forth across my room while Derek and I look on silently. Finally, she stops and glares at the laptop screen. "What a bunch of jealous pricks!" Emily will never be accused of beating around the bush.

"Marcus's friends or the gossip sites?" I'm not sure which infuriates her more.

"*All of them.*" She's so angry she's growling.

"Calm down, baby," Derek says, tugging on her hand as she paces by him.

"I will not calm down!" Stopping suddenly, she slides onto his lap. "Derek, please do me a favor." She nuzzles the side of his closely-shorn blond head and his eyes close.

"Anything."

"Please beat the shit out of Marcus."

"Except that."

Sitting straight up, she folds her arms over her chest and glares at him. "What the hell good is having a muscly boyfriend if he won't beat people up for you?"

I'm glad the text from Reid comes after they've gone.

Reid:	You went to prom with some other guy? I'm hurt.
Me:	Very funny
Reid:	Our little act is a success. I've already been contacted for comment.
Me:	Crap
Reid:	It would help if we go out to dinner and look happy
Me:	I don't think that's a good idea
Reid:	Sure it is. One happy outing in the face of those stories will put an end to them.
Me:	You know I'm 400 miles from los angeles, right?
Reid:	I'm visiting a friend in san fran tomorrow. Drive in, stay over. We'll go somewhere cool.
Me:	I'm not meeting you in san francisco, reid
Reid:	Fine, i'll come to you

Graham is as supportive as Emily, though far less violence-craving.

"I should have just backed out of prom," I sigh into my webcam, scrubbing my hands over my face. "Marcus wasn't going to be happy no matter what I did, and now the whole world thinks I'm a stuck-up bitch who wouldn't lower herself to speak to regular folks."

"I'm sure no one believes a word of that." His voice is so warm and soothing that I almost believe him.

"People do believe it! And you know the most annoying part? Before now, I was a middle-class *nonentity* to most of the people from his school. Marcus and I have run into classmates of his several times, and every time I felt exactly like I do when Chloe eyeballs whatever I'm wearing and gears up to mock my entire sense of fashion—or lack of it."

He smiles reassuringly. "I happen to like your fashion sense."

I barely hear him. "And what about the rumors that I'm cheating on *Reid* with *Marcus*? I'm not *dating* Reid, but the studio wants everyone to think I am... so of course I'm a cheater if I go out with anyone else. What will that mean when *you're* here? We'll have to sneak around. If we're caught, I'll look like the biggest slut in Hollywood."

He laughs and shakes his head. "Emma, love, you've got a long way to go to win *that* crown."

I smile goofily at my screen. "You called me love."

He smirks, chin tucked low, staring at his screen through his lashes. "You okay with that?"

"Yeah." I stare into his beautiful warm eyes and wish for the hundredth time in two days that he was standing in front of me. "Are *you* okay with me meeting Reid for dinner?"

He nods and says, "As okay as I *can* be." Which seems cryptic, but I don't push him. I can't expect him to be thrilled about it.

Chapter 7

Brooke

"This is the part where you'll either start gaining her trust or you'll blow it." Obviously, Reid hasn't gained *my* trust. I'm fully expecting him to blow it.

"Who died and made you all-knowing?" He's barely got the words out before I want to strangle the ability to speak right out of him. I don't know if Reid and I are capable of ever *not* wanting to rip each other to shreds. That desire lingers right under the surface of every conversation we have.

"I'm not kidding, Reid, if you touch her or pressure her in any way before I do my part of this, it's over and we're screwed."

"Or not," he quips.

"Ha. Ha." *God*, I have had just about enough of his horseshit.

"Look, I'm not stupid." He pauses and I know he's thinking he left that wide open. I would dearly love to deliver the retort he expects, but it's just *too* easy. "Everything else in my life is boring the shit out of me. This is the only thing remotely stimulating. I'm following your orders, because you're the most successfully conniving girl I've ever known, plus I can *smell* how badly you want Graham."

If it wasn't true, how much I want Graham, I'd end this here and now. But Reid makes it sound like wanting him is dirty. It's not. I'm simply ready for something more serious and meaningful than all of the faceless boys and men I've been with in the last few years. None of them were worth half of Graham, and I'm willing to be whatever he wants me to be to get him. What's so wrong about that?

I've always been a crap judge of character. Graham was the only exception to that, though the existence of our friendship was all due to him. When I met him, I was reeling from Reid breaking my heart, and I just wanted to hook up. I was bouncing off guys like the shiny silver ball in my father's vintage pinball machine— *ding-ding-ding.* I guess Graham could tell that about me. He was one of the few who turned me down, but he didn't run away when my humiliation that any guy would reject me morphed into uber-bitch mode. He stuck around and became one of my best friends. Something I didn't deserve, and something I've always hoped would grow into more.

Graham has this quiet, steady aura about him, and of course I'm drawn to a disposition so completely opposite of mine. I thought we'd balance out, like a relationship seesaw. When we both scored roles in *School Pride,* I was sure my chance had come. Close quarters for three months, and my very real need for emotional protection from Reid that only Graham could provide.

Then he met Emma.

At first, I assumed she'd screw him over for Reid. She was obviously not immune to him, and he focused exclusively on her. I remembered all too well how *that* felt. When Reid and I first met, he flashed those blue eyes at me—*baby* blues, because holy shit he was what, fourteen then?—and I was a goner. Fifteen years old, and I was sure I'd met my soul mate, the guy I wanted to spend forever with. God, what a naïve idiot I was.

Unlike me, though, Emma figured him out. I have to give the girl props, she resisted long enough to witness him doing what he does, and then she dropped his ass. It would have been a joy to behold, if not for Graham. I'd never seen him so crazy infatuated before. Every time we hung out, I made careful plans to seduce him, but all he wanted to talk about was Emma, if he *talked* instead of brooding over her—which he was more prone to do. I don't think he even noticed my seduction efforts. Now, I'm glad he didn't.

Because this time, those efforts are going to work.

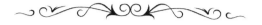

REID

Choosing a restaurant in a city you've never visited is tough. Since Emma lives in Sacramento, I asked her to choose whatever she'd like. This one will do, though not for my calculated purpose of being observed together *in* the restaurant. The windows are draped, probably thwarting the cozy paparazzi photos Brooke and I were anticipating. For actual intimacy, though, it's ideal—corner table, flickering candles, semi-tasteful décor (points deducted for the acoustic tile ceiling and likely-artificial paneling on a far wall).

"So what's the deal with this Marcus character? He seems like an ass. I thought when you dumped *me* you were trying to move away from that type." I smile, bumping Emma's arm lightly, and she rolls her eyes.

"Yeah, well, I guess that's harder to avoid than I thought." She returns my smile, but pulls her forearm away from mine, slowly, putting an ever-so-slight distance between us.

I lean back, pretending not to notice her withdrawal while she examines the menu. The waiter, introducing himself as Chad, is so uneasy he's twitching. He also punctuates practically every sentence with either *heh-heh* or *Mr. Alexander*. After taking our drink order, he scurries to the back through a set of double doors where the rest of the wait staff congregates. They've all been not-so-sneakily casting looks our way since we walked in. Typical.

A fun fact about celebrity: If you get carded, there's no such thing as a fake ID. They already know your real name. All anyone has to do is hit up IMDb or Wikipedia to get your *exact birthdate*. I rarely get carded, especially in LA or New York, or really anywhere we're filming. Most restaurants, bars and clubs are so freaked at having celebrities show up that they just don't give a crap. Apparently this place, which passes as "upscale" for Sacramento, gives a crap. I can't help my reaction, though, when Chad the waiter comes back a few minutes later all sheepish and asking to see ID for the bottle of wine I ordered.

"Dude, are you serious?" I say, and his face goes scarlet.

"My manager, heh-heh," he subtly inclines his head towards the back. "I'm *really* sorry, Mr. Alexander."

"It's okay," Emma says, giving him a reassuring smile. "I'll just have water." The breath wooshes out of the poor guy and he looks back at me.

I shrug. "Yeah, me, too." Chad rushes off and I shake my head. "I guess I'm not in LA anymore, Toto."

Emma laughs. "No, definitely not."

"So I heard through the grapevine that you were in New York recently, visiting colleges. Chosen one yet?" I'm curious about whether or not she'll ask which grapevine I got that from. What might she think to know it was Graham-to-Brooke-to-me?

She doesn't take the bait. Either she doesn't see it, or she's too smart to pick it up. "I'm leaning towards NYU."

"Tisch." I nod. "Cool."

"You know it?"

I laughed. "You don't have to sound so surprised. I was up to my eyeballs with paying work by the time I got close to finishing my high school coursework. College was never really on my radar. But that doesn't mean I don't know all the major theatre programs. You know, just in case."

She tilts her head. "In case what?"

That's right, Emma. Follow the crumbs. "In case I decide to take my career in a more serious direction at some point."

A crease appears on her forehead and my finger itches to smooth it out. "But I thought you said something about wanting the *crazy famous* and *ton of money* route?"

Wow. She remembers what I said months ago. Suddenly I'm recalling why I found her so unusual. She's outwardly focused, in a way few people in this business are. Including me. I smile. "Maybe the critical acclaim is more important to me than I let on." Total lie, of course.

"Huh," she says, and then for some reason she blushes.

Chapter 8

GRAHAM

Me: Touching down now. I'd call but i'm afraid of the flight attendant.
Emma: Lol why?
Me: She has a mustache. And sideburns. And perpetual anger.
Emma: Be careful...
Me: I'm taking my life in my hands to text that i'm only a few hundred miles from you
Emma: Wish I was there now
Me: I want to see you so bad it hurts

The second I hit send, I'm rethinking—too late—that last text. Because how desperate can I seem? It's been so long since I've felt this way. No. I've *never* felt this way. I was lovesick over Zoe, but I didn't rearrange my life in my head to make room for her everywhere. In a matter of what—less than two weeks?—Emma has gone from the girl who got away to the girl I see in every moment of my future. I'm starting to enter panic mode and second-think everything when my phone plays its text tone.

Emma: Me too

And just like that—relief. Muscle-flooding, breath-releasing, mind-calming relief. Laughing to myself, I stare out at LA as we taxi up to the terminal. I was sixteen the last time I felt so jerked around by my own desires. I'm out of practice.

I won't see Emma until tomorrow, when she checks into the hotel in LA, and I'm already craving the sight of her like I used to crave the feel of a cigarette between my fingers, between my lips, inhaling, exhaling, the nicotine flooding my system and making everything right with the world, thirty seconds in.

I definitely shouldn't tell her that thinking of her makes me wish for a cigarette to take the edge off, for the first time in months. Not that I'm sure it would even work.

Me: Heads up, seeing you will not be enough.
Emma: Consider me warned and ready
Emma: OMG *blushing*
Me: :)

My next text is to Cassie, to let her know I've landed, to ask how Cara's doing. Most of the time she's fine when dropped at her aunt's, but sometimes not. My sister reports that currently, Cara is dancing in front of Caleb's battery-powered swing and eating Cheerios from a cup.

My family has been supportive from day one as far as Cara goes, *day one* being the day I brought her home. Before that, they were divided—Mom and Brynn on one side and Dad and Cassie on the other. Mom and Brynn were not in favor of me taking custody of Cara. We'd had a family meeting to make the decision, and even though my sisters were both in college and no longer lived at home, they were both given a vote. Mom was tight-lipped, but Brynn was livid.

"*Why* would you do this to yourself?" Her hand smacked the pine-planked kitchen table where we all sat, me at the head like the accused. "She told you she's absolutely not keeping it, thank *God*, so you're off the hook for eighteen years of child support. Let her take care of it in whatever way she sees fit and go live your life! You're *sixteen* for fuck's sake!"

No one said anything. I don't think Dad and Cassie disagreed with her. They just thought I should be given the choice, and I'd made it.

I stared at my hands, splayed on the table. They weren't as big as my dad's yet. They weren't the hands of a man. They were the hands of a boy. I knew in that moment that I could reclaim my adolescence and walk away from this with my family's full support.

My voice was low, but sure. "It's *my* baby. I can't just let her give it away—"

"Graham, honey, we can all appreciate your sense of responsibility." Mom's placating tone annoyed me even more than Brynn's anger had. "But Zoe is accountable for not protecting herself, too—"

"We didn't know antibiotics would screw up her pill."

"And you weren't using *condoms?*" Brynn yelled. "What the hell were you thinking?"

My face flamed. I was sitting in the kitchen while my entire family discussed my sex life and stared at me like I was the biggest idiot on the planet. Unquestionably the most awkward moment of my life.

Dad cleared his throat, and everyone waited for his tie-breaking assessment. My father is a man of few words—a trait I inherited. His eyes met those of Mom, Cassie and Brynn, one by one. "I think Graham's made his decision, and if Zoe agrees with this, we'll have another member of the family, and we'll all adjust accordingly." He turned to me. "Graham, I want your word that you'll handle this like a man. No running away when it gets hard. No changing your mind later."

I nodded. "I know, Dad."

He returned the nod, as though I was an equal, and I sat up straighter.

"Talk to Zoe. Keep us informed. This will all work out." He offered a half-grin to my mother, who sat stoically across from him. "It's not like all three of *you* were planned, after all." Mom smirked back at him. That was the end of the family meeting.

Zoe was convinced she was going to be "just like *Juno*." We told her parents our decision, and since they'd given Zoe everything she wanted since the day she was born, it was easy enough to convince them to go along. There were moments during the next few months when she was pissed and blaming me for talking her into having the baby. Like the weeks she spent part of second period in the bathroom, throwing up, every day. Or when she got a new stretch mark. Or when she realized she'd gained forty pounds and the baby wouldn't weigh more than eight.

We weren't together-together, but Ross Stewart was no longer hanging around (which somehow confused Zoe), and I was convinced that part of everything *working out* would include Zoe and me getting back together. That didn't happen, of course.

Once Cara was born, Zoe handed her over, signed the legal papers terminating her parental rights, and went to spend a month in the south of France with her parents. When she returned to New York, she spent several weeks in the Hamptons before heading off to Florida for college. She never called or came by. It was like Cara never happened. Like I never happened.

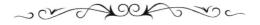

Emma

Once I've pulled my suitcase across the threshold of my room, I speed-dial Graham to tell him my room number. Waiting for him, I pace the length of the suite, door to window, window to door, my stomach in knots and my face as flushed as if I had a fever.

As he predicted, we've texted and talked and Skyped for the past ten days. I know so much more about him than I did a month ago. I didn't know him at all last fall. I only knew the comfort I felt in his presence, as though he'd always been a part of my life, a part of me. Maybe this is how it feels to lose your memory—only impressions and shadowed inclinations remain, with no factual signals to back them up.

A knock sounds at my door and my heart stops and falls to my knees, starting back up violently as I walk to the door and pull it open. For the barest moment we stand there drinking each other in, before I take a step backwards into the room and he follows as though there's a cord attached to his chest. The door snaps closed behind him.

Every detail about him has sharpened, my brain having played my mental pictures of him over and over. His dark hair is messy and falls over his forehead. His eyes are deep caramel in this late afternoon room, but they'll be black in low light. Slight stubble on his chin, and across his jaw. His mouth is set—if I was a stranger to him I'd think he was angry, but I know he's not. His nostrils flare just the slightest bit and I back up another step.

"Is it... okay... if I lock the door?" His voice is so low, and I recognize it as the voice he uses when we're talking late at night.

I nod, and he turns to twist the bolt and slam the interior lock home, the sleeve of his black T-shirt drawing back to expose the taut, defined muscles of his upper arm. My mouth goes dry with a longing so strong it makes my breath catch. When he steps towards me, I'm stock still, torn between swaying towards him and taking another step back.

His arms slip around me as he bends and buries his face in my neck. "I've missed you." His voice hums along my collar bone, soaks into my shoulder.

"I've missed you, too," I say, my voice a whisper, like smoke.

He pulls back, his arms still locked at my lower back, and grins. "I've missed you more." I remember this promise from him as he walked away from me last fall in the airport, after we exchanged goodbyes and I told him I'd miss him. *I'll miss you more*, he'd said.

I give him a mock-stern look and flash my eyes to his. "I don't believe you. I think you should have to prove a statement like that."

His mouth turns up on one side as he stares down at me, that expression so familiar and beautiful it impedes my breath. "Oh?" he says, one eyebrow angling up.

My hands have been inching up his arms, which are tensed and tight around me still. He's not loosened his hold since he slid them around me. I take fistfuls of his sleeves on both sides and revel in the feel of his shoulders, broad and solid and so different from mine that I feel soft and small.

Pulling me closer, Graham lifts me onto my toes as his mouth crashes down on mine. The feel of his lips, insistent and giving no quarter, stuns me for a split-second, and then I'm matching his movements, opening my mouth, a restrained moan building in my throat as our tongues meet. My hands glide into his hair, the dark strands like ink spilling over my fingers as I urge him closer. "Emma," he breathes, wrapping one arm around my lower back, his fingers stroking over the skin at my waist as his opposite hand cradles my head, thrusting through the hair at my nape. His touch gentles then, kisses shifting to slow-motion, pulling me along like a subtle current, unhurried.

Without realizing I've even moved, I feel the mattress pressing into my calves, and he breaks his mouth from mine long enough to lift me onto it, rising over me in the center of the bed. "I just want to kiss you," he murmurs, his lips tracing a path from under my chin to my ear before he rolls onto his back and pulls me across him. My knee is between both of his, anchoring him to the bed as his hands run over my back and my shoulders before framing my face and pulling me down for a long, languid kiss.

Capturing his wrists, I mash them into the mattress, my hair falling over my shoulder and tickling along the side of his jaw. "That's all you want? Are you sure?" I ask, brazen in a way I've never been. Because this is Graham, and he's real and here and touching me—not a face on a screen, thousands of miles away.

He chuckles, his eyes closing as he turns his head and nuzzles my forearm, leaving soft kisses on my wrist, grazing my skin with his teeth and igniting an eruption of goose bumps straight up my arm. His eyes open and he stares at me, all heat. "No. I want everything from you, with you." He turns his hands until they imprison my wrists, curving over me until I'm under him again. "But right now, I'm just going to keep kissing you until you make me stop."

If he's waiting for an objection, he isn't going to get one. I lick my lips, a signal for *kiss me please*. And he does.

Chapter 9

Brooke

I scroll to *Reid* and hit *talk*. Just when I think he's letting it go to voicemail, he says, "Yeah."

"Time to bump up the interference," I say. "His flight landed a couple of hours ago, but he's not answering his phone."

There's a pause. Reid never looks at his phone before answering, and obviously, he's not yet reacquainted with my voice. A rather unreasonable hostility bubbles to the surface, though I suppose I should feel privileged—his skanks don't score his phone number at all. He learned *that* the hard way, I'm sure. Not that I can talk. I had to change my number half a dozen times before I finally comprehended that hot guys can turn as psycho as any girl. "Brooke?"

I puff out a sigh. "For chrissake, Reid, who do you *think* it is? And haven't you put me into your contacts yet?"

"Yeah... It just says *Satan*, though, and I forgot I'd assigned that title to you."

I would dearly love to choke the ever-lovin' life out of him. "That's very funny. You're hilarious. Can we move on from the juvenile name-calling?"

"Sure. But really, you should consider it a compliment to your level of evil."

"*Anyway.* I think we should check into the hotel. Recreate the atmosphere from Austin last fall."

He laughs once, condescension saturating his tone. "Because *that* worked out so well for each of us."

True, asshole. But beside the point. "We weren't working *together* then—*hello*."

He sighs into the phone. "I'd venture to say that at least on your end, we were doing the opposite of working together. I might even suggest that one of us was actively engaged in *sabotage* of the other."

I knew he could hold a grudge, justified or not, but hell's bells. "Okay, *fine*, I helped screw it up for you. But I couldn't have if you hadn't done most of it to yourself. You could have salvaged it."

"Says you."

I grip the phone tighter, bound by my own designs for reconnecting with him in the first place. If he doesn't go along with this scheme, it could prove impossible. Who am I kidding? It *will* prove impossible. "Reid, if you don't believe me on this, then you won't trust what I tell you to do to get her back and we might as well give up now. In which case I might just have to kill you."

"Harsh."

"Yeah, well." I don't hear any noise on his end, which strikes me as odd. "Where are you?"

"Driving. Going to pick up a couple of guys, do some clubs…"

"Do some girls, you mean."

He barks a laugh. "Hey, I consider tonight my bachelor party. You told me I have to be good once I'm luring Emma into my lair, right? This may be my last night to get laid for a while."

"Classy." I throw his assessment of me back at him.

"Well, you asked. So. You think we need to check into the hotel where everyone else is—even though we both live in LA. Proximity to the victims makes sense, I suppose."

Victims? "Shit, Reid. Talk about harsh. I don't just want to screw Graham, you know."

"I guess I *don't* know. Especially considering your MO."

For half a second, I consider hurling my phone at the wall. "*Look*, I've had it with the snide comments. I'm not any more of a slut than you are, so just *lay the hell off*." Dammit, there goes my stupid twang. I can be a cold bitch all day long and sound like the perfect LA native, but get me *actually* pissed and I go all Texan, which just pisses me off more. If he mentions it, I swear to God…

"Okay, okay. I'll stop. And Brooke?" His voice has turned husky, and the sound of it slams me right in the solar plexus. "That accent still gets me *hot*, damn you."

I take a deep breath and shake it off. I'm not playing that game with him. "Enjoy your last night of freedom, ha ha. I'll set up reservations for both of us at the hotel. Our story is that the studio wants us there with everyone else. No one will question it. Text me once you're in tomorrow morning and we'll review strategy. You remember morning, right? That brightish space of time between eight and noon when you're usually sleeping off a hangover?"

"I'm saluting, in case you're wondering."

I imagine clearly the exact gesture he's making. "Put your middle finger down, asshat, before someone thinks you're flipping them off and drives your ass off the road. I need you."

"No comment."

"None expected."

GRAHAM

It's been a long time since I've been this content. Not that I don't want more. Because *God*, I do. But I'm not desperate enough to forsake the need to hold her close, to feel her heart beat against me, to require nothing more than the exquisite fusing of our mouths and the stroke of our fingers over each other.

We lie entwined in the center of the bed, spent from a couple of hours of kissing that set fire to every emotion I've ever felt for this girl. I know she can tell that I've held myself in check a couple of times, physically—a small crease appears on her forehead, or she affects a marginal withdrawal of her own. I hope she knows there's no need for her worry. As much as I want her, I've been falling in love with her for months, and sleeping with someone you're in love with shifts everything to a more complex level. I can't go there alone. I have to know she's going with me.

As if sensing my heavy thoughts, she turns her face up from my shoulder and stares into my eyes, silent. My fingertips continue caressing her arm, up and over her shoulder, down her back, and I shamelessly examine the distinctive facets of her gray-green eyes, savoring the unguarded way she allows me to study her. My head tells me it's far too soon to tell her everything my heart wants me to blurt out. The last thing I want to do is scare her away. I'll take as long as she needs, be more patient than I've ever been, if it means she'll be mine in the end. I'm not afraid of my own feelings. I'm only afraid of misjudging hers.

The words lay on my tongue, unspoken. Waiting. My fingers have wandered up her back, rising and falling over each tiny arch of vertebrae until I reach her neck. Shifting, I lean over her and kiss her gently. My lips are sore and I know hers must be, too, though I've tried to use restraint. I smile now, knowing that any restraint I've employed didn't last long. I've practically devoured her for the past two hours. From the bedside table, our phones have beeped and buzzed a couple of times each, but neither of us made any move towards them.

"What are you smiling about?" she asks, her voice rasping between regular speech and a whisper, a tentative answering smile on her red, red mouth.

"I was thinking about how sore my lips are, and wondering if yours are, too."

She nods, her smile expanding. "I don't think I can feel them."

"Can you feel this?" I ask, leaning closer to run my tongue over her swollen lower lip, dipping inside her mouth when she opens with a sigh.

"Mmm-hmm," she says, raising her hand to my face and holding me just so, mirroring my effort. When her small tongue slips inside my mouth, I release a moan that sounds more like a growl and then I'm rattling off baseball statistics and diagramming sentences in my head. (I was so sure last semester's Advanced Structures of Modern English would never come to any practical use.)

"Maybe," my voice breaks and I clear my throat, "Maybe we should get dinner… or something."

She blinks, and I'm glad to see she's as affected as I am. "Room service and a movie?" She gestures to the television, reading my mind.

"Sounds perfect. I don't want to leave this room. Well, I mean, not until I have to. Um—"

"Would you... want to sleep here?" Her eyes fall, watching her own hand where it lays on my chest, rising and falling with every breath I take. My heartbeat accelerates with her words; she must feel it pounding under her palm. "We only have a couple of days, and I'll probably fall asleep if we're up late..."

She doesn't mention the biggest impediment—the fact that thanks to the ruse she and Reid are perpetrating, she and I can't be demonstrative in public. Her room—and mine—are like private islands. The only places we'll be safe to touch unguardedly.

"And you want me here when you wake up?" She nods, and I kiss her carefully. "I would love to stay with you tonight, Emma." Tipping her chin up, I look into her eyes. "And I'm not taking that as an invitation for anything other than sleeping next to you."

After dinner, I walk to my room to grab a toothbrush and clean stuff to wear tomorrow, checking my phone messages on the way. No calls from home, but one missed call and a text from Brooke. Basic Hi babe, are you here yet? stuff. Texting back that I'm all checked in, I tell her I'm going to bed early—using the three-hour time difference as an excuse for my exhaustion.

True to her word, Emma's out cold before the second movie is over. Cuddled up against my side, she sleeps on her stomach, a pillow flattened under her face and chest, one of her knees drawn up against my thigh and the other sprawled behind her. I grin and shake my head that such a small person can take up so much of a queen-sized bed. Her face angled towards me, her lashes lay across her creamy skin and her lips are parted slightly... and they actually do look a little puffy.

That thought has me contemplating noun phrases (Emma's lips) and verb phrases (are swollen) and prepositional phrases (from hours of kissing)... which does absolutely nothing to help me. When a groan escapes me, Emma moans softly in response, shifting without waking, her arm stealing across my abdomen. Oh, man. I am *never* getting to sleep. Still, I wouldn't trade the feeling of holding her like this for anything.

It's midnight in LA—3:00 a.m. New York time—and I'm staring at the swirling patterns on the ceiling, trying to concentrate on anything but my T-shirt loosely bunched in Emma's fist. A few minutes later, or half an hour, she stretches, pulling my shirt askew at the same time. When I glance down, she's awake, sort of. A drowsy, slowly-blinking stage of awake.

"Hi," she whispers.

"Hey," I whisper back. My arm has gone to sleep under her head, so I'm grateful when she moves to lay her face on my chest. "Checking for a heartbeat?" I ask, stretching my arms out, returning one to pull her closer and tucking the other behind my head so I can see her more clearly. Her eyes go to my bicep and I feel like an idiot boy, wanting to flex it and be impressive. She props herself on her forearms, chin on her hands, and stares at me.

"I can't believe how comfortable I feel," she says, a confused note in her confession. "How do you do that?"

I raise an eyebrow, equally confused. "How do I do what?"

She breathes out a sigh, her fingers scraping over the underside of my jaw. "Make me feel like... like I can trust you with everything. I haven't felt like that in so long, with anyone. I'm always afraid of being left. I always hold something back."

I shrug. "You're cautious. Maybe... losing your mother did that to you."

Her fingers still on my chin, she's quiet for a moment before saying, "Maybe so."

"Thank you for trusting me, Emma. I'll be worthy of it. I swear." In my ears, this seems a too-solemn promise, but somehow it seems necessary in this moment. She doesn't reply beyond another sigh.

Running my hands over her, I spread her hair across my chest, fingertips trailing the sides of her face, hands kneading her shoulders and folding over her like a blanket. I have no problem falling asleep this time, with her locked in my arms.

Chapter 10

REID

Damn Brooke and her hangover comments. I'd say she knows me well, but I'm no different than any other eighteen to twenty-five in LA, especially the celebrity subset. I suspect she's the same; she just likes being high-handed with me.

Her orders, texted to me last night: Check into the hotel by TEN. The cars are picking everyone up at 11:30. Look hot. Don't flirt. Be friendly and sweet. Make her think you've forgotten about her rejection.

Rejection. Way to twist the knife there, Brooke... almost as if she doesn't know she's doing it. Damn, she's good.

I check into the hotel at 11:15, after not bothering to answer her texts and calls all morning. She's got to get one thing straight—I'll follow her dictates to a point, but only to a point. I don't trust her enough to blindly obey everything she says, and I'm not stupid enough to ignore the fact that she'll hit her goal first. For Emma to fall into my arms, Graham has to fall into Brooke's. And I have no illusions about how much help Brooke will be to me once she gets what she wants. I'll be on my own.

After checking into my suite, I text Brooke: I'm here.

The lobby is one big Austin déjà vu, and after I step off the elevator, I stop to observe the interaction of my former costars before joining them. Tadd spots me first.

"Reid, you've *got* to come to Chicago and hang out." He walks

65

over and we exchange a fierce hug. "My new place is awesome—penthouse right on the river. Oprah is just down the street."

"I'm sure you'll be painting each other's toenails in no time, man," I laugh.

"So, what's up?" He tosses his straight pale blond hair out of his eyes, his clear blue eyes flicking to Emma and back.

"Not yet, dude. I'm getting there, though."

Both eyebrows rise now. "Interesting."

My eyes trace over Emma. She stands a foot from Graham—nothing outwardly betraying anything between them, though an alert observer would say the way they seem to avoid touch or eye contact is conspicuous. "The studio wants us to maintain an illusory thing until the film's released. I want less *illusory* and more *thing*."

"Hmm," he says. "A warning, then." Shoulder to shoulder, we stand watching everyone else. "There's a little, I don't know—chemistry? Going on between her and Graham."

No need to fake ignorance with Tadd—he's had my back too many times to count. He likes Emma, but I'm sure he'd come down on my side if it came to that. "Yeah, I've been made aware."

He smirks through the fringe of hair that falls right back down over one eye—a look that probably gets him whatever guy he wants, whenever he wants it. "By who?" he asks, and I glance in Brooke's direction. She's deliberately snubbing me, still pissed that I ignored her texted commands, I'm sure. "*Really.*" Tadd's eyes widen. "*More* interesting."

Emma

Remaining hands-off with Graham is more difficult than I expected. I'm drawn to him, as though there's some sort of gravitational attraction tethering us to each other. I want to press myself into his side. I want him to slide his arms around me like he did last night as we slept. I want to run my hands over him like I did an hour ago in my room, pushing his shirt up and counting his abdominal muscles out loud while he laughed, self-conscious and proud at the same time. *This belongs to me*, I thought, touching his hard stomach and biceps, kissing his mouth. *And this. And this.*

When I woke up in his arms this morning, I spent five minutes staring at his flawless, sleeping face. The world had tilted overnight, and everything had fallen into place. I slipped carefully from his grasp and tip-toed to the bathroom to brush my teeth, and when I came back and snuggled against him, he came slowly awake, kissed the top of my head and excused himself.

When he came back to bed and kissed me, his minty breath echoed mine. I giggled when he rolled me flat on my back and smiled. "Good morning," he said, mischief in his eyes.

"Do I snore? Or talk in my sleep? Or drool? Or something worse?" I asked.

He laughed. "Not that I know of. As far as I know, you're perfect."

Turning my head back and forth, I stared up at him. "No, I'm not."

Intertwining our fingers, he pushed my arms above my head, holding me prisoner. A bolt of pure liquid fire shot through me and pooled where our bodies pressed together. "Oh yes. You are," he said, kissing me.

By the time he left the room and I got into the shower, I had only half an hour to get ready. My hair is wavy and damp now because I didn't have time to dry it, let alone style it.

"Emma." Brooke snatches my attention back to the lobby and my costars. She arches a flawless brow as her eyes dart over my hair. "You could have borrowed my flat iron if you needed one. I owe you, as I recall."

As was her intent, I'm reminded of the night she borrowed my straightener in Austin, when Reid took me out to dinner and I thought I was falling for him. I glance over at him, and he smiles like he knows exactly what night I'm thinking about. Sliding his eyes away, he greets Meredith and MiShaun.

He must be over our breakup last fall, and our exchange in Austin just a few weeks ago—when he said *I could be different with you* and I refused to be that girl. This is the third time we've seen each other since then, and he doesn't seem at all resentful. He hasn't really flirted with me, either—not any more than he does with everyone. Maybe the coming month won't be so bad.

When I turn back to Brooke, she's staring at Graham as he

listens to Quinton relate some amusing story in his usual animated manner. Graham laughs, arms crossed loosely over his chest, and Brooke's eyes roam over him in a way that makes me want to stomp on her foot. She and Graham have been close for years. He says she's never been more than a friend, and there's no reason for me to distrust that. I can't tell Graham who to keep as friends; I wouldn't accept any guy doing that to me. Despite all of these reasons, I don't think I'll ever be relaxed around her. Not when she's looking at him like he's a steak and she's starving.

I clear my throat and her ice blue eyes snap to me. There's no guilt in them, but maybe she's just incapable of feeling any. I remind myself that she was sympathetic, even supportive, when everything blew up in my face with Reid. "How've you been, Brooke?" She's a couple of inches taller than me, plus she's wearing spiked heels—a true LA girl. Not for the first time, she reminds me of my stepmother.

Her smile is pretty and calculated, like a magazine cover. "Very well, actually. I've got a little rom-com thing lined up for the end of the summer, and my agent's gathered new scripts for me to look at after that's done. How about you?"

I'm sure she and I discussed the fact that I'm going to college in the fall, but people seldom remember personally unimportant things. Although, Reid remembered. "I decided on going to college. I'm starting this fall."

She laughs in that throaty way some girls do that attracts all male attention within hearing distance. "Oh that's right. Personally, I wouldn't want to back up and do college now... but I forget how young you are."

Graham hears this last bit, and his lips flatten just barely. What the hell does she mean by *how young you are*? She seems to be ridiculing my age in relation to her own—or Graham, but I don't know if he's even told her anything about us. As new as this all is, we haven't discussed who to tell or when. Emily and Dad know, of course—and Chloe by association. Graham's sister knows, and possibly the rest of his family...

They're both staring at me and I realize I zoned out. "Oh. I'm sorry—what?"

"Hmm, looks like someone didn't get much sleep last night..." Brooke's grin is full of comprehension, and my eyes flick to

Graham, who shakes his head almost imperceptibly. Whatever he's told her didn't include where he spent the night. *What exactly is she assuming I was doing? And with who?* My face burns as I scramble for something to say.

"Hey, baby," MiShaun says, touching my arm. I smile and turn to hug her, grateful for the interruption. "I hear you're going off to college in the fall?"

"Yes, I am. In New York."

"That's awesome! I expect to see you on Broadway in no time, headlining, dating some hot leading man, or maybe some sugar daddy Wall Street type." My glance bounces off Graham's. Judging by the semi-smirk of his lips, he's amused. When he catches me staring at his mouth, his eyes heat and I have to look away.

"So, MiShaun… are you still visiting Austin occasionally?" I ask with a conspiratorial smile, and she waggles her brows.

"I'm actually considering a permanent relocation there," she says, tapping her chin with the index finger of her left hand.

"Ohmigod, MiShaun! Is that an *engagement* ring?" Brooke grabs her hand and squeals as though she's just won a beauty pageant and the rhinestone-studded crown to go with it.

MiShaun's ring finger sports a near-flawless marquise-cut solitaire.

I know this because Chloe dragged me along to shop for a tenth anniversary gift Dad didn't know he was giving. After hours of babbling cut-color-clarity basics, she found the perfect diamond, and then pouted until he bought it. I borrowed *Blood Diamond* from Emily that weekend, but Chloe totally missed the insult. *What a depressing movie*, she commented, yawning as she left in the middle of it to take a bubble bath. *Nice try*, Dad smirked at me.

"This settles it—we're all going out after the shoot is over tomorrow night—we have to celebrate!" Brooke beams at her.

Graham and I glance at each other. Tomorrow night is our last night together until the premiere, and it appears we'll be spending the evening in a group, out in public. Crap.

Chapter 11

GRAHAM

The first shoot is in the studio—the layout: a stylized schoolroom. Everyone is made up, hair is runway-model-styled, and the clothes are exclusive labels—fitted to us with pins and clips. If people got a 360°-view of us, we'd all look a hell of a lot sillier.

Like the shoot in Austin, the majority of pics are Reid and Emma, separate or together. Emma's hair is teased and coiffed and I can tell by the set of her mouth and the way she holds her head that she hates it. Her eyes are darkly lined and shadowed, her lips filled in, and she looks closer to twenty-eight than eighteen. I know she hates this, too, though she looks beautiful. Not as beautiful as she did this morning when I woke up to her face snuggling against my chest, but beautiful in a different way—aggressively sexy. The photographer has her biting on the string of pearls around her neck, invoking the memory of her nipping my earlobe last night.

I've never in my life gone over so many sports statistics in my head so frequently. I didn't know I *knew* so many sports statistics.

Batting averages for Jose Reyes become unnecessary mental fodder a few minutes later, when Reid joins Emma and I'm trying to psyche myself for the positions in which they're about to be placed. They've put him in a navy pinstripe suit, crisp white shirt and loose red tie. Next to him, Emma's outfit is an elegant compliment—a very short, very tight, strapless red dress, which she hitches up at the bodice between shots until the photographer's assistant pins it tighter down her back.

Why do photographers insist on putting her in his lap? The guy from *Vanity Fair* had her wrapping her legs around him, though her posture screamed how uncomfortable she was doing it. Now, she perches on his thighs with his hands splayed at her waist, and then he leans her back like he's about to kiss her. My entire body is rigid with irritation. The audible photographer instructions would negate this if I wasn't imagining—if I didn't *know*—that they've done this before, in private. All illusions that I'm keeping these deliberations under control are shattered when Brooke leans closer, her brow knit, and whispers, "You okay?"

I nod, failing at pretending to be unconcerned as Reid pulls Emma up and turns her so that she's facing out from him, her legs straddling one of his. His arms are wrapped around her, his head on her bare shoulder, their faces jammed together as the photographer hops around, babbling words like *sexy* and *hot* and *baby*. Is this photo shoot for a PG-13 movie, or an ad for high-priced escort services?

Emma's eyes find me and her gaze immediately falls to my thigh, where Brooke's hand sits. She stares, puzzled, her brows furrowing until the photographer asks her in an annoyed whine why she's frowning and she wrenches her eyes from my leg.

I'm smoldering from my head to my toes, watching Reid's hands move over her body like they belong there, and she's annoyed that Brooke's hand sits passively on my leg.

I suppose one could argue that there's no photographer ordering the placement of Brooke's hand. Removing it to her own knee, I shoot up and walk to the back corner where bottles of water and snacks are located. Grabbing a bottle and twisting the cap from it, I wish I could just pour it over my head. It's not that I don't trust her. I don't trust *him*. And I don't trust his history with her.

"Hey," Brooke says, appearing next to me, one hand on my back, stroking down. I take a deep breath, her touch calming me. "What's the matter?"

I shake my head and laugh once, turning and looking down at her with a grim smile. "Nothing out of the ordinary. I just really hate photo shoots. The makeup. The crap in my hair. The clothes." I gesture to the black suit that screams either "church" or "funeral," depending on your mood. Anyone could guess mine right now—at least Brooke certainly can. I hope it's because she's known me for so long and not because I'm so ridiculously transparent.

She tilts her head to the side a bit, glancing back at Emma and Reid. I don't follow her gaze. I'm still just trying to *breathe* while Reid Alexander practically makes out with my girlfriend in the live version of photos millions of people will see. Many of those people already think they make an attractive couple. Against all better judgment, I glance towards them and get confirmation of this fact. They're both beautiful. Of course they look good together. How could they not?

"Is there... something going on between you and Emma?" Brooke asks, her LA-smile, as I call it, firmly in place.

"Why do you ask?" I hedge, and she does that low-laugh thing, still smiling up at me.

"I don't think I've ever seen jealous Graham before." She squeezes my bicep and arches a brow. "Mmm, very alpha-male."

When I scowl, she laughs at me again and I take a deep breath, feeling years less mature. "God, am I that obvious?" I start to run a hand through my hair, but can't. The styling for the shoot looks better than my *Bill Collins* helmet-do during filming, but it doesn't matter. Either way, it's untouchable. "Aauuugh," I say, and Brooke laughs again.

"So you and Emma, huh?" She selects a Perrier from the ice bucket and fingers through the snacks, choosing nothing. "How long has this been going on?"

I shake my head once. "Not long."

The photographer calls us for group shots, and I'm happy to end this conversation. Talking to Brooke has had a dual effect. I'm less tense, but instantly worried by the jealousy accusation. *Alpha-male?* Good God, no. Mom and Brynn would lecture me until my ears rang. Possessive men are at the top of their lists of to-be-scorned things. "A self-possessed man is what a psychologically healthy woman wants," preaches my mother, the psychologist. "Not some guy who dispenses orders and punishment—whether physical or emotional—and distrusts her every move."

She brought home enough codependent client stories, a few complete with stalking—two of which turned criminal—to scare my sisters away from those type of guys and scare me away from that type of girl. The type who wants—*needs*—the jealous boyfriend to prove she has worth. My eyes are on Emma as she talks and laughs with Jenna and MiShaun, and I know she's not in that category. Compromising and generous, yes. Forgiving, too, I think, watching as Reid moves near her and joins the conversation.

Her response to being held too tightly would be a quick exit.

Her eyes swing to meet mine, and everything in me snaps and sings with pleasure. A slow burn begins at my core and I know it will build until we're alone in her room again, the rest of the world shut out. There's a line at the edge of possessive, and she makes me want to walk it. This three-second glance between us reinforces what I know. I love her. Everything else—the ins and outs of my feelings and hers in conjunction with what it all means—can be deciphered in due time. I love her. That's all that matters, and in this moment, that's all I am.

Brooke

Well, shit. This is more serious than I thought. He may actually believe he's in love with her.

I've put far too many years into this relationship to lose him like this, to *her*. I care about Graham deeply, but if he pairs up with Emma, what we have will be over. For some reason, I know this. My intuition is screaming it at me—that I'm losing him. I could be what he wants. I could be sweeter and softer with him. Not so hard. God, I'm tired of being so uncompromisingly *hard* all the time.

If I backpedal and stop this now, linger forever off to the side as his friend and confidante, I could convince Emma that I'm not a threat. I could hold onto his friendship, which means more to me than he'll ever know.

But, no. Friendship isn't enough. I want him. *All* of him. He's exactly the type of guy I need, and all I have to do is get Emma out of the way and convince Graham that I can be what he needs. Somewhere between Reid and myself there's enough deviousness to pull this off. And if this has to be an all-or-nothing battle, then so be it. No time to be squeamish. I've lied my ass off for worse causes than landing the perfect guy.

Chapter 12

Emma

Getting out of that tiny dress and the five thousand pins they used to fit it to me like a glove took *forever*, so I'm the last one out of the studio. Three black cars idle at the curb, waiting to transport the nine of us to the hotel. Brooke climbs into the first car behind Tadd, and I'm both relieved and annoyed at myself for *being* relieved that Graham isn't with her.

Brooke is a force of nature. The last thing any sane girl would want is to get into a tug-of-war with her over a guy. Graham says they're just friends, and I have to trust him if this is going to work. No matter how beautiful she is. No matter how familiar her casual touches seem to be. No matter how many times I catch her looking at him like he's on her room service menu.

As I'm standing near the last car, scanning for Graham as covertly as possible, someone says, "*Pssst.*" I bite my lip to stifle a yelp when Graham snakes an arm around my waist and drags me into the car. MiShaun, chatting with Jenna a few feet away, raises an eyebrow as I disappear into the back seat, backwards. She bends to see who's snatched me off the sidewalk. When she spots Graham, her wide eyes tell me I can expect to be quizzed about this later.

"Graham," I hiss, laughing. "You just made me look like that hapless character in every horror film who's dumb enough to stand right next to the darkened basement doorway."

Grinning mischievously, he kisses the back of my neck, withdrawing his arm before anyone else sees. Thank God for opaque windows. "So you're the expendable cheerleader, and I'm the demon, or werewolf...?"

"Or the mentally unbalanced guy with the chainsaw, yeah." Aware that I'll have to sit up straight and keep my hands to myself once someone joins us, I press back against him for a moment, leaning my head onto his shoulder and tracing the top of his hand with my fingers.

"I was wondering if you'd want to check out Griffith Park in the morning." His question is a breath in my ear as Jenna moves to stand by the open door, still talking to MiShaun. He flips his hand over and my index finger maps the lines of his palm. "We'd have to go early to get back in time to leave for the second shoot."

I nod. "I've been to Griffith, but not for years. My family used to go hiking there."

My memories of hiking in Griffith have been augmented with photos my parents took there when I was very young. Some are from weeks—days perhaps—before Mom began to get sick. To be honest, I'm not sure if my memories of Griffith Park—or my mother—are genuine. Almost every clear recollection I have of her was caught on film. Perhaps the real memories faded away long ago, supplanted by the unchanging photographs.

"If you climb high enough, you can see all of Hollywood," I say. "And the sign."

My childhood scrapbook contains a series of photos Mom took of me near my birthday every year, standing in the same exact spot on some unspecified trail of Griffith. In each of these, the Hollywood sign is stark white against the hill in the background, my own personal growth chart. In the last one, I'd turned six. Her quick downward spiral didn't allow her to return, and Dad either forgot the tradition or didn't have the heart to keep it up.

"That's what I read—sounds cool. I'll rent a car and have it brought around at, say, 5:30? We can pack coffee thermoses and catch the sunrise." He takes my hand in his, fingers stroking the back of my arm. His eyes catch and hold mine. "Unless it would be too painful for you to go there."

I shake my head, twisting my mother's ring around and around on my finger. "No. I'd like to go with you."

When Jenna starts to get in, I straighten from leaning against Graham, my hands folding primly in my lap. I feel more than hear him chuckle at my suddenly proper posture. Just before Jenna sits down, I hear Reid's voice. "Hey, Jenna—Brooke wants you to ride with her. Wanna switch?"

"Oh. Okay, sure."

I'm wondering at the oddity of Reid delivering a message for Brooke as he slides in next to me. Graham's thigh tenses against mine.

"Hey," Reid says, sticking a hand out to Graham. "How're you doing, man?"

"Good," Graham answers, reaching over. I sit for two surreal seconds with their hands clasped just above my lap, tension radiating from them both, though neither one's expression betrays it.

Swinging his hair from his eyes, Reid glances at me and winks before returning his attention to Graham. His knee presses against mine as he leans forward. "Got any new projects lined up?"

My face warms as Graham's fist clenches and unclenches once before settling on his leg. "Not right now. I'm finishing up my last semester at Columbia. You?"

"Nothing 'til fall—just trying to get into decent shape before then. I'm supposed to do some of my own stunts in the next flick. Hopefully the ones that won't kill me." One side of his mouth turns up and he glances at me again.

"Cool," Graham says.

Reid clears his throat, looks back at Graham. "So—theatre degree?"

"English Lit."

"Ah."

Having reached the end of conversable topics, Reid sits back and they both fall silent while I sit mutely between them, contemplating how the hell I got myself into this incredibly awkward position.

When we reach the hotel, Reid slips out, turning and offering his hand. Without thinking, I take it. Pulling me alongside him, he places his opposite palm at my lower back as he smiles for the paparazzi gathered around the entrance while our bodyguards ensure that we get to the door unmolested. I have no chance to look back for Graham until we reach the lobby, at which point Reid drops his hand from my back. "We're all meeting in my room in a little while—you're coming, right?"

Before I reply, he turns and looks past Graham, whose eyes connect with mine. Our hours to be alone are dwindling down. Brooke walks up behind Graham, her hand coming to rest on his arm, arguably unintentional, if she didn't do it so habitually. "Hey," she says.

"Brooke, you told Emma and Graham about tonight, right?" Reid asks, no trace of the hostility—let alone the desire to maim each other permanently—that usually colors every word they say to each other.

Graham appears as astonished as I am at this friendly exchange, especially when Brooke replies, "Oh, shit, I forgot," without biting Reid's head off first. Linking her arm with Graham's, she smiles up at him, her perfect faux-tan and red-nailed talons standing out against his paler skin. "Mixer in Reid's room! *You* have to come." She turns her toothpaste-ad smile on me, saying, "Oh, and you too, Emma," like an afterthought.

The desire to stomp on her foot returns, a hundred times stronger than it was this morning. Worse, her calculating smile says she's more than aware of it.

REID

Watching Brooke and Emma face off is possibly the most involuntarily hot thing I've ever witnessed. They're subtle, and perfectly civil to each other, while under the surface lurks a biting, kicking, hair-pulling, bitch-slapping violence. The only thing that would have made it better—much better, in fact—is if *I* was the inspiration for those vicious feelings. But no. It's all for Graham.

I sort of get it. I mean, he's good-looking. And he's got that mysterious element about him that chicks are drawn to. I know his protectiveness is attractive to Brooke. When she and I were together and I got the slightest bit possessive of her—which, granted, has never come naturally for me—she loved it. In fact, the more jealous I was, the more controlling I acted, the more she liked it. Kind of freaked me out a little, actually.

"You're flirting with her too much in front of Graham." Brooke walks through my door a quarter hour early, issuing unrequested critiques of my progress. "If you make him jealous before anything happens between Graham and me, you'll *never* get her away from him."

I smirk. "Thanks for the vote of confidence. And that's not what happened *last* time."

She turns, arms crossed under her breasts and wearing her patented I-know-better-than-you expression, stopping when her eyes flick over my bare chest. I haven't yet buttoned the shirt I threw on after my shower. Clearing her throat and averting her eyes to anything in the room but me, she retorts, "Last time, he was fighting falling for her. Now he's not. The only way he'll give her up is if she falls into bed with *you*. And since you were a big *fail* on that last fall—before she even knew what a man-whore you are, I think we can safely assume *that* isn't going to happen easily."

I take a slow breath. No way am I letting her know how much I want to test the challenge she just threw down, just because she tossed it at me. She's probably correct, though—neither of them is going to cave easily. "Shit, Brooke, if you think it's so impossible, why bother?"

She glares at me. "I told you. I want him. I'm *right* for him, and it's not impossible. It's just going to take shrewd planning and careful execution, and I don't want you screwing it up."

The combination of a hot ex-lover alone in my room and the cleavage-flaunting way her arms are crossed is killing me. With effort, I cut my eyes away from her heaving chest and deceptively flawless face and pour a shot of whatever the hell is sitting on my dresser.

"How much attention have you been paying to following your own orders, Brooke? Emma has *definitely* noticed the fact that you can't keep your hands off him. As far as condemning your ingenious plan before it gets off the ground, that will do it. If she feels threatened and talks to him about his relationship with you, this whole little plot could be toast."

I watch her face in the mirror over the dresser. A crease appears between her brows, her self-confidence slipping faintly. "How do you know? That she's noticed anything, I mean."

What I wonder is how Brooke *hasn't* noticed. I thought girls were better tuned to each other than that. "I was standing right next to her, and I'm observant." She makes a noise of derision I choose to ignore. "She's *noticing*. So cool it yourself, or you may have to give *my* bed a try if you want to get laid." If the objects of our affections weren't showing up in five minutes, I would give that proposition a more enthusiastic effort.

"Another offer to sleep with you? How sweet. I'm flattered. Have you forgotten what I told you last time?" It's almost impossible to associate this Brooke with the girl she was when I met her. Almost.

"I remember." I saunter closer, but she doesn't budge. She's always been tall and thin—willowy, George would say. When I was fourteen and she was fifteen, we were almost eye to eye up close. I've got several inches on her now. With her arms locked under her breasts, the view from my vantage point is greatly improved. "I also remember what we were like together, even if we were just inexperienced kids." I shrug. "Well, *one* of us was inexperienced."

She's silent, but her eyes are furious. Every time we start to get into it, I want her to feel what I felt when I saw the photos and read the story that ended us. But that's not possible. She has no heart, and she managed to stomp the shit out of mine years ago. I'm playing games with a viper and I damn well know it. I should feel sorry for Graham, but I don't really know him, he's got a girl I want, and I'm in the mood to be petty.

"Look. We've got time before the premiere. She and I have an interview schedule from hell, but that means we'll be around each other, a *lot*, without Graham's interference. I suggest you work on him from the same angle. He can't hang around LA—he's got school. Isn't he graduating or something? Why don't you show up in New York for that. Hang around after."

She nods, her poker face firmly in place. "I'd already considered doing that."

"Good. Let's do it, then. Divide and conquer."

She's so outwardly cool, but her breaths are too shallow. "I still say don't push her until I get to Graham. She'll turn you down on principle."

"Gotcha." We're six inches apart, and still she isn't backing away.

"I'm serious, Reid." She puts one hand up, to stop me, I suppose, but her hand is on bare skin and her eyes widen and I know we both feel the surge.

"So am I."

She stares up at me like I'm some sort of twisted riddle, and then a knock sounds on the door and she jumps, muttering, "Jesus," under her breath.

I button the shirt as I walk to the door. There's something gratifying about making an ex want you, even for a second.

Chapter 13

GRAHAM

I didn't sleep in Emma's room last night.

There were no let's-get-hammered games in Reid's room since we have the final photo shoot today, but Brooke had no trouble convincing Tadd to man the bar and shake up margaritas. Even though straight-up shots were out, everyone had enough tequila to tamp down inhibitions and loosen tongues. And Emma and I had just enough to be hazardous.

I took one look at her half-mast eyes and knew I'd fail any test of having her in bed with nothing but boxers and T-shirts between us. Worse? I *wanted* to fail it, and we'd spent the whole evening not touching.

My sexual history began with Zoe, followed by a self-imposed dry spell waiting for Cara to be born, and Zoe to come back around—which didn't happen. Next up, a sampling of indiscriminate college hookups. Nothing has been ultimately satisfying, and while I was capable of feeling turned on and wanting a physical connection, I never felt anything more intense. Nothing deeper, nothing emotionally linked. Not until Emma. By the time I left her standing in that airport last October, I wanted so much with her that it scared the hell out of me. I hoped it would fade with time, and after the *VF* photo shoot in March, I felt confident I was getting over it.

And then there she was, a month later—standing in that damned coffee shop, our eyes locked over Cara's head. My daughter had demanded hot chocolate after her dance rehearsal, shoving her cold little fingers under my sweater to prove her need for it. If we'd not stopped exactly there, exactly then, Emma and I would have never crossed paths when I didn't have my guard up. I'm not sure if I believe in fate, but this could be evidence of it.

They call it *falling in love* because it's less like stepping and more like tripping. Tripping is the part where you're still trying to remain upright. I hadn't fought it with Zoe. I just fell right in, head first. With Emma, I fought it all the way down, and now, I've lost.

Emma: Are you sleeping here?
Me: Not a good idea tonight

She didn't answer for several minutes, during which I called myself all sorts of idiot, because that was an open invitation, as was the progressively unreserved look in her eyes all evening. I only wanted to be sure of her feelings, not make her wonder about mine.

Me: This has nothing and everything to do with how much i want you. If i was in your bed tonight...after the alcohol...i want you. Trust me.
Emma: I kind of feel like a hussy now
Me: NO, that isn't what i mean. It's me. It would be too difficult. Tomorrow night, no drinking, and i can be good.
Emma: Well dammit you should have told me this before margaritas. I would have practiced my just say no. To alcohol that is. :(
Me: God how do you make me laugh through this. Hussy, indeed. I'm one nudge from coming to your room and ravishing you to hell.
Emma: I want you to
Me: OMG emma...
Emma: I'm sorry

Two rings. Three rings. *Please don't go to voicemail* was running through my head. She answered talking. "Graham, I'm sorry, really, I—"

"*No*, please don't be sorry. That's why I'm calling you." I lie back on my bed, eyes closed. The alcohol buzz was diminishing, but not gone. "Don't be sorry, Emma." My voice was almost a whisper. "Do you remember those things I said I wanted to do to you?" A few of our calls and Skype conversations over the past couple of weeks had reduced both of us to mush.

Her reply was an exhalation of a pant. "Yes."

"None of that has changed. Increased, maybe. Some of those things are looking quite tame, in fact."

"Oh, God. I'm not even sure what that—what that means…"

I pictured her lying back on her bed exactly as I was on mine. "Yes. I *know*. Which is why we're waiting a bit."

"But you're going back to New York."

Her sulky tone made me chuckle. "Yes. And I'm coming back to LA in three weeks."

Her sigh was faint. Not relieved, or exasperated. Just… accepting. "Okay," she said, sounding so much like Cara when she doesn't get her way and she knows she isn't going to.

"I just don't want to take advantage of you, or push you—"

Lies, lies, lies—I wanted her so bad I could conjure up her scent, imagine the feel of her skin under my fingertips...

"But Graham, I'm pushing *you*."

"Yes." My voice is like a growl—so appropriate to the feral hunger coursing through my body. "And in three weeks, I'm going to let you. If you still want to."

"I will."

At 5:30 a.m., we meet in the lobby—which is deserted except for a bored desk clerk who gives us a disinterested once-over. Flashback to our mornings in Austin, up before everyone and heading out to run. I remember stepping out of the elevator and seeing her waiting in the lobby, or getting there first and waiting for her, looking up at the soft chime, stainless steel doors swooshing open and delivering her to the ground floor. I loved those mornings.

I hand her a thermos when she comes to stand next to me, fighting the urge to slip my arms around her and kiss her. "Ready?" I ask, and she nods. Tossing the backpack onto one shoulder, I take her hand. This is a risk, if only to cross the lobby. I don't want her mortified over stories of multiple hookups like she was in Austin, so we have to remain a secret until after the premiere. I get that, but it still sucks. "I packed water, bagels and a blanket. I figured this morning was more about watching the sunrise and less about exercise."

Her hand squeezes mine. "Sounds perfect."

The Jeep is ideal for the early morning drive and the cool weather but not conducive to quiet conversation. We have to yell over the road noise to hear each other. Falling silent after a few minutes, we just hold hands and watch the street lamps start to pop off as the sky begins to lighten. I spent an hour on the Internet last night, making sure of the route to Griffith and the trail to take once we get there. The sun is already a half-orb above the horizon by the time we get to the spot I mapped out and spread the blanket.

Pressed together, we sip the coffee and watch what's left of the sunrise. Perhaps I should say *she* watches it while I watch her. I've seldom been this close to her and allowed myself the pleasure of staring, of drinking her in—all the seemingly trivial details. The indistinct image of a webcam never revealed the fine blondish hairs at her temple, and the darkness of her bed hides the freckle behind her ear and the blush across her cheeks when she realizes I'm examining her.

Leaning to her, I tell her softly, "You're so beautiful."

Her lashes lift as she glances into my eyes before closing hers. "No, *you* are."

My mouth pulls up on one side. We're a little off the beaten path, but not so far that we can't hear people walking by, talking. "God," one of them says, stopping just out of sight where there's a perfect view of the sunrise. "So beautiful!"

Emma and I suppress our laughter, attempting to avoid detection. I kiss her softly. "See, he agrees with me," I whisper.

She leans up, her hand on my jaw. "Maybe he agrees with *me*." When she starts to giggle, I cover her mouth with mine, partly to silence her but mostly because I can't escape the need to kiss her again.

REID

It hadn't occurred to me what a huge advantage this photo shoot is for getting Emma used to me touching her again. Not that she's particularly responding to it. I mourn the loss of that wistful, spellbound look she had back when we first began filming *School Pride* last August, but then again the fact that she's less affected by me makes up for it.

Yes, I'm one of those guys—more turned on by what I can't have than anything else. When you think about it, though, how surprising is that? When getting girls is as simple as deciding that you want one—no different, really, from deciding what to have for lunch—of *course* the ones who stand out will be the ones who don't come when called. Emma is like that pizza I can only get in one hole-in-the-wall place in the middle of Brooklyn, and nowhere else. If I lived in Brooklyn, maybe it'd be no big deal. But I live in LA, and goddamn do I hate it when I think about that pizza I can't *have*.

We're on some estate in the LA hills, but the backdrop is very middle of nowhere. The grounds are rustic and native, but carefully cultivated to look that way rather than just left wild. My parents would probably hate it. Our lawn looks more like it belongs in the English countryside—bordering hedgerows and shaped shrubberies and roses, etcetera. It's impressive but sort of laughable and out of sync at the same time.

Emma is perched on the wooden-slat seat of a swing attached to a high limb of a stories-tall tree. Staring straight up through the branches, I wonder how they got the ropes attached that high—if someone climbed this tree like they might have done a hundred years ago, or if they brought in a truck with a ladder or one of those bucket things like the guys who work on telephone lines use. While the photographer reframes the shot for what feels like the hundredth time and we wait for instructions, I grip the ropes just over Emma's hands, my pinkies grazing her index fingers.

"If we don't get a lunch break soon, I'm going to start nibbling on *you*," I murmur, careful not to lean too close. "I'm freaking *starving*." Emma's stomach growls just then, which makes both of us laugh. The photographer's head snaps up and he starts taking shots. Damn if I'm not thinking about that pizza now. And then Emma telling me *yes* in my room that afternoon last fall, hours before everything went to hell.

"Reid, go ahead and give her a gentle push." I pull the swing back and let her go, and she swings out and right back to me.

I've never tried to win a girl over by feigning friendship-only intentions, mostly because it seems counter-intuitive. Brooke's plan isn't infallible, but if she succeeds in getting Graham in her bed, Emma *will* be distraught. And I'll be right there to assure her she's desirable and provide emotional support—the sort of support everyone needs after discovering infidelity. She was attracted to me before. There's no reason those feelings can't be revived, with Graham out of the way. All I have to do is be patient.

Not exactly my forte.

Chapter 14

Brooke

"Okay people!" Elevating my voice above the music and general bar noise, I clank a spoon against my daiquiri glass until everyone looks my way. "We're here to celebrate—or mourn, depending on your interpretation of the event—the fact that our friend MiShaun has decided to take this smokin' hot body—" I pull her up from her chair and pirouette her in a circle "—and give it to *one guy* for the rest of eternity."

"*Booooo,*" Tadd says, hands cupped around his mouth, and everyone laughs.

"Tadd Wyler, what the hell do you care what I do with my body?" MiShaun asks him.

"I'm objecting on general principle," he answers. Standing, he takes her hands and holds them out to her sides, scanning her curves in the tight little black dress she's wearing. "Plus, it seems a shame to deprive the straight end of the male population of this sort of perfection."

MiShaun shoves him back into his seat with a laugh. "The male population has mostly *been* deprived of it on *personal* principle." Smoothing her hands down her hips and cocking one eyebrow at him, she adds, "This body is more discriminating than some *others* seated around this table."

"Hey now," Tadd says. "There's no need to talk about Quinton that way."

Details of Quinton's on-again, off-again relationship with his childhood sweetheart, along with allegations of a few casual hookups around LA, have been plaguing him for the past month. Apparently, Mr. Hottest Up-and-Coming Star played the field too close to a designated "*on*" period, and his girlfriend—who's close friends with his *sister*—caught wind of it and went on a tell-all rampage. *Boys.* They never learn.

"Dude!" Quinton says, shaking his head. "*Low.*"

"*Anyway,*" I say, rolling my eyes and raising my glass. "To MiShaun. May she be happy with her computer guy, and may he be freaky in hot and stimulating ways."

MiShaun hides her face behind her hands as everyone clinks glasses.

One of the bodyguards walks up behind Reid and leans over to speak to him in a low voice, pointing to a couple of girls—women, actually—standing off to the side. They're early twenties and hot. Not good, and no way for me to telepathically threaten him because he's *pointedly* refusing to look in my direction. As he slides from his chair and strolls over to his drooling fans, I try not to watch too closely because I don't want to call Emma's attention to him.

Too late—dammit, she's already watching him. He's smiling that easy, sexy smile, and the women are all stupid-melty at the sight of him so close, in the flesh. One of them asks to squeeze his bicep—hello, *creepy*—and when he consents, flexing, they both coo over him. *Ugh.* Directing the bodyguard to take their phones, he poses with each of them separately and together, their arms wrapped around his torso like seaweed. And then, still grinning, he shakes hands with each of them before turning and walking back to the table.

I have to admit, I'm astonished. He didn't pull out his phone, or jot a number on a napkin, or confer with the bodyguard to escort them back to the hotel to await his pleasure. *Nothing.*

Emma's head leans at the slightest angle, observing him. Glancing her way as he pulls his chair out, Reid smiles at her. When Meredith asks her a question and she turns to answer, he turns those stormy blue eyes on me, one eyebrow rising in a quick non-verbal *See?*

I incline my head. *Well done.* Smug son of a bitch. I signal the waiter for another round of daiquiris for MiShaun and me, and scan everyone from my vantage point at the head of the table.

Reid sits at the opposite end, now chatting with Quinton and knocking back another Jack and Coke. Jenna sits next to Quinton, and then Graham, next to me. MiShaun is on my right, then Tadd, Emma and Meredith. My eyes shift back to Emma, who's having a silent exchange with Graham as she sips her drink. I thought she'd ordered a Long Island iced tea, but from the looks of it, it appears she's drinking an *actual* iced tea. And Graham is either drinking straight-up vodka on the rocks or *water.* What the hell?

"Some reason you're going teetotaler tonight, Graham?" I smile, chin in hand. "Not planning on driving anywhere, I assume?"

His glance towards Emma and back is rapid, but not rapid enough for me to miss it. "Mmm, no, just not in the mood. I have an early flight tomorrow morning. Nothing worse than flying hungover."

He says this as though he's ever in his life flown hungover, which I doubt. I've seen Graham under the influence, but never smashed. This is just another of his always-in-control qualities— one that used to bother me, when I was in my phase of going hard and getting as trashed as humanly possible. I wanted him to join in. I didn't see then that getting liquored up and trying to seduce him was never going to work. Graham doesn't do drunken hookups.

Ding.

Oh shit. Are he and Emma hooking up tonight? Is that what this is about? Is this the first time, or a repeat? This could affect my best laid plans—so to speak. I can't imagine how to discover the answer to that question, though. Damn, damn, *damn.*

I fight to keep my voice even while my brain is going a hundred miles per hour. "So you're going back home tomorrow, then. Did you miss class this week?"

He rests his chin in his hand, too. "Yeah, but two independent study, and the other two gave me a pass because I completed research papers early. So it's all good."

We're in this mirrored pose, a foot apart, over the corner of the table. I ask him about his final classes, as though I'm interested in the specifics of them—and perhaps I would be, if I knew enough about literature to know what the hell he's talking about. I'm listening just closely enough to reply and form questions while I'm cataloguing details I haven't had the chance to savor in a while.

I've said that Graham is the best-looking guy in the cast—a towering claim considering the fact that Reid, Quinton and Tadd are no fugly ducklings and are constantly publicized as Hollywood's hottest young celebs. Quinton is solid, cut musculature while Tadd embodies the buff surfer look, and Reid is so beautiful that sometimes *I'm* jealous of the perfection of his face.

But Graham is all dark, smoldering male. In the hazy, subdued light of the bar and against his lighter-toned skin, his dark chocolate hair and smoky eyes are almost black. He's wearing his usual expression—cool and easygoing, but shuttered. My God, he's hot, and though he must have some idea of this, he rarely exhibits that cocky veneer that comes second nature to Reid.

He's rattling off something about Dostoyevsky and existentialism when suddenly he stops mid-sentence and runs a hand through his hair. One lock of hair sticks straight up in front. "Sorry. That can't possibly be as fascinating to you as your acting skills indicate." His smile is self-deprecating, lashes sweeping down as he sighs. "You should stop me before I get that far."

"Hey," I say, "just because I can't even *say* Dosty-Dosto—"

"Dostoyevsky."

"Right, *Dostoyevsky*, doesn't mean I don't find something you're that enthusiastic about interesting." That adorable cowlick is begging me to reach out and blend it in with the rest of his hair, but I recall what Reid had to say about my casual touches in front of Emma and I keep my hands to myself with immense effort. Having raised the thought of her in my head, I have to fight the urge to check if she's even watching.

Graham clears his throat and glances down the table at her. I'm crossing my fingers that he at *least* forgot all about her for the space of that little literary exchange, even if he's recalling her existence now. When he smiles and winks at her, I want to emit a sharp little scream and stomp like I used to do as a small child whenever someone told me *no*. His eyes swing back to mine and I swallow that outburst and smile instead.

Emma

Graham is leaving California in the morning. I'm enjoying interacting with everyone, celebrating MiShaun's engagement to David, but I'm hyper aware of the hours and minutes ticking away. His wink is a tiny electrical zap, darting a zing of pleasure through me.

He's sitting at the other end of the table, with Brooke hanging on his every word, and I'm trying not to be jealous—or concerned.

That attempt isn't going so well.

I tell myself that I'm only jealous of the time I'm losing with him, which rings half-true and half-hollow.

"Emma, I hear you and Reid are doing *Ellen?*" Meredith snaps me out of my gloomy trance.

"Yeah, in a couple of weeks. I'm scared to death."

"No need to be scared," Reid says, swinging his attention to our conversation. "She's just as nice in person as she seems."

"You said that about Ryan," I accuse, smirking. "Are you going to tell me that every time?"

"I was right, wasn't I? And no, if someone's going to be tough, I'll give you a heads up."

"Promise?"

He hooks my pinky with his. "Promise. And for the record, I've never broken a pinky swear."

"And how many pinky swears have you made, Mr. Alexander?" Meredith asks, arms folded loosely over her chest as she leans back to watch our discussion play out in front of her.

"Meredith," he says, "that's classified information. Top secret. Plus I tried the Boy Scout promise on her months ago, and she promptly accused me of never having been a Boy Scout. Imagine." He blinks innocently and we can't help but laugh. This far away from the humiliation of last fall, his wicked reputation feels less personal.

Lips flattened, Meredith says, "Yes, *imagine*. I'm thinking this is *numero uno* pinky swear for you, buddy."

Our fingers are still hooked on the table in front of Meredith, who angles one eyebrow in question before I withdraw my hand

and give Reid a stern look. "Okay, I'm choosing to believe you *and* your pinky swear. Don't blow that trust."

He looks back, steadily, suddenly more serious than he was seconds ago. "I won't."

It takes forever for the hallway in front of my door to clear. Graham's room is on the same floor, but two turns and a couple dozen rooms away from mine. I text him when everything grows quiet and I haven't seen a soul pass my peephole in five minutes. It's nearly 2 a.m.

When he walks up to the door, I swing it open silently, and try to close it just as quietly. He's wearing jeans and canvas flip flops and holding the ice bucket from his room. "This is your idea of subterfuge?" I whisper, pointing at the bucket and trying not to laugh.

He pretends offense. "The vending area *is* between our rooms, so I thought it made more sense than pretending to be lurking in the hall for no apparent reason."

I take the bucket from his hands. "It's still empty."

He rolls his eyes. "Well, duh, I wasn't going to waste time getting actual *ice*." I've left one small lamp glowing in the corner, and his black eyes regard me in the dim light. While waiting for the hallway to clear, I changed into a dark violet shorts and tank set from Victoria's Secret that Emily gave me before I left town. *Purple is the I'm-a-woman version of pink*, she cautioned, fixing me with a knowing look. Graham's slow perusal is like a caress, leaving me breathless and feeling somehow powerful and vulnerable at once. He raises one eyebrow. "Unless we need it for something kinky."

My blush is immediate, and I turn to put the ice bucket on my sink counter in an effort to hide it, in case the low lighting isn't low enough. His arms slide around me from behind, his cheek nuzzling and stroking my hair back from my neck. His lips are warm and I'm glad he's supporting me, because my legs feel boneless as he places light, sucking kisses from the curve between my shoulder and neck to the sensitive hollow behind my ear.

"If I traced an ice cube along this line," he murmurs, "it would melt instantly, because your skin is so hot." I gasp lightly, imagining his tongue following a line of icy water sluicing down my neck. Turning me gently, his hands are in my hair and then his mouth is on mine, so gentle and slow that kissing him feels like a dream. I don't want to wake up.

A minute later, I find my calves hitting the edge of the mattress as they did two nights ago. I scarcely have the capacity to register the question of how he manages to transport me all the way across a room without my notice before he lifts me into the center of the bed, still kissing me.

Rolling to his back, Graham's strong hands pull me halfway over his body, one palm on my thigh and the other cradling my head. His jeans are rough against my bare legs, but he's kicked off his shoes somewhere between the door and the bed. My knee falls between his legs as he angles up, never breaking his mouth from mine for more than half a second. His hand runs along my back from shoulder to waist, lightly over my hip and down the leg that presses between his.

His heart hammers beneath my hand, matching the tempo of my own, and I'm not content to lie here and let him find his equilibrium. When I lift my hand from his chest and slide it under his shirt, he makes a noise between his teeth—*tsss*—like I've burned him. "*God*, Emma." His hand covers mine with the T-shirt between us. I spread my fingers over his abdomen and his breath catches.

At first, he doesn't loosen his hold, stilling my hand with his. Distracting him with kisses, I wait until his grip goes slack, and when it does I set my fingers to roam slowly over his sleek skin and hard muscle, moving under his shirt soundlessly. He holds himself very still, but when my fingers glide lower to the waistband of his jeans, his eyes flash open and stare into mine, his hand clasping mine again.

"You can't sleep in your jeans," I say, repressing the urge to giggle at this deceptively rational argument for why he should remove his pants in my bed.

"I probably should." We're both whispering, as though everyone in the hotel will be able to hear us if our voices rise to regular levels.

"Graham, I'm not going to take advantage of you. I promise." I hold up two fingers, Reid's silly months-ago vow still front-and-center from our conversation earlier tonight. "Scout's honor."

"Oh my God," he says, laughing softly. He caresses my face, his thumb moving over my lower lip as his expression transforms from amusement to want. "I can't promise the same thing. And that's why." My eyes slide from his and he takes an unsteady breath. "Besides, I didn't bring anything with me tonight—as in, ah, protection."

He didn't bring condoms, which means he wasn't just *assuming* we weren't going to, he was actively *planning* that we weren't going to. I bite my lip. "So you don't want...?"

"I want. Hell *yes*, I want. Three weeks, remember? I need to, um, get tested when I get home, too." When my eyes widen, he adds, "I'm sure everything is fine, because I've *always* been careful." His mouth twists. "Well, ever since Cara I've been careful. I was a whole lot of stupid before that, because you always believe that stuff is never going to happen to you, until it does."

I find myself wondering how many girls there've been. And then I wonder if Brooke was ever one of them, even if it didn't result in a relationship, even if it was casual. I want to ask, but the questions are stuck in my throat and won't get near the surface. I shouldn't be surprised—he's much too good at this to have been celibate since his daughter was born. He hasn't asked me about my sexual history at all, and I wonder if he doesn't care, or if my inexperience is just that freaking obvious.

"Hey." He takes my chin between his fingertips, obliging me to look at him. "I just... I need both of us to be sure." His finger traces the frown line on my forehead. "Please don't worry whether this has anything to do with wanting you. It doesn't."

I don't ask about the multitude of girls I imagined parading through his bed. I don't ask about Brooke. I just sigh and curl up against his chest, though I don't remove my hand from under his shirt. Gained ground is gained ground. "Okay." I feel distinctly pouty.

Laughing quietly, his arms encircle me. "Hmm. I'm not ready to stop kissing you, you know," he says.

"I didn't know," I mumble into his shirt.

"Well, now you do."

I lean my head back on his arm, my eyes meeting his. "So many warnings, so little action..." I sigh.

He growls and flips me onto my back, and we don't fall asleep until close to 4 a.m. In the end his jeans are in a heap on the floor and my tank is decidedly askew and he's taken at least three very serious breaks. Inexperience or not, I'm reasonably certain this adds up in my favor.

Chapter 15

GRAHAM

I was convinced Emma would cause me to internally combust last night.

It's a lucky thing my sense of responsibility is so unswerving, because at some point between arriving in her room and falling asleep, I no longer cared whether or not she loved me—the desire was so powerful and overwhelming that my sense of emotional self-preservation was prepared to toss itself out the window and to hell with it. I must have suspected that weakness skulking below the surface, which was why I left my wallet (and the condom inside it) in my room when I went to hers. I know myself that well, at least—using protection is second nature. Not once since Zoe have I had unprotected sex.

I promised Emma three weeks, and I'll willingly keep that promise, as worried as I might be that she doesn't feel as strongly as I do. I suppose love is never a sure thing, no matter what words are spoken. Love requires a leap of faith into the abyss, every time.

I scribble a sappy note to leave on her nightstand. My sisters call me an old-fashioned boy. Perhaps this is the result of too much close-reading and analyzing of eighteenth century literature. Even still, there are romantic, old-school sides of myself I've never fully unleashed, and for some reason Emma brings every one of them to the surface.

Zoe didn't care to be courted. When I left notes in her locker or under her windshield wiper, she asked if she had to respond in kind, and also why couldn't I just text her like a normal person? And though she appreciated having an armful of carnations delivered from the Choir Cupid on Valentine's Day, she paid little attention to the attached poem that took me a week to write.

Relatively sure that I was past such unmanly silliness by the time I met Emma, my feelings for her slammed into me, unexpected and inspiring. All of a sudden I found myself rivaling Keats and Rilke for romantic musings.

The first note I left for Emma was in Austin, after she told me about her mother's death and we fell asleep watching television. That one was the result of several longer, more maudlin versions. I left the abbreviated edition on her night table, and threw the others away in my room. Since then, I've crafted poems to her in my head (discarded without being jotted down), written her two letters (put through the shredder in Mom's home office), and tapped out multiple soul-baring texts (deleted without even being saved to drafts).

As I pull her door shut and it locks behind me, I have a two-second panic attack about the note I just left for her before I take a deep breath and head for my room. There's no taking it back, apart from the fact that I don't actually want to.

I round the corner and inexplicably, Brooke is standing in front of me. "Graham?" Her expression is bemused, head at an angle like a bemused puppy. She frowns at the ice bucket in my hand. "Are you... getting ice?" She points back to where the vending alcove is, which I'd have passed if I was coming from my room.

"Um. No?" My mind is blank. I have no idea what to offer as an excuse. Thank God I'm wearing pants.

She glances behind me towards Emma's door, but thankfully, she doesn't voice the question that flashes through her eyes, because I'd have to tell her it's none of her business, which would answer her curiosity in any case. For some reason, she directs her best faux-smile at me. I seldom get the faux-smile from Brooke. "Are you about to check out?" she asks. Her Louis Vuitton overnight bag is slung over her shoulder, D&G sunglasses perched on her head, and I'm not sure what label the stilettos are, but I'd be willing to bet they're the ones with the red undersides. She's a walking LA-girl stereotype.

"Yeah. I've gotta grab a quick shower and then get a taxi to LAX."

"I can take you." She shrugs and turns to walk to my room with me. "It's not like I have a booked schedule. And we didn't get to hang out much this trip."

I *have* been focused on Emma for the past three days. I didn't consider that Brooke might want face time, too. "Oh. Okay, cool. Thanks."

When we get to my room, I tell her to make herself at home while I shower. Twenty minutes later we're crossing the lobby as Reid is coming in with his bodyguard. "You two leaving?" he asks, unnecessarily, since we're both holding luggage.

I'm anticipating Brooke's sure-to-be acerbic answer when she says, without a trace of condescension, "Yeah, I'm taking Graham to the airport."

"Cool." He shoves his mirrored shades up and sticks a hand out. "See you guys in three weeks, eh?" I shake his hand, and then he gives Brooke a quick hug as I begin to wonder what kind of twilight zone I've entered.

When he walks off, I'm staring at her, perplexed. Sunglasses in place, she says, "What?"

I shake my head. "Oh, I don't know—possibly the hug and friendly banter with a guy I nearly decked in the middle of a nightclub for you a few months ago."

She shrugs. "I guess we needed to get that shit out of the way. It was all a long time ago. I'm trying to move past it. Okay?"

I nod. "Sure. Okay."

A valet pulls up with her black two-seater Mercedes, and I put our bags in the trunk while she tips him. I've barely clicked my seatbelt in place when she pulls into traffic. "So tell me... just how serious is this thing with Emma?" Her tone is very nonchalant.

"We're not really revealing anything about it yet." My attempt at being evasive earns me a smirk.

"Yeah, I figured that much. Because of the studio edict for Reid and Emma to look like a real-life love-match?"

"Who told you about that?"

She flips her hand off the top of the steering wheel. "He did, I guess. I don't remember."

This is more and more odd. So now they're chatting? "Hmm."
Glancing at me through her sunglasses, she says, "You can tell me, right? You know I won't say anything to the freaking *media*."

In four years of friendship, Brooke has never given me a reason not to trust her.

"All right. It's semi-serious."

She shoots me a look over the top of her sunglasses.

I shrug and look out the window. "And I want it to be more than semi."

Her faux-smile is back, but she's directing it out the windshield. "That's new for you."

Isn't it though. "Yes."

REID

While I'm packing up, I text John to find out if he wants to go out tonight, and he calls me back while I wait in the lobby for the valet to bring my car around.

"Hell yeah, you know I'm game," he says. "Any ideas?"

"I was hoping you had something. No clubs—I've got studio orders of exclusive coupledom until the premiere. Can't risk taking anyone home if it could get leaked." Not to mention the fact that Brooke will hang me up by my balls if I screw up this elaborate scheme of hers. "Any private parties?" John's network includes plenty of the bored rich kids of LA's most prominent cosmetic surgeons, Hollywood execs, and professionals like our dads. He's even better connected for that shit than I am.

"Yeah, sure, there's at least one or two that might not prove lame. Pick you up at ten?"

"Cool."

John and I have known each other for three years, ever since a party during which I thought I was going to die.

I was hitting on this girl, and she was hitting back like a pro. We found a shadowy spot near the pool waterfall to make some semi-stoned explorations and get better acquainted—all fine and good until someone yanked me away from her with the clear intent of ripping my arm from its socket. Apparently she had a boyfriend who was a bit disappointed to find her with her shirt hanging open and one hand down the front of my jeans.

"What the *fuck* do you think you're doing?" he screamed, eyes crazy and swinging back and forth between us. His hand was still clenched around my nearly dislocated arm as she stumbled backwards. He was smaller than me, but older and *really* pissed off.

When he let go, I tried to just retreat and take the loss. No sense getting my ass kicked for some girl who hadn't bothered to volunteer her name or ask mine, as far as I could remember. "Nothing, man, seriously," I mumbled, still high but sobering up fast. Unfortunately, my unzipped jeans and the fact that she was fumbling to rebutton her shirt contradicted my words.

He stepped closer to me, his wiry neck muscles bulging. "I'm gonna kill you."

That's when John popped up next to me. I'd never seen him before. "*Hey!* Do I know you?" At first I thought he meant me, but a quick glance told me he meant pissed-off guy.

"Back off, dickwad." The guy stabbed a finger at me. "This is between me and *him.*"

"Oh yeah? This is *my* house. So why don't *you* back off." John was smaller than both of us, but he was gushing righteous indignation.

That's when pissed-off guy's six-foot-four, linebacker-width friend materialized. Gaping at him, I thought: *I'm dead. Holy shit, I'm totally dead.* Expressionless, he stared back as I contemplated whether or not it was even remotely possible for me to get in one punch that might stun him long enough for me to make a run for it. I couldn't look away from his glassy-eyed gaze until he cracked his knuckles.

I swallowed, trying one last stab at conciliation with the pissed-off boyfriend. "Hey, uh, sorry, dude—I didn't know she was taken."

"Not good enough, *dude,*" he sneered, unappeased. He didn't want apologies. He wanted blood. *Mine.*

That's when John sidestepped me and meaty guy, all 140 pounds of him barreling straight into pissed-off guy. Knocking the guy flat on his ass, he commenced to beat the shit out of him, fists flying. *Great,* I thought, my eyes sliding back to the huge thug whose *neck* was the size of one of my thighs, *now I'm definitely getting my ass kicked.*

I stood straight, fists clenched, certain that if that guy landed one punch, I was going to be (a) unconscious and (b) not nearly as attractive as I began this lousy evening. And then meaty guy breathed a deep, frustrated sigh, rolled his eyes, and leaned down to grab his friend out from under John. Making for the side gate, he towed his bleeding, stumbling comrade along. Without a word, the girl followed.

This all happened in the time it took me to blink twice.

Like a prize fighter, John rocked his head back and forth a couple of times, popping his neck, and then looked at me. "Come on, man, I've gotta ice my knuckles." He grinned idiotically as he pumped his hands open and closed as though that would help the pain. "God *damn*, that hurts."

I shook my head at him. "Uh, thanks?"

"No prob. That guy was a dick." I followed him into the house, where he opened a drawer in the freezer and rummaged through ice packs of various shapes and sizes. "My step-mom does kickboxing," he said, in explanation of the ice packs. I tried and failed to imagine my mom kickboxing. Pulling a hand-sized pack from the freezer drawer, he said, "So, you're Reid Alexander, yeah?"

At sixteen, I was still on the outer fringes of celebrity. "You know who I am?"

I had no idea then how much everything would change, or how quickly. Meeting John was one of the earliest indications of the approaching shift in my social status. John is one of my closest friends now, but he's always been conscious of who's who, and I've wondered if our friendship would have ever occurred if he hadn't known who I was that night.

"I know Karen and Olivia, and they said they were bringing you tonight."

The last glimpse I'd gotten of Karen and Olivia, they were dancing together and driving every guy in the vicinity nuts. Too bad for the guys, because neither girl would be interested in any of them. They were much more interested in each other... which is why I'd gone looking for my own amusement.

Taking two beers from the fridge with his uninjured hand,

John handed me one.

I twisted the cap off and shook my head. "Guess I got lucky that big guy wasn't in the mood to fight, eh?"

John shrugged. "The smaller guy was the douche. I figured, take him out, problem solved."

Risky guess. "Yeah, well, thanks."

Chapter 16

Emma

I wake up alone, with bits and pieces of last night and this morning floating back to me. The first thing I remember is the last thing that happened—Graham leaving a piece of paper on the night table before he leaned over, hands on either side of my head, and kissed me goodbye. I drifted back to sleep with the taste of him on my lips.

I sit up a bit, scooting back against the pillows and rubbing my eyes, and the note is there, where I remember him leaving it. The clock reads 11 a.m., so he must have left three hours ago. He's somewhere between California and New York, probably flying over a patchwork quilt of corn and wheat fields. The room-darkening draperies seal out the sunlight completely, so I have to switch the lamp on to read his note. I run the pad of my finger over his familiar scrawl, my name at the top and his at the bottom.

Emma,

I'm sitting next to you with a directory balanced on my knee, watching you sleep and striving to compose something profound and passionate that will express how I feel. Something that will make you breathless waiting for me to return. Instead, I'm the breathless one, recalling the feel of your mouth opening to me, the stroke of your fingertips everywhere you touched me, the perfect weight of you in my arms. The thought of time away from you is torture. I haven't even left your room and I already miss you. Tonight, we'll talk, and I'll tell you a story of exactly what I plan to do to you in three weeks. Or perhaps you'd prefer to tell me what you want—like a list of resolutions, or a treasure hunt, or crumbs along a pathway... I'm very good at following crumbs. Or instructions, directions, entreaties...

Yours,

Graham

Reid: Are you still at the hotel?
Me: Yes, leaving for the airport soon
Reid: I'll drive you and we can talk about the interview schedule on the way
Me: k

"Your car is really… yellow." Yellow or not, this is the fanciest non-limousine vehicle I've ever been in. This even beats out Marcus and his Sacramento-rich-kid Volvo. I'm afraid to touch anything.

Reid's eyes are invisible behind the sunglasses, but I can tell he's rolling them. "Ugh! Don't start, woman. I'm replacing it soon anyway."

I click the seatbelt in place and he takes off. "Why? It looks brand new."

Smirking, he says, "Because it's yellow."

I laugh, confused. "But didn't you *choose* it?"

Shrugging, he looks at me and smiles. "Semantics." Taking a

sharp right at the corner, he says, "Hold on," and I'm suddenly glad for the molded seat and multiple interior handles.

"Were you a race car driver in a past life?" I ask after he weaves through several cars like he's James Bond.

"Too fast for you, Emma?" he asks, laughing. "Damn. I'm *always* going too fast for you. I've gotta learn to rein it in…"

Lips pressed tight, I glance at him, and he flips me a patented Reid Alexander smile, decreasing his speed and moving into the right lane, his hand smoothly working the gear shift between us. "I'm just teasing, you know."

I shrug in reply, hoping we aren't going to rehash what happened last fall, hoping he isn't going to renew his request for another chance. Everything with Graham is too new, and I'm not ready to share it, or defend it to Reid.

He's quiet for several minutes, tapping his fingers on the wheel along with the beat of the music. Finally, he clears his throat and says, "So, we have a few semi-local radio and TV appearances to do—something scheduled every day next week."

I sigh, relieved at the change of subject. "I guess I'll be back in LA Monday, then."

He nods once. "Most are morning shows beginning at *totally* unacceptable times of day—starting with Monday morning at six."

"Six *a.m.*? Crap."

He shakes his head. "That word is nowhere near strong enough for anything that begins at six a.m. The first one's at a local LA station, though. I'll drive, or get a car, and pick you up at your hotel, so don't worry about transportation. Actually I might as well handle that for all of them. We don't want anyone talking to us separately if at all possible, what with our romantic charade." He smiles at me again, but playfully. No reason for alarm.

The coming week will include lots of one-on-one time with Reid. Not long ago I'd have been euphoric over a chance like that. Now it makes me nervous in a whole different way. Though I no longer want a relationship with him, he's still charismatic and curiously easy to be around—most of the time. I should feel more distrustful and wary. That's the problem, really—I'm not totally on guard when every logical cell in my body tells me I *should* be. But then that's the sort of thing at which Reid Alexander excels— faking trustworthiness.

The rest of the trip is filled with small talk. He asks what I'm planning to study in college, and I ask about his upcoming project—an action film opposite Chelsea Radin, small-town weathergirl turned hot celebrity. He doesn't bring up last fall or our conversation in March. When we arrive at the airport, he hops out to retrieve my bag from the trunk. Pulling the handle up and out, he presses it into my hand, and before I can react, he leans in close and brushes my cheek with a kiss.

He's sliding his sunglasses back on and getting into his car, calling, "See ya Monday morning," while I'm standing on the sidewalk, blinking. The kiss was an unexpected shock, even if it wasn't on the mouth and seemed oh-so-casual. But his mostly-harmless kiss isn't what has me frozen.

On the other side of the multiple one-way lanes in front of my departure gate stands a girl with a camera aimed directly at me. This is no cell phone, and no touristy three hundred dollar Kodak. It's a big, black, professional-looking piece of equipment. *Damn. It.* As I turn away, her face breaks into a happy, *evil* grin before she turns, too, quickly disappearing into the parking garage.

I know what just happened between Reid and me on the sidewalk: an innocuous kiss. I also know exactly how it will look on every celebrity gossip website to which that girl can upload and sell a photo.

Brooke

I'm not as afraid of the paparazzi as some celebs. Very little of my life *isn't* an open book, anyway. Aside from my one ginormous secret—that somewhere out there is a (most likely) blonde, blue-eyed, beautiful three-year-old with a mix of genes from Reid and me. (God help whoever's trying to raise that kid if there's any truth to the "nature" end of the nature versus nurture debate.)

I have a secret weapon in my paparazzi back pocket. Her name is Rowena, and she's a female jackal amongst the pack of a male-majority profession. I chose her for that reason, in fact. Anytime I can give a woman a leg up over a man, I'm on board—as long as the woman in question isn't competition, because then all bets are off. Rowena didn't trust me, at first. Not until she got two or three photos that would have never been possible without my help. Since then, when I call she only has one word—*where*.

I use her for "candid" shots of myself, of course. That's how I got her hooked originally. I convinced her to give me her number, and then I'd call when I stopped by Starbucks for a Frappuccino with a hunky costar. I'd text where I'd be shopping with my mom. Since I control the scenarios, I appear how I want to appear, and Rowena looks like she knows how to catch hot celebrities out on the town, trying to be inconspicuous. Now the gossip rags eagerly take her calls, and I stay in the public eye—looking like a normal (attractive) person, rather than a bag lady flashing her underwear—or lack thereof—to the world.

Some celebs think they're above such maneuvering, or they're just too stupid to comprehend how to work it to their advantage. I'm not high and mighty, and I'm *not* stupid.

When I called Rowena this morning and told her to get her ass to LAX for a Reid Alexander and Emma Pierce exclusive, she asked the gate number and was off like a well-trained greyhound.

"Don't worry about looking for her," I told Reid last night. "She's a pro. You probably won't even see her until she's already gotten the shot, if you see her at all."

"You are a devious little bitch, Brooke."

I couldn't take much offense because there was admiration in his voice.

"FYI, I'm *not* telling you to try anything that could backset our plan… but the more you look like you're dropping your lover at the airport after a torrid night, the better."

He laughed. "Okay, yeah, I'll see what I can do."

His kiss on her cheek was brilliant. He and Emma both know it was quick and innocent, but the photos that started popping up a few hours later could be interpreted a million ways, and very few of those interpretations are *innocent*.

Me: I just found out I'll be in nyc the week of your graduation. I don't want to invite myself…but can i invite myself? Would your family hate me to intrude?

Graham: No, i'm sure that would be fine, if you're sure you want to go. Might be a long boring ceremony.

Me: Is that a jab at my sometimes limited attention span? Cuz i promise i'm
           proud of you and can sit still for the WHOLE THING.
Graham: Haha, ok sure. That would be cool.

I am *not* content to wait a week and a half to pop up in New York… With Emma safely stuck on an LA publicity tour with Reid, it's the perfect time to pay a friendly impromptu visit to Graham's home turf. The romantic comedy I'm filming there in the fall calls for a short-term apartment, I think. One that could become long-term. My stated purpose for being in town will be meetings with producers—entirely feasible, so it won't be questioned.

If I'm going to be with Graham, I'll have to win over his mother, his condescending sisters and his kid. I've only seen Cara once, and it was a couple of years ago so there's no way she remembers me. That trip also included a disastrous, drunken kissing incident that (luckily) Graham decided to play off as though it never happened.

Life's a Beach was filming an episode where several characters go to New York. (LA beach characters in New York—what the hell, right? But hey, it was ratings week, and I do what I'm paid to do.) I'd somehow contrived to stay with Graham while I was in New York, so when I got word of a party in a Union Square penthouse apartment owned by the friend of one of my costars, I invited him along.

We'd been dancing and got hot and ended up on the rooftop, stargazing. Or he was. I was gazing at *him*. I was accustomed to guys like Reid, who take advantage of opportunities like girls drinking themselves stupid, or pretending to, in order to land some hot guy. I should have known Graham wouldn't respond to that.

Not that he was unresponsive. When I moved into his arms and kissed him, for a few mind-blowing seconds, he kissed me back. I thought I was going to melt, it was so good. And then he grabbed my shoulders and held me away, saying, "Brooke, no." I was just wasted enough that I didn't realize what he was doing, at first… and once I figured it out, I was just sober enough to be humiliated. And pissed.

God, I was pissed. I stormed back inside, shaking and furious, and grabbed the first decent looking guy I encountered. Backing him against a wall with the thump of the music pounding through the sheetrock and into us both, I closed my eyes and pretended he was who I wanted. I don't remember much about that part, just that I couldn't fool myself, no matter how hard I tried. Moments later, Graham separated me from the guy, who nearly slid to the floor because I hadn't really allowed him to breathe. "Let's go," he said, his hand gripping my arm.

I yanked loose, crossed my arms and glared. "I'm not finished with this party."

"Yeah, you are," he said, leaning in so I could hear him. "You're completely trashed, and you're going to do something you'll regret if we don't leave now." His proximity was killing me.

"I already did," I mumbled, my eyes filling. I blinked back the tears and pinched my own forearms, determined to stay enraged.

"What?"

I snapped my arms straight, fists at my side. I felt hard, but brittle, like I was made of concrete. One solid whack and I'd crumble into dust. "I said *I already did*. You're going to hate me now, and I've ruined our friendship." My voice broke again and I realized I was more angry at myself than I was at him. "I just want someone to care about. Why is that so wrong?"

He closed his eyes. "It's not wrong." When he put his arm around me and led me to the door, I didn't fight him. We walked a couple of blocks before I pulled to a stop and whined that my feet hurt and I was tired, and he hailed a taxi to take us back to his parents' house.

It was late, and the house was quiet. He stopped outside the guest room door, his voice hushed. "Brooke, you haven't ruined anything." He sighed. "Can we just forget this happened? You mean a lot to me. You're one of the few friends I have who even know about Cara. You had a lot to drink. It was a silly mistake. And I could never hate you."

For a moment, before I call my travel agent and make reservations for a Tuesday flight, I mull over that sentence: *I could never hate you*. What it meant to me at the time. What it means to me now. And I almost chicken out.

But I'm right for him. I know it. I just need the chance to prove it.

Chapter 17

REID

No matter how many times we've woken up hungover, or how many times we've mumbled *I will never do that again* to ourselves and each other, John and I tend to slam back drinks until we can't see straight the next time we go out. The exception is when we get high instead.

We didn't even bother with a hangover Saturday morning—we just went straight into the next binge, making Sunday's hangover a real bastard. It's late afternoon before either of us can move, and somewhere in the back of my mind is the nagging philosophical question of the moment—was it fun if I don't remember it?

There's some chick passed out on John's couch, and neither of us remember who was responsible for bringing her back to his apartment, or what was done with her once she was here. For all I know, we all fell asleep. Her makeup is smeared to hell and she's lying on her stomach with her skirt and top weirdly twisted, lots of skin exposed, and all four limbs extended as though she was tossed there.

"She's kind of tall. Probably yours," I say, due to John's known weakness for models.

"She's kind of blonde. Probably yours," he returns. He prods her hip with his foot. "Hey. Wake up." She releases an annoyed grunt but otherwise doesn't react.

This is really, truly wrong, and insanely hilarious. Unfortunately, it hurts my head to laugh. "Shit, John, she's not a bum."

He exhales and blinks slowly, his eyes squinting at her in the not-that-bright light of day—the blinds are still shut tight. "Dude, I beg to differ. She's unconscious, somewhere she doesn't belong, where nobody knows who she is. That's pretty much the definition of a bum." He leans over and tries nudging her shoulder—with his hand this time. She moans again and he recoils. "Oh for chrissake, her *breath* sure smells like a bum's."

I dig my phone out of the jeans I was wearing last night, which I find slung over the back of a nearby chair. "I'll call a cab. You find some ID. We'll load her in, throw some twenties at the cabbie and send her on her way."

Holding his head, John casts around for a purse while I make the call. "Wallet!" He says finally, his hand emerging from between the sofa cushions. "Okay, who are you..."

"The taxi will be out front in five." I collapse into the chair just as John utters a string of curse words at a much too elevated volume. "Dammit John, shut the hell up," I hiss, pressing my palms to my temples.

"Yeah, okay. Look." He hands me her ID.

I don't recognize the name or address, but the taxi sure as hell won't do any good. "Shit—*San Diego*? We can't send an unconscious girl to San Diego in a cab."

John shakes his head minutely. "No man, that's not the problem." He lets loose with another string of curses, softer this time, staring at her like she's a zombie and any second she's going to wake up and attack.

"*What*, then?" I ask, and he hands me another ID. I didn't really look at the photo of the first one, or the age. I do now. The photo could be her—twenty-one year old Amber Lipscomb... Until I look at the second ID, which is *clearly* the girl on the sofa—seventeen-year-old April Hollingsworth. "Oh, shit." I knew the club was a bad idea. I *knew* it.

"We are so screwed." He stares at zombie girl, no longer making any effort to wake her up.

My phone launches into its ringtone, startling us both. "Yeah?" I croak, mouth parched and heart rate spiked. And I thought my head was pounding before. Ha. "Okay, thanks." I look at John. "The taxi's here."

His eyes swing to me. "Put your pants on and get out of here, man."

"Are you serious?"

He's staring at her again, wary. "I'm nobody. She can't prove shit about who she was with last night, and there's only so far she can get with a damned good fake in her possession, and being in a 21-up club. We're nineteen, which makes this a misdemeanor at worst. No one will do anything to *me* for such a minor offense— but someone would find a way to make *you* pay for it. So get out of here."

John and I have been in tight spots before, but this is probably an all-time low. If this goes poorly, his father will torch him. I never could have imagined John throwing himself on that grenade for me. I can't wrap my brain around it. "Look, you woke up in your room, I woke up in the guest room, and clearly she hasn't budged from the sofa since she landed there. Maybe nothing happened."

"Maybe," he snorts. "*Reid*. Take that taxi and go home. And perform some sort of ritualistic sacrifice once you get there, man. I'll call you later."

Emma

Derek and Emily picked me up at the airport Friday afternoon, and almost forty-eight hours later, they're dropping me back off.

Riding in Derek's Jeep gives me a déjà vu of my excursion to Griffith Park with Graham. I pull my hair into a ponytail and recall the pleasure of huddling together to watch the sunrise, and the feel of his mouth on my neck as he murmured *you're so beautiful*. I've reread his note several dozen times, and only the fear of it being ripped from my grasp by a gust of wind keeps me from pulling it out now. Our three weeks are counting down.

I didn't know, last fall, in my back-and-forth skirmishes with Reid, that *this* is how it's supposed to feel. Not relentless internal questions of *should I give in* or *am I ready yet*, not a constant feeling of defending my borders—but yearning for this next step, this connection. An inherent trust that it means everything it should mean.

From the back seat, I watch Derek and Emily communicate without speaking, something they've probably learned to do of necessity in this open-air vehicle. Their hands are clasped over the center console—his strong, tan forearm brushing against her paler, fragile-looking skin. I can't help but smile. Thanks to the Jeep and a host of new outdoor activities, Emily has actual tan lines. They're the faintest tan lines ever, due to her liberal all-over use of sun block, but still.

Derek has gotten my best friend into rock-climbing recently—something that made Mrs. Watson stop speaking to him for a week except for under-her-breath asides about *danger* and her *baby girl* and *imminent death*. Emily says he finally made a concerted effort to explain all the details of the pulley system and the fact that as a novice Emily was *always* hooked up to it, in the end convincing her mother that he would allow absolutely nothing to happen to the girl he loved.

"It was all very sitcom-sappy," Emily told me Saturday morning as we lounged in her bed. "I told Derek he wasn't allowed to speak to my mother that way—all that mushy stuff—which of course bonded them immediately." Her sly smile made me laugh out loud, and I wondered how Dad and Chloe would handle the news of Graham and me.

By Friday night, photos of me with Reid outside LAX were plastered all over the Internet, along with rampant speculations about our possible relationship. "I figured that this crap falls under need-to-know," Emily sighed, turning her monitor to face me. The time of day he dropped me off, some sites insisted, confirmed the probability of our having spent the night together.

I texted Graham so he wouldn't be caught unaware, again, of a seemingly intimate photo of me with Reid. He texted back: Vultures. Thanks for letting me know.

Emily wasn't the only one who kept an eye out for incriminating photos of me. I should have known right away from Chloe's patronizing questions over dinner last night that she'd discovered them, too, but my mind was so occupied with thoughts of Graham and his promises for our Skype-time later that I was running on auto-pilot answers and all but ignoring her.

When she passed the vinaigrette, she said, "Emma, you sneaky thing … how was LA?"

I dribbled dressing over my salad, vowing to squeeze in a long run in the morning. "It was fine. Pretty clear this trip, actually," I said, alluding to LA weather and the always-welcome lack of haze.

As I passed the bottle to Dad, Chloe gave him a self-satisfied *see there?* sort of look, which made him frown.

"Everything is definitely *clearer* lately." This was a Chloe attempt at being cryptic, but nothing about my stepmother is ever obscure or even vaguely mysterious. Her thoughts and designs are transparent, unconstrained by silly social constructs like tact or poise. I've learned to count this as one of her positive traits, in the same way you know a shark is capable of biting your arm off because you can see the teeth.

First, I registered the fact that she called me *sneaky*. And then the *clearer* comment.

Recognition dawned. "Ah. You've seen photos." I turned to Dad's concerned eyes. "You know how Dan said that the studio wants Reid and me to look like a couple until the premiere? Well, that's what we're doing—just so you know. *Nothing* is actually going on between us."

"Why in the world not?" Chloe was incredulous. "He's gorgeous!"

Dad's frown turned into a scowl. "For God's sake, Chloe, I don't want my daughter hooking up, or whatever, with that adolescent Casanova."

I almost choked on a tomato hearing my father say *hooking up*, which he air-quoted.

Chloe sighed heavily and rolled her eyes like she was twelve. "I'm just saying that since she's *abandoning* the film industry, she's not likely to get a shot at anyone like him *ever again*."

"All the better!" Dad countered, following that with a harrumph as he stabbed a forkful of salad and stuffed it in his mouth.

I glared at both of them. "Excuse me. *I'm sitting right here.* And in case you've both forgotten, I'm a legal adult, and I'm perfectly capable of conducting my own affairs... such as they are." My face warmed, matched by Dad's. Now probably wasn't the time to bring up my new relationship with Graham. I cleared my throat. "I'm, uh, going to finish my salad in my room."

Graham devoted time to me late each evening, but he was otherwise engaged in being a dad to Cara and studying for finals. He warned me that he'd be busy reviewing for exams and finishing up final edits on research papers over the coming week, and then his mouth quirked adorably. "But as of Friday, I'm all yours."

I'm content to have something to distract me, even if it means hotel rooms, getting up before dawn, and spending time with Reid, driving around LA and the surrounding areas. There are a lot of hours to fill outside of the hour or so I'll spend each night, swapping life stories with Graham and asking him in whispers to compose his alternate stories of us—fairytale lives we would have had if we'd met under different circumstances, or if we'd never been actors at all.

The story he devises tonight, my first night back in LA, supposes that we'd met as regular high school students—something neither of us had ever been.

"I'd have been a senior at seventeen, instead of a college sophomore. And you'd have been fourteen—so, a freshman—wide-eyed and innocent. Though I guess that sort of describes you now, too." His smile is teasing, but warm. "So maybe it isn't so difficult to imagine."

I lean my head in my hand, my eyes drinking in his face on my laptop screen. "You would have been popular, though. Why would you be interested in a freshman when you could have had your pick of any girl in the school?"

He shakes his head. "I would have seen you the first day, trying to get your locker open." He's referring to the first time he saw me, in the hallway of the hotel in Austin. "Immediately intrigued, I'd have walked over, acting all cool but shaking inside, thinking *who is this beautiful girl?* 'Need some help?' I'd say, and you'd look at me, all suspicious. I'd brush your fingers aside, gently, and say, 'What's your combination?' but you'd be too smart for that."

"I would?" I laugh. "I think maybe I'd just forget it on the spot, if you talked to me."

He laughs, too. "Nah, you'd say, 'But I'm not supposed to tell anyone my locker combination.' And then I'd say, 'Don't worry, I'm safe.'" His smile is positively wicked. I'd have melted to a puddle on the floor if he'd said any such thing to fourteen-year-old me.

"After more assurances and against all better judgment, you'd give me the combination and I'd open the locker for you. Then I'd lean on the adjacent locker and say, 'I require a small fee for damsels in locker-opening distress, you know.' Your suspicion would come back full-force, your eyes narrowing, waiting for me to tell you this supposed fee. I'd tell you that you had to go out with me Friday, because there's a mandatory orientation party. And since you *have* to go, so you might as well go with me."

"Oh, *smooth*."

"You'd get that little pensive frown you get sometimes, and you'd say, 'Huh. No one said anything about a mandatory orientation...'" He taps his finger against his chin and I laugh at his reference to my favorite habitual word.

"So then I'd say, 'Oh, it's only for special freshmen—you have to be invited by a senior.' Now you're completely convinced that I'm full of crap. 'Sounds like a hazing charge waiting to happen,' you'd say. 'No, no—would I lie to you?' I'd say, oozing seventeen-year-old boy charm."

"Were you this cheesy when you were seventeen?" I ask.

He grins. "*Emma*. I'm trying to tell a story here. And I plead the fifth."

"Sorry."

"So then you'd floor me. You'd say, 'I don't know. *Would* you lie to me?' And I would look into your eyes and see everything I could ever want. I'd say, 'Let's skip the party. I'll take you to dinner. And then I'll take you somewhere private and kiss you until you tell me to quit.' What would your answer be, Emma?"

I could barely breathe. "Oh... I think, for the sake of the story, I'd probably be okay with that."

"You think?" His mouth turns up on one side and I can tell he's watching me on his screen as closely as I'm watching him.

"I don't know. I need more information about the kissing."

He chuckles softly. "Let's say you tell me yes, and we go to dinner. We talk, and we're both surprised at how comfortable we feel. And then we get into my car and drive to a secluded spot overlooking our sleepy little suburban town. Totally private, dark but for a sky full of stars… and tomorrow, I'll tell you what happens next."

The noise that comes from my throat is half-growl and half-whimper, and he *hmms*. "I need to study a bit more tonight—if I even *can*, now—and you have to get up before five a.m. and be animated and personable on camera."

I couldn't care less about being animated or personable. "Mmm. More tomorrow? You won't forget?"

"Hell no, I won't forget," he says, grinning. "At this point, I'll be lucky if it doesn't work its way into my essay on the Lost Colony of Roanoke during my final for Early Settlements of Colonial America. I can see it now: *No evidence of what happened to the 114 colonists was ever found… but in my dream last night I took Emma parking and got to third base.*"

"Graham!" I laugh, hands over my mouth.

"I'm kidding. I wouldn't go for third on the first date—maybe second?" He laughs softly when I cover my face completely. "It's probably just as well you didn't meet me when I was seventeen. I was kind of a horn dog. But I think I'd have known enough to be careful and slow with you. At least, I will in this story, to be continued tomorrow…"

I'll never get to sleep now.

Chapter 18

Brooke

Rowena and I don't make eye contact as she shuffles through first class on her way to coach, her bag of camera equipment weighing her skinny shoulder into a sharp downward slope. She looks like a lop-sided scarecrow. I can easily imagine her slipping into narrow, impossible spaces, getting shots the large, aggressive men of her kind—the ones who scare the crap out of celebs with their obnoxious belligerence—could never get. The only thing unnerving about Rowena is her eyes. They're not empty like some psycho killer—they're just flat-out ruthless.

Not that I can talk.

She generally doesn't have to leave the LA area to make a living, but she understands the strategic part of doing personal favors for the right people, and I'm one of those people. Graham and I may not be A-listers, but we're close enough to make news if the story is juicy, especially with the movie premiere a couple of weeks away. I've made it clear to Rowena that this favor is non-negotiable if she expects a continuance of tips like the Reid-n-Emma bonus that probably paid several months' rent. I'm paying her airfare and hotel, plus she'll be compensated for the photos themselves.

Now all I have to do is get Graham into the picture.

I hate long flights alone because there's nothing to *do*. God knows I'm not going to chat up the middle-aged CEO or whatever he is sitting next to me. He reminds me of my dad—from the stereotypical Rolex and custom-made suit to the trainer-maintained body and bleached teeth.

Daddy dearest is on his fourth marriage to someone too young for him. As I get older, they're getting closer and closer to my age. I just turned twenty—how can he be okay with the fact that his newest Mrs. Cameron is five or six years older than his youngest daughter? I think my oldest sister is actually *her same age*. You'd think he'd at least have the awareness to be embarrassed.

My mother was the idiot second wife—the younger woman who attracted a powerful married man away from his wife and two daughters and got knocked up with me, probably on purpose. By the time his divorce was settled and the pre-nup my unwitting mother agreed to was inked, I was a month old. Inexplicably, I was in their farcical wedding photos (which my mother filed through the shredder when my father left her for wife number three—*hello*, who didn't see *that* coming?). Why didn't either of them think I'd eventually grow old enough to look at those framed photos and figure out that I'm *beyond* illegitimate, or that my friends wouldn't come to the same conclusion?

Mom is currently prowling for Husband Number Four. Number Two, Rick, was actually okay. I sort of miss him. Number Three was a huge douche and I was more than happy to get my own apartment in LA when Mom moved back to Texas with him—good riddance. She now says that her third marriage was the "fifteen minute" variety. In actuality it lasted around a year, but maybe fifteen minutes just refers to how long either of them remained faithful.

Mr. CEO keeps peering at me, and I'm not sure if it's because of my hot little LA body or if he actually recognizes me. I don't particularly care. Grabbing the satin sleep mask, I shove it on, lean my seat back and settle in to pretend sleep. I don't want to contemplate forty-something lechers, or my parents and their meaningless relationship histories. I just want to think about Graham.

I don't want to screw this up. I know I'm about to manipulate him in deplorable ways, but I'm a practical girl. The ends justify the means. This is something my parents have never, in either of their pathetic lives, done—plan for the future, rather than living in the moment. Graham is not a momentary whim, though I admit he was at first. But that was a very long time ago. I've known for a while now that he's exactly the kind of stable guy I need. He's one of only two people in the world I can comfortably talk to about what happened with Reid.

God, *Reid*. What a tortuous mess that was.

When we met, he was fourteen, and I was fifteen. Both of us were recurring extras on the set of a soon-to-be-canceled sitcom. I'd catch him staring at me sometimes and he'd blush, or vice versa. I thought he was the most beautiful boy I'd ever seen. We talked a few times, but in short, nervous sentences on meaningless subjects—not in any substantial way.

Then, a month later, we both managed to land minor parts in the same movie. It was like fate, in a way—though to what purpose, I have no idea.

The cast was on location in Idaho, living in trailers. With no one else our age around, Reid and I had our tutoring sessions together, and we grew close fast. Our parents were too uninvolved to be around much, and the notion that production babysits underage kids is ludicrous. Yes, we were somewhat separated from the older cast mates because that sort of slipup would spell legal disaster, but for Reid and me the situation was akin to being thrown into the same playpen. We could mess around with *each other* all we wanted to. And we did.

I'd moved to LA with Mom when she married Rick, and the sitcom had been my first acting job. When the movie Reid and I were filming was over and we were back in LA, we kept seeing each other. Neither of us was old enough to drive, but we were privileged kids of clueless parents. We hired cars and hung out frequently at each other's houses, which weren't too far apart.

We were too young and irresponsible to be sexually active, but eventually, going all the way felt like a natural progression. Reid looked at me like I was a goddess come to life in his bedroom. He was reverent and adoring. I loved the feel of my hair spread across his pillow and his weight pressing into me and the expression on his face when he stared into my eyes and whispered, "I love you."

God, we were stupid. We used protection most of the time, but occasionally we'd forget, especially if we'd been drinking. Reid resisted drinking with me most of the time, or he'd have one beer or one shot and quit. Something to do with his mother. And then came the night of the screwdrivers. We must have downed half a bottle of vodka between us, and we were both violently sick most of the night. The next morning, his dad discovered us in his room, passed out and hungover. After delivering a harsh parental lecture, his dad called my mom.

Loving mother that she is, she sent a car around to collect me. (Had she even noticed that I never came home the previous night? Who knows.)

When I staggered through the door, the only thing she asked—derision in her tone, not concern—was if I needed a morning-after pill. The last thing I wanted to appear was dumber than my mom. "Of course not," I told her, trailing my hands along the hallway walls on the way to my room. "*We* use protection."

She narrowed her eyes at me, and if she'd had any sense she'd have never believed me. Instead, she snapped, "You don't get to be all high-and-mighty just because you know how to use a rubber, missy."

"Why the hell not?" I returned, my head throbbing. "If *you'd* known how to use one, I wouldn't be here to bother you."

She slapped me then, and it wasn't like seeing stars, it was like sparks erupting and everything blacking out at the edges. Rick rushed in and said *That's enough, Sharla* and steered her out of my room as I stumbled onto the bed. He came back minutes later with ice chips and pain pills. My ears were still ringing when he sighed, "Just sleep it off, Brooke. You'll feel better later." In his kind eyes was the concern missing in my mother's. He was weighing something he never got a chance to say, because Mom began calling his name in that petulant tone. Patting my arm, he sighed and left the room.

She preferred me to be invisible to him. I was starting to look like a woman, and all of a sudden, I was a rival, or at least something conceivably prettier than her. She didn't like it.

I don't remember what Reid and I fought over the night we broke up. We're so similar that if we both happened to be in a pissy mood at the same time, we would inevitably end up in a vicious argument. At first, he seemed shocked at the things I'd say, trying to hurt him, to get a reaction. But his temper was as bad as mine—he just had a longer fuse. When he'd finally lose it, we would say cruel, spiteful things to each other and accuse each other of all manner of sins.

I confess that making him that angry was a turn-on at times. If I could get him to lose it and then rein him in at just the right moment, the passion he unleashed was insane. He'd pin me to the bed and kiss me so hard it hurt, choking back his anger and redirecting it gratefully to something more satisfying than screaming obscenities at each other.

Sometimes I missed the mark and pushed him too far. That night was one of those. And then, for the first time, he didn't call me an hour later, crying. That reaction from him always made me cry, too, and we'd blubber apologies and reaffirm our love and the need to see each other even if it was 3 a.m.

I waited, but he never called. Two days later, I was in a panic. I didn't want to call first and appear weak, but I was breaking down. I missed him. I wanted his forgiveness. I also wanted him to need me more than anything, and if he was staying away, that wasn't the case.

So I went out to a club with a couple of costars from the last film—girls in their early twenties who felt sorry for my little fifteen-year-old breakup woes. I had no problem passing myself off as legal with the right makeup, clothes, attitude, and a top-notch fake ID. Being fawned over by older guys didn't help like I thought it would, though.

I was close to grabbing a taxi to Reid's house and begging his forgiveness when I noticed a guy with a camera. Failing in his attempt to be subtle, he was hiding behind a post that didn't quite conceal his girth. I knew he'd be spotted and shown the door any second. As he zeroed in on my friends, I decided on a different, stronger course of action. I would make Reid crazy with jealousy, and then he'd come back to me.

I found a hot guy, pulled him onto the dance floor and performed every degrading dirty dancing move I could think of on him. I incorporated things I'd seen my mom do on the stripper pole she had installed in the extra bedroom for "exercise," and the photog recorded it all. Reid and I weren't big time, but we were cute together, and Hollywood liked us. I had no idea that being idolized also meant people were salivating over the moment we'd split up and how it would happen. I was just desperate to make Reid cave first.

The article online the next day made me out to be the biggest whore imaginable—*so sad, she's so young*—while Reid was cast as the naïve boy who had no idea what his slutty girlfriend had been doing behind his back.

Out that night, and the next, and the next, Reid was photographed leaving clubs, parties and hot spots with a swarm of different girls until there was no doubt in my mind that we were done and he was over me.

I cried for two weeks. I barely ate. I couldn't sleep. I wanted to call and tell him I hadn't been with anyone else, that it was all a ruse. But I was hurt and resentful, knowing that was no longer true for him. My mother, fresh into her separation from Rick, sat me down and told me that the only way to get over a guy like that is to get a new one. I heeded her advice, but couldn't settle down to any one guy. And I couldn't exorcise Reid from my head.

That's when I met Graham, who resisted and spurned me. *No one* rejected me, not when I was offering straight up no-strings screwing around. We were on location not too far from LA, just beginning to film a movie. I'd known Graham for a week, and I already detested him for his high-handed dismissal.

And then I figured out that it had been a while since I'd had a period. I peed on a stick and was stunned to find out I was pregnant. Abortion? No problem. Sign me up. Until the doctor said how far along I was—almost ten weeks.

Which meant it was Reid's. Absolutely Reid's. I told them I couldn't do it. Not when my mother pleaded with me not to ruin my career. Not when my father was called in to order me to comply (because yeah, *that's* always worked on me).

"I've made the appointment, and we're going tomorrow," Mom said, as though I had no opinion in the matter.

"Be a good girl and listen to your mother," my father added.

I hated them both.

Graham heard me crying in my trailer that night, and knocked on the door. I don't know why, but I took one look at those warm brown eyes and I told him everything.

Holding me while I cried, he told me that he and his ex-girlfriend were having a baby in a few months. She was planning to hand it to him and walk away, but he was hoping for a reconciliation.

"Brooke, this might be the most important decision you ever make. It doesn't matter if you didn't plan this—there's a choice to make, and *you* should make it. Decide what's right for you, *whatever* that is, and then *do* it."

No one had ever said that to me before, and here was this boy, who wasn't quite a year older than me, sounding so wise and sure. Of course, I know now that in that moment, Graham still had completely undeserved faith in Zoe, so he wasn't exactly the soul of discernment he appeared to be. Still, he had a point about taking over the decisions for your own life. That was the moment I started doing just that.

If I'm capable of loving anyone, it has to be Graham.

The ends justify the means, right? The ends justify the means.

Me: I'm in town for a couple of days. Meetings over that fall project. Dinner?
Graham: Bad week. I've got finals and papers due through friday. When are you leaving?
Me: Early friday. :(
Graham: Damn, not the sad face! I could maybe get away for an hour or so tomorrow?
Me: Yes please! :) Text me your address and I'll pick you up at eight.

REID

Brooke: We're having dinner tomorrow night. Photos should be up thursday. Make sure she sees them.
Me: Yep
Brooke: That answer doesn't leave me with warm fuzzies
Me: Are you capable of warm fuzzies? I'm thinking cold ice shards.
Brooke: Do you ever STFU??
Me: Quit freaking out. I'll handle it.

Emma and I are on our second day of local television morning show interviews. These are like an annoying, unnecessary rehearsal for the ones that matter—the nationally syndicated talk shows, the late night network and cable shows.

Most of these local morning anchors will never make it out of their thirties in front of a camera, especially the women. Not because they can't do the job, but because there's always some fresh-faced, ambitious twenty-something who wants that job, will take less to do it, and will look hotter doing it. No wonder some of them look at Emma and me like they'd give anything to just punch us in the face.

I may be exaggerating a bit.

This morning, though, the female anchor is interrogating Emma as though she's personally responsible for a host of swept-under-the-rug hate crimes. Leaning so far forward that Emma moves closer to *me*, Wynona narrows her overly-lined, heavily-mascaraed eyes. "Emma, you can't tell me there isn't *something* going on between you two. Look at the photographic evidence!"

Without her eyes ever leaving Emma's face, she points to a huge monitor in between her chair and our small sofa. I stifle a laugh. The cell phone photo I suspect Brooke of taking during Walt's show? Really? *Everyone* saw and picked apart that photo, *months* ago. "Um…" Emma says, and I lean up, chuckling slightly.

"Wynona." My voice is like honey and her attention swings to me. Professional thirty-something women aren't quite sure how to react when I take such a familiar, somewhat condescending tone. "That's a really old, really fuzzy photo." I shrug. "As we've said in previous interviews, the whole cast got along really well during filming. We were all very close." When Emma almost turns to look at me, I press my knee against hers and she freezes in place. Good girl.

"Reid, I believe you had an *old flame* in the cast, as well?" Wynona clicks the device in her palm and the photo on the wall is suddenly a four-years-younger me, leading Brooke by the hand as we leave some LA hotspot. Both of us are smiling—me, right into the camera, and Brooke, looking at me. I haven't seen this photo in a very long time.

"Yes." My smile is similar to that of the boy on the screen, if Wynona doesn't look closely enough. That boy is not yet the uncaring bastard sitting in front of her.

She scoots an inch closer. "Were you and Ms. Cameron in contact between your *tween* romance and the filming of *School Pride*?" I can tell from her cold eyes she knows damned well we weren't *tweens* in that photo, but I ignore her pointless taunt.

"Sure," I lie.

Ignoring me, she asserts, "Because there are rumors that the two of you had—*issues*—on the set of your recent film."

I laugh complacently and match her icy gaze. "There's a reason they're called *rumors*, right?"

She looks like she wants to bite me. And not in a good way. "What about now? Do you consider yourselves to be—*friendly*—now?"

What a *bitch*. I decide to throw her a fast ball, which turns out to have perfect timing. "Yeah. We hung out this past weekend, in fact."

Thank God I'm occasionally truthful, because just as I admit this, she click-clicks and up pops a photo from three days ago in which I'm entering Brooke's apartment. She's clearly visible in the doorway, admitting me. I wonder if Brooke knows about this. I wonder if she even set it up with that photog girl she has on payroll. How else would this shot get into the exclusive hands of a common local news station when *Star* or *Us* would have paid a shitload of cash for it?

Wynona's façade crumbles a little at the edges at losing the element of surprise, but she rallies and turns back to Emma. "So if you and *Reid* aren't involved... is this due to your involvement with a—" she glances at a card "—Marcus Hoffpauer?"

The photo on the wall changes to Emma looking bored to death, arms crossed, standing next to that conceited prick at his prom. That *must* have been a pity date.

Emma is speechless, so I laugh and gesture to the photo, grinning conspiratorially at her. "Ah, I remember this—the community theatre guy, right?"

Emma nods, her lips compressing when she glances at the photo. "Yes, at his prom."

I shake my head, smiling and staring daggers into Wynona. "If he wanted to score points, he could have—I don't know— introduced her to his friends? That's what *we* do when we invite non-celeb friends to *our* parties." A glance at Emma makes it clear that she's grateful for my interruption.

I turn and give Wynona a mesmerizing smile. "So, about *School Pride*. We're both really excited about the upcoming release and ready to talk about the film. We brought several clips—I assume we can show your viewing audience a couple of them now?"

Emma breathes out a deep sigh the moment we shut the car doors and I start the engine, letting it idle and purr for a moment. "Wow, her face..." Her mouth turns up on one side. "I kind of expected her head to start spinning around at one point."

Wynona was tough, but I've had more hostile question-answer sessions than that. No need to pass that info on to Emma, though. "Courtesy never works with people like her, so I don't bother. If you want to shift topics, you have to force it. With a smile and an angelic look, of course."

"Of course."

We pull into traffic and I'm glad for the heavily tinted windows. The last thing either of us needs right now is more public scrutiny. "You looked miserable at that prom. Anyone talk to you at all?"

Shrugging, she says, "The waiters were nice." I laugh and she gives me a grim smile in return, her head angled. "How did you know? I mean, practically everyone fell for the story that I'm so conceited that I wouldn't lower myself to speak to regular people."

I make a disgusted sound. "*Please.* You're one of the least conceited people I know. Your best friend is a non-celeb girl—that's evidence enough that you're not above mingling with commoners."

She smirks and I smirk back.

"Let me guess—you told him you're moving across the country to go to school, so you can't imagine a relationship between you going anywhere—something like that—and he got pissed. I wouldn't be surprised if he wanted you to give him a leg up in the industry and he saw his chance at that falling away."

She blinks in surprise, and her hands open on her lap. "I can't blame him for being disappointed about that, if that was the case."

I'm shaking my head before she stops talking. "Why should he put forth no more effort than cozying up to the right girl? Yes, there's a lot of luck and who-you-know, but we both had to work like hell to become successful actors. We didn't just get it handed to us. Even if you *are* planning to toss it all aside to become an ordinary little co-ed."

She clears her throat, a light blush across her cheeks.

In the silence, I begin ruminating over John's usual phenomenal luck holding steady with that under-aged girl. Once I was gone and he got her to wake up, she was more than happy to be given cab fare to get to a friend's house so her parents wouldn't find out she was at some strange guy's apartment overnight.

"I'm 99 percent sure we all passed out when we got to my place," John said.

"What about the other one percent?"

John sighs, passing on a rare piece of insight. "Dude, I hope we never have daughters."

My best friend doesn't know about the possible kid with Brooke. I love John, but unlike Brooke, I don't trust *anyone* with that information. Thanks to her, Emma and Graham both know about it.

"Do you mind if I ask you about your relationship with Brooke?" Emma asks. I'm glad she can't see my eyes behind these shades. I mean *damn*, does she read minds? "You don't have to tell me anything. It's not my business. But you guys weren't friendly a few months ago and now you're, uh, hanging out together."

I shrug, exiting the freeway in a split-second decision that will keep her with me a little longer today. "You know that old photo of us that Wynona put up this morning?" She nods. "I guess I can't blame either of those kids for what they did back then. Growing up in the spotlight, as you know, isn't all that easy to handle."

"So, you're what—*friends*—now?" I can't blame her for being incredulous. The idea of Brooke and me ever being friends *is* ludicrous. She glances out her window and adds, "And where are we, by the way?"

I chuckle. "We're stopping for breakfast tacos at this very authentic place I know. And let's just say Brooke and I have reached an understanding."

Her brow knits as she takes in the East LA scenery. "Is this a safe spot for us to stop?"

"This car is like the Batmobile. It's bulletproof."

She peers at me. "Is that true?"

"Um…" I laugh at her gullibility and she swats my arm.

Pulling into a patchy, fissured parking lot and trying to avoid the potholes, I park and pull out my cell. Emma stares at the row of multi-ethnic businesses while I make a short call. With a limited Spanish vocab stemming from a lifetime of Hispanic caregivers and housekeepers, I request my usual order, doubled. Five minutes later, a tattooed guy in a wife-beater and a loosely-tied apron exits the restaurant storefront with a paper bag and two coffees. He makes a beeline in our direction. The Lotus would stand out in this lot even if it wasn't yellow.

My window slides down noiselessly. "Gracias, Raul," I say, passing the coffees to Emma and swapping a twenty for the bag.

Raul pockets the money and tips his chin up once, murmuring, "*De nada*," before sauntering back inside.

Handing off the cream containers and sugar packets to Emma, I unwrap one of the small stuffed tortillas, suddenly starving. I've already finished one and am starting another while she's mixing her coffee. By the time I'm backing out, I've finished a second burrito and Emma is taking her first tentative bite.

"Good?"

She nods. "Potato? And—?"

"Cabrito." I hope she doesn't know what that is.

Her brow furrows. "Is that… goat?"

Damn. "I said it was authentic…" She doesn't look *too* disgusted. "Not as bad as tuna, huh?" I remind her of our first official onscreen kiss. MiShaun had admonished me for eating tuna sandwiches beforehand, and I'd played cool about it in front of them and then sprinted to my PA and demanded a toothbrush and toothpaste before we did the scene.

Emma laughs while finishing her bite, holding a hand over her mouth. "I can't believe you remember that."

My answer is an indirect smile and nothing more, because all I'm remembering right now is the sweetness of her kiss. Brooke can't get her half of this insane arrangement completed quickly enough for me.

Chapter 19

GRAHAM

My research paper boasts a formidable title concerning Flannery O'Connor and didacticism… and not another complete or coherent thought. I've completed the research and bits of draft, but my deductions and conclusions are a jumbled mess. Thank God this one isn't due until Friday—I still have 48 hours to finish it.

I decide to take a break and see what Mom and Cara are doing when I catch myself staring at nothing and composing a new story for Emma. She seems fond of the steamy narratives I've been feeding her every night.

After which I take freakishly chilly showers.

I committed to dinner tonight with Brooke, and I shouldn't have—not with everything I have to do. I suffer from a vague sense of guilt where she's concerned. At times I sense that she wants more from me, but she never says so. Leading a girl on isn't something I've ever knowingly done, and that's exponentially true for someone I consider to be a friend. But she's only pushed me for more once during the course of our friendship, and she was very drunk at the time. Ignoring that whole episode seemed like the best way to deal with it.

Brooke regards her hard shell as strength. In reality, it's nothing more than a shield, though I can't say I blame her for it. I'm one of the few people she allows behind that barrier, and I've always felt the need to prove to her that relationships, including friendships, can survive without manipulation or exploitation. Whether I've been successful at that attempt is debatable.

Until last fall, I was sure Brooke's damage was mostly Reid's fault. I still believe their relationship had a lot to do with it, but having met him and watched them interact, I think they're just too similar. Like their impairments run parallel, and some subliminal recognition of that similarity was the reason they were originally drawn to each other.

Mom always warned my sisters and me that having been raised by a psychologist, we'd all know just enough to be dangerous; I guess I should lay off the amateur analysis. In reality, I have no clue how to help Brooke beyond preserving our friendship. So that's what I do.

I meet Mom and Cara on the staircase. My daughter is obviously ready for a nap; when I pick her up, she drops her head on my shoulder after one huge yawn. Mom continues up the stairs and I turn and follow.

"I've got that emergency client in about fifteen minutes, and then I *have* to start grading these damned finals." The stack of Blue Books in her arms is at least four inches thick. "And don't forget I have that faculty retirement party tonight, and I'm dragging your father along with me."

Crap. I forgot about the party, *and* the client appointment—which I'm not telling her since it looks like I was on my way down to retrieve Cara because of it. "Um, I'm supposed to go out to dinner tonight... I totally forgot to ask about that, didn't I?"

She hands me Cara's bunny. "Call Brynn. Maybe she's free." Watching me from the doorway as I lay Cara in her bed, Mom tries to pretend like she's not dying of curiosity. *So* not working. "Er... who did you say you're having dinner with?"

I tuck Cara under her nap blanket with the stuffed toy. "I didn't. It's Brooke."

Mom's face falls. "Oh."

I can't help but laugh as soon as we're out of the room. "Come on, Mom. You haven't even seen her in what, two years?"

She harrumphs. "Has she made positive changes in her life since then? Started therapy? Gained some maturity or had a personality adjustment?"

Sighing, I tap out a text to Brynn to see if she can watch Cara. "Mom—*try* to remember that you're a professional therapist."

She takes my arm, a tactile connection she's always used when she wants to make sure I'm listening. "I'm also a mother, and I can't help wanting what's best for my children."

I frown down at her, knowing exactly what she's implying. "Mom, I'm not *dating* her."

One of her eyebrows crooks up in the expression we share.

"I'm seeing Emma now. I could have sworn Cassie would spill the details of that." When we get to my room, I start reorganizing the mess of books, journals and paper on my desk and bed as she leans on my door frame.

"Oh, she did. I was just waiting to see if *you'd* tell me about her." I crook an eyebrow back at her and she sighs. "Cassie liked Emma quite a bit." A smug smile creeps across my face, and then she adds, "But watch out for Brooke. I think she has an agenda, whether you see it or not."

I'm trying really hard not to roll my eyes like a ten-year-old girl. She makes it sound like I'm incapable of seeing Brooke in a realistic light. "Mom, I know *you* think I'm awesome, but not every girl I meet *wants* me. Plus, I've known Brooke for four years. Don't you think I'd have seen some evidence of scheming if it was there?" I never told her about that drunken mistake of a kiss, of course, and I don't plan to.

"Are you sure you haven't?" She inclines her head as though she knows I'm withholding.

"I'm sure," I say, in the interest of placating her.

She sighs, walking up to me. "It's your life, honey." Frowning again, she pushes the hair off my face, something she's been doing to me for about a dozen years now. She likes it styled short, but has always deferred to whatever style I prefer—usually a little shaggy, unless I'm required to cut it for a film role. Cupping my chin, she stares up into my eyes. "Just don't make me say I told you so, because you know I can't resist saying it."

I shake my head and smile. "Duly warned, Mom."

Brooke

Graham: Can't do dinner tonight. No babysitter. I'm sorry.

A million things pound through my brain, starting with *Goddammit*. And then I recognize what an opportunity this is. I can't freak out at a kid-related set-back or I might as well give up now. I have Rowena all set to go. If Cara tags along, we'll look like a charming little family. The speculations could be even better than photos of us alone.

And Graham's secret would be outed—which will happen as soon as he gets the slightest bit more well-known, but doesn't need to be tonight. Tonight is about how level-headed I can be about his daddy obligations. Rowena will just have to work a little harder for her photos.

Me: Why don't I come over? We can order in, and I can help with Cara so
         you can get back to studying sooner.
Graham: That would be cool. You sure?
Me: Absolutely.

"Hey you." I smile up at him when he answers the door.

His eyes are warm and his smile is genuine, as always. He pulls the door wide, saying, "Hey, Brooke, long time no see." Such an adorable nerd.

He probably napped earlier in his jeans and slightly rumpled navy v-neck T-shirt. That one little strand in front sticks up from his disheveled mop of hair. Smiling, I reach up and make it blend with the rest. I'm wearing heels, but he's still inches taller, even barefoot. He looks good enough to eat, and my stomach flutters when I note his eyes scanning me head to toe. These jeans fit me like a second skin, and the silk top is fluid enough to flash curves and cleavage without explicitly doing either.

"I'm sorry we're staying in," he says. I move past him into the foyer, and he shuts the front door and leads the way across the slate flooring. "I'm sure you had hopes of showing off that outfit." He takes my bag and light scarf, our fingers brushing—sending a zap all the way to my toes. When he turns to hang them on a brass hook in the entryway, I draw in a deep, silent breath.

"What, *this*? You know me, Graham—heels and silk are

comfort clothes." I haven't been in this house in two years, but it hasn't changed. His family is fond of cozy décor, a warm color palette and natural elements. Pretty much the direct opposite design of my place. This setting suits Graham, though—a fact I'll keep in mind while apartment hunting tomorrow. I want him to feel at home when he's there.

Without warning, Cara pops up at my feet and stares up at me, all huge dark eyes. I know from posing the question years ago that his family insisted on a paternity test when she was born, but those eyes are unmistakably Graham's. Her strawberry blonde hair must be from her mother. It's in need of a trim. And a flatiron.

"Are you a Gossip Girl?" she asks.

I laugh. "Um, no. I wish! They're all very pretty."

She nods, her eyes never leaving mine. "So are you. And you dress like them. You could be one if you want." This kid is as observant and direct as her father.

"Oh, well, thank you. Maybe if I let the producers know that you said so, they'll let me be on the show. Hmm." I tap my finger to my chin. "Which boy should I date?"

Nose scrunched, she says, "I don't like the *boys*. Boys are kind of yucky." She glances at Graham, who's trying not to laugh. "Except for Daddy."

He shrugs as I arch a brow and smirk at him. "I agree completely. Boys *are* yucky, except for your daddy."

We order Chinese, and I'm impressed when Cara rattles off what she wants and then eats her whole meal with chopsticks, as though she was born with them in her hand.

"Wow. I don't think I ever even *had* Chinese until I moved to LA." As far as Mom had been concerned during my first fifteen years of life, *ethnic* meant either Tex-Mex or a jar of Ragu. Dad made a failed effort to broaden my cultural borders during obligatory weekends and parts of summers that I detested giving up for him. I resisted anything he suggested just to spite him, and arrived in LA with a hopelessly unchic palate. Reid was the one who introduced me to the broad array of the ethnic foods I'd missed growing up.

"That's what you get, growing up in Manhattan—a multi-cultural appreciation and an innate knowledge of take-out." Graham steals a snow pea from Cara's bowl, and without missing a beat, her chopsticks snatch a broccoli floret from his. Chewing, they smile at each other and I marvel that even *this* interaction makes me want him.

By the time I leave, we've put Cara to bed and Graham and I have had all the chitchat I can stand. Unfortunately, now isn't the night for me to slide onto his lap and beg him to carry me to his bedroom. The signals he's sending are still wholly friendship-based, and I know what comes of pushing him for something he doesn't know he wants. Patience is one virtue I have in abundance, when I have a target on which to focus. My goal with Graham isn't just sex and morning-after guilt (on his side—I'd feel no such thing). I want it all.

Without warning, I hear my mother's voice in my head, referring to a man she recently started seeing: *I'm not gonna be some quick lay in the hay. If I want the cha-ching! lifestyle, I have to be patient. I want it all.*

I lay my head back against the taxi seat and close my eyes. I'm. Not. *Her.*

I support myself. *Entirely.* I have my own money. I *make* my own money. Unlike my mother, who hops from one man's bank account to another's, I don't now and won't ever need a man for financial support.

I'm not her. I'm not her. I will *never* be her.

Chapter 20

Emma

"I had no idea how often you *eat*." After this morning's interview in San Bernardino, Reid and I set off for San Diego. We'll do our last early-morning interview of the week there tomorrow, and somehow he talked me into letting him drive us instead of flying.

He's already claimed to be starving to death twice, though he admits to having eaten breakfast. First stop: two hash browns, three eggs and orange juice at McDonald's; second stop: a grande caramel macchiato from Starbucks and a protein bar from the glove compartment. Now we're keeping our eyes peeled for an In-N-Out somewhere just off the I-15, right before we get into San Diego, and it's not even noon.

"I need a few thousand calories a day or I'll start losing muscle. Right after I pass out."

I scowl at him. I haven't so much as looked at a fast food burger in three months, and I've already planned a room-service salad for my lunch. "I hate you."

He laughs. "You're going to get something this stop, right? Burger? Chocolate shake?"

My mouth drops open. "Are you serious? We're going to be on *Ellen* next week. Don't you remember what the media did to me last fall when I ate *bread* one day?"

Crap. I can't believe I just reminded him of that.

He gives me a wicked grin. "Ah, yeah, the infamous baby bump week." He chuckles when I roll my eyes and cross my arms. "Emma, you can't take that stuff personally—it's just meaningless gossip."

"How can I not take it personally when people all over the world are discussing which cast hottie knocked me up?"

He makes a *psshh* sound, dismissing my argument. "A bunch of stupid speculation, all proved to be fictional in the end."

I sigh heavily. "That's exactly what I mean—why should I have to prove that sort of thing to anyone? It's nobody's business."

He's staring straight out the windshield and I'm wondering if he's going to respond when he points and says, "Ha! There it is." As he exits the highway, he opens the center console, pulls out a Lakers cap and shoves it over his trademark dirty-blond hair. He grins, his blue eyes well hidden behind his mirrored Ray-Bans. "Whaddaya think—regular guy?"

Of course—because a Lakers cap and Ray-Bans are automatic regular-guy camouflage. We'd been lucky on the other two stops—the person at the window each time was older and hadn't recognized him. "Reid, we aren't in Beverly Hills or even Long Beach, and you're driving a yellow—whatever this is."

Pulling into the parking lot, he shakes his head. "It's a Lotus. And we're cruising around So-Cal, not *Kansas*."

I shrug, suppressing a laugh, wondering if he's actually this clueless about *regular* people or if he's just screwing with my head. "Whatever you say, Mr. Regular Guy."

Once he lowers his window, the aroma of fries is overwhelming, and my stomach gurgles in protest. I haven't eaten fries since the last time Emily forced half of hers on me in her typical manner: *Get your ass back, would ya? It's practically nonexistent back there.* Reid orders a burger with three meat patties and no cheese, wrapped in lettuce instead of a bun, and a gigantic vanilla shake. "Are you sure you don't want something?"

Clenching my jaw, I shake my head, willing myself not to breathe through my nose.

When we pull up to the window, the girl working the register tells Reid the total as she turns towards him, and then she nearly stops breathing. He hands her a fifty and her hands shake as she pulls bills and coins from the cash drawer. She has to start her tally over three times. Finally, she hands him his change, but forgets to count it back. Wide-eyed, her hands still trembling, she just shoves the money into his hands all at once.

"Thanks," he smiles, and she looks as though she might faint.

"You're welcome," she squeaks, backing away from the window before disappearing around a corner.

Reid stuffs wadded bills into the front pocket of his jeans and tosses the coins into a cup holder as we wait for the food.

"This is just a guess, mind you—but I think she *may* have seen through your elaborate *Regular Guy* disguise."

His mouth twists up on one side. "Smart ass."

"Just sayin'."

Three girls and one guy, all four of them stuffing into the tiny window space, deliver his food, which consists of one small paper bag and one large Styrofoam cup. Our original cashier hands him the shake as four pairs of eyes shift back and forth between us, and the guy hands him the bag. It doesn't take long for them to figure out my identity, too—I hear my name whispered amongst them.

"Would you like extra napkins?" a second girl asks, handing out a stack two inches thick without waiting for an answer.

"Here's your straw!" the third girl waves it out the window, blinking rapidly as Reid reaches to take it from her hand.

"Will there be anything else?" the boy asks, beaming.

"No thanks, this is perfect." Reid turns his smile on them again, and four sighs come from the window. I roll my eyes behind my sunglasses, not that anyone notices.

We park near an exit, windows down, so he can wolf down the unwieldy beef and lettuce burger. He tries to hand me the shake. "Have some."

"No."

Toggling it back and forth, he turns on the full-wattage Reid Alexander smile. "I got the large so there would be enough to share."

"*No.*"

He takes a sip, peering at me over the top of his sunglasses, his blue eyes full of amused mischief. "Mmm, *so* good. No?" I shake my head. "At least hold it for me while I eat, then."

With the cup holders full of change and empty Starbucks cups, I'm tricked into taking the shake by my own courteousness. *Crap.*

His stupid bunless burger smells good, coupled with the heady aroma of fresh fries from the restaurant behind us, and my mouth is watering from full awareness that the cup I'm holding is filled with several hundred calories of *evil*.

"Emma," he says, his tone coaxing, "a sip isn't going to hurt you."

By the time a couple of shifty-looking guys pull into the parking lot in a beat-up sedan, eyeballing not so much the Lotus as who's *in* the Lotus, Reid has lured me into taking a couple of bites of his burger (which isn't bad) and sipping enough of the shake that I just told him he's the devil.

He watches the two men for about twenty seconds before murmuring, "Hmm. Time to go." I barely have time to rebuckle before he's revved the engine, reversed out of the end spot and accelerated straight out of the lot with the sedan in pursuit.

I look back and they're right behind us. A maniacal smile spreads across the passenger's face right before a large black camera obscures it. The last thing we want to do is lead the paparazzi directly to the hotel. I spin forward. "They're right behind us."

Reid glances in his side mirror, smirking. "Not for long." We hit the entrance ramp and he's going ninety before we're fully *on* the freeway. Gliding around slower-moving cars—by which I mean *all* other cars—he loses the sedan in the thickening traffic. Reaching for the shake, he curls his hand, still warm from holding the burger, around mine, and leans close to sip from it rather than taking it from me. "Mmm. Damn that's good."

I clear my throat and try to slip my hand out from under his, but he transfers his hand back to the wheel, releasing me. Checking his mirrors, he grins. "Rule number one of tailing a Lotus: don't attempt it in a Hyundai."

REID

We're almost to the hotel when I get a text from Brooke. It's a link and nothing more, and I'm pretty damned sure I'll find photos of Brooke and Graham getting cozy when I click on it. I'll check it out once I'm in my room.

"So, dinner tonight?" I say to Emma, noting that she's checking her phone as well, and frowning. She doesn't answer. "Emma?"

"Hmm?" She glances up, worry in the downward slope of her brows and the unfocused gaze of her gray-green eyes.

"Everything okay?"

Blinking, she shutters her distressed expression. "Oh. Yeah. Fine."

My lips twist. "Convincing."

She blinks again and shakes her head. "It's nothing, really. Just… it's nothing."

Someone must have alerted her to the photos. I haven't talked to Brooke in a couple of days, so I have no idea how successful she and Rowena were last night—but if Emma's response is due to those photos, Brooke's personal paparazza must have nailed it.

The traffic is bottlenecking as we get into town, so I can't do any more than glance at Emma a couple of times to gauge her level of turmoil. Staring out the window, her reflection is no longer scowling. While I don't get any pleasure from upsetting her, she'll need to be upset enough to break things off with Graham for this to go down as planned.

Speed-dialing my manager, I tell him we're almost there. "According to the Garmin, we'll be there in five to ten."

"Good. A bodyguard is waiting in the lobby. I'll have him move outside, just in case." George is always cautious, which I appreciate. Very little sneaks up on him. The exceptions to that are my occasional dumbass activities… like that under-aged girl I didn't have to mention to him (thank God and John for that). I hate disappointing George.

At the hotel valet stand are a couple of bored-looking guys in red vests. A dozen feet behind them, our bodyguard for our stay in San Diego exits the hotel—big and badass, arms crossed over his chest and wearing the characteristic intimidating scowl. He could be one of those Ultimate Fighter competitors. I don't see any paparazzi or fans—a relief after the hasty departure from the In-N-Out.

The valets perk up when they spot the Lotus. Normally, I feel possessive of my wheels and hate turning it over to valets, but I'm so over this car that I don't care. I told Dad to arrange available funds for me to car-shop as soon as the premiere is over. I definitely want a Porsche. John suggested a 911 GT3.

As Emma and I exit the car, the bodyguard steps up ahead of the valets. They hang back, daunted by his tank-like size. "Mr. Alexander, Ms. Pierce, I'm Alek. I'll be joined by another security team member within the next hour, in case either or both of you need to leave the hotel for any reason, separately or together. Otherwise, we'll occupy rooms near your suite and are at your disposal during your time in San Diego."

Emma's eyebrows rise. "Um, thank you, Alek. It's nice to meet you." He shakes her hand, giving us each his card and telling us to call him before leaving the suite, so he or his colleague can accompany us wherever we want to go.

The valets exchange looks, clearly unsure if they're even allowed to approach us. "Heads up," I call before tossing the Lotus keys to the one nearest me.

Alek has all the luggage except Emma's laptop bag, which she's sliding onto her shoulder, and mine, which she hands me as she shuts the trunk lid. "What does he mean, 'your suite'?" she asks as after I pass a couple of twenties and instructions to the valets and follow her inside.

I shrug. "I guess we'll find out in a minute. Production set up the reservation." I don't plan to tell her I was contacted for the specific arrangements of said reservation, so I know *exactly* what 'your suite' indicates.

The chrome and glass entry doors slide open soundlessly as we walk up to them, and the concierge meets us just inside. "Good afternoon, Mr. Alexander, Ms. Pierce. Right this way, please."

The suite is a two-bedroom penthouse. A bellhop transfers the luggage upstairs while we're getting our keys and I'm signing my name and halfway listening as the concierge rattles off the various rider-required items he's handled for us ahead of time.

For me: grilled chicken and hardboiled eggs from room service available at any time, a shower with a clear glass door—not a curtain, minimum 1200 thread-count Egyptian cotton sheets, ten goose down pillows, two 700-fill down comforters, fresh flowers daily, dry cleaning picked up and returned twice daily, a full gaming system and games (type TBD), wireless controllers and batteries, minimum 52" flat screen television, four new toothbrushes per day (different colors), a lint roller, and a box of Crown condoms.

Emma's list: cold bottled water and a bowl of fruit. Shit. In comparison, I come off sounding like J. Lo. Fortunately, she doesn't seem to be listening, staring at the key in her hand and looking apprehensive.

Once we're in the penthouse elevator—which requires one of our room keys to enter—I lean against the pebble-flecked wall, arms crossed loosely. "Are you okay with us sharing a suite? I guess production fell for their own buzz. Just so you know, I've stayed here before, and the bedrooms inside the suite are completely separate."

The elevator deposits us directly into the living area, the wall of windows opposite displaying an unobstructed ocean view. "Wow," she says. I don't think she's going to object to the suite.

"Come look." I walk to the window. When she follows and looks, I point left. "Mexico."

"Wow," she repeats.

"What time do you want to have dinner? We can go out, or have a chef come up and cook for us." I have to laugh at the look on her face—eyes wide and mouth slightly ajar. "Are you sure you want to give all of this up to go to college, Emma? I'll bet your agent is already getting daily requests for roles someone wants you to consider…"

She turns and walks into the Asian-décor seating pit, plopping onto a sofa. "He is. And I admit it's tempting." She gazes around the room, her fingers brushing the soft leather under her hand. "*This* is tempting. But there are things I don't want to give up, even for all of this." I sit opposite her. "I've never been able to choose my own direction. My own future. What I wanted was assumed, based on other people's opinions. My dad meant well, but meaning well isn't really good enough, you know?"

I can't follow her reasoning about wanting to study theatre instead of becoming a huge film star, but it's easy enough to understand the motivation to direct her own destiny. "There's only one problem with making all of your own decisions," I say, and she waits for me to elaborate. "If you make a mistake, whether career, relationship or *wardrobe*-related," I smile and she does, too, "it's no one's fault but your own. You take all of the responsibility, all of the consequences."

She nods. "True."

"So. Dinner. I vote for trying the chef. Like, *soon*."

She laughs. "How can you be hungry enough to think about food again? I'd look like a side of beef if I ate like you do."

I flex a bicep at her. "Are you saying I *don't* look like a side of beef?"

The text from Brooke is almost exactly what I thought it would be—photos of her with Graham. But instead of the two of them out together, she's standing on the stoop at his house, smiling up at him and running her fingers through his hair. And then they go inside. The accompanying article is all conjecture about what they were doing for the three hours and fifteen minutes she was there. There's a perfect shot of her leaving the apartment with her Cheshire cat smile.

Me: So operation graham went as planned?
Brooke: His kid was there
Me: Um, what
Brooke: Shit
Me: He has a kid??? Calling you.

"Does Emma know? Of course she knows... what the hell, Brooke?" My head is spinning. I'm trying to keep my voice down since Emma is somewhere in the suite with nothing more than my flimsy bedroom door between us, but I'm pacing like crazy.

"Reid, you *cannot* say anything about this to anyone," Brooke hisses.

"He knows he can't keep this a secret right?"

"Of course, but you have to promise me—"

"I'm not going to say anything. He knows about *our* secret indiscretion, after all. That's why you told him, isn't it?" Obviously. It even makes a weird sort of sense. "What about your photographer flunky? No way would *she* not reveal this."

She releases a sigh. "She doesn't know and I'm not telling her—yet. I want the first public photos of Cara to be the three of us, together."

I come to a solid stop. She has this more intricately planned out than I gave her credit for. "You are beyond frightening. You realize that, right?"

"What do you mean?" She knows exactly what I mean.

"Nothing." Nothing except I'm glad she's not manipulating *me*—without my knowledge. "Emma and I are in San Diego. Next week we do a couple of San Fran stations and *Ellen*, and the week after that *Conan*, and then the premiere. She's a little too comfortable at the moment. I'm going to throw her off balance a bit, make sure she knows I'm still interested."

"Meaning?"

"Brooke, you know I don't kiss and tell."

"Reid—don't you f—"

Yeah, I don't really need to hear that tirade.

Chapter 21

Emma

Over grilled ciabatta and brie, Reid asks me about Marcus. I admit that we were dating, and that he was correct in assuming I'd broken things off with him right before the disastrous prom night.

"Why'd you even go with him, then?" He tops off our wine glasses and sets the bottle back into the ice bucket. A chef arrived to make our dinner. She's in the small gourmet kitchen, so we're sitting close together on the sofa and talking quietly.

"I felt guilty."

His mouth turns up on one side and he lowers his chin—a look that would have melted me not so long ago. "Go on."

I shrug, concentrating on spreading the brie evenly over the surface of the bread. "It's always hard to break things off with someone."

He takes the cheese spreader from my hand when I'm done. "Why not wait until after his prom to do it, then? You gave him too much of an opportunity to be an asshole, and he took it."

My face warms. "I was worried that he was expecting... things to become more serious." I glance up to see that he's mulling over the back and forth that occurred between *us*. "I thought it was better to be honest up front."

He laughs softly. "The honesty policy doesn't always work out so well, huh?"

I purse my lips. "Well, actually, it did. I didn't feel guilty any more after that. I knew from how he reacted that I'd made the right decision about him, even if it was a wretched night."

My words apply to him last fall as well as they do to Marcus two weeks ago, and his eyes tell me he knows it.

"I am sorry, you know," he says. I swallow and ignore it when his gaze dances to my mouth and back.

The server who arrived with the chef exits the kitchen and stops several feet away. "Please excuse me. Dinner is served." He indicates the small table adorned with linen, china, and a romantic cluster of candles. I worry again that Reid arranged all of this while pretending that production was responsible, and the repetition of his apology from March does nothing to contradict that concern.

Just when I think he's dropped the subject, Reid leans back in his chair, twisting the wine glass in his hand and watching me, his eyes as dark as Graham's in the low light. "So why'd you break it off with Marcus so suddenly?" He tilts his head. "There's someone else, isn't there?"

Graham thinks I have an effective poker face, but that's not the case tonight with Reid. Either he's been spying on me, or my thoughts are as clear as glass to him. I could lie right now, but he'd know. He's already smiling as though he does. "Who is it?" He leans up, waiting.

I'm saved by the server again as he removes our salad plates and delivers the main course of pappardelle pasta and roasted mushrooms, but the reprieve is short-lived and Reid isn't letting this go.

"Well?"

I sigh. "It's Graham."

His eyes widen slightly and fall away from mine momentarily. "Really." And then those eyes flash to mine and away, as though he knows something I don't. "Hmm. Interesting."

"Interesting, why?"

He shakes his head minimally, his attention on his plate as he slices a bite. We dine in silence and I wait for him to elaborate, but he says nothing more. Finally, he rests his silverware on his plate, folding his arms in front of it. He stares at me. "I have one request."

147

Request? "What?"

"If he fucks it up, I want another shot." Before I can sputter a reply, he holds up one hand and adds, "I don't want an answer. I just want you to know where I stand. And I'm not going to interfere with whatever you two have going on," he smiles then, his expression far from angelic, "unless you ask me to."

Graham told me two days ago that Brooke was visiting New York—meeting with people about the movie she plans to film late summer. They had dinner together last night, and he was late Skyping with me because of it—but he was completely open with the fact that she'd come over and had spent a couple of hours with him and Cara. And I was fine with it.

Until I got a text from Emily earlier today, with a link to the paparazzi photos of the two of them. Suddenly his devoted friendship with her isn't as easy to stomach. On one hand, they've known each other for years and have a mutually supportive history I can't hope to challenge. On the other hand, my best friend is spitting nails and telling me he's no better than Reid. Her last text asks the question I can't answer: He never told you he had a KID. What else is he hiding?

It's true—I know only what he tells me, and my heart has no problem trusting every word he says. But I was stupid about Reid. I was stupid about Marcus. What if I'm being stupid about Graham, but I just don't know it yet?

All I could hope was that the photos wouldn't look as bad on a full-sized screen as they did on my phone. Once Reid and I checked into the hotel and I shut myself into my room, I brought up the links on my laptop. On my 15-inch screen, they're definitely worse. Graham stands in the doorway to his home—a place I've never been—smiling down at Brooke as she runs her fingers through his hair, her breasts brushing against his chest. There's no awkwardness or irritation on his face. He seems fine with her touching him that way.

I'm *not* fine with it.

Knowing I had hours before our appointed Skype time, I spent the afternoon napping, reading, and watching Reid play video games, followed by dinner and ending with Reid's out-of-nowhere declaration. He'd asked me not to answer, and I hadn't.

He seemed almost confident that Graham would screw up. At best, he's seen the photos; at worst, his new and improved relationship with Brooke makes him privy to information I don't have. His indirect allegation planted a seed of doubt that I can't reject entirely, as much as I want to.

At 9:00, I sign on and am so happy to see Graham's face that I almost want to ignore the whole confrontation. "Hey," he smiles.

At 9:01 I get a text from Emily: You are not allowed to ignore this btw. ASK HIM.

"Hi. All done with finals?"

He heaves a deep sigh. "Yeah. One more paper to wrap up and I'll be finished. How are you? Snug in your hotel room, I see."

"Yes. I'm so ready to get up *after* sunrise again. I've been up before 5:00 every day this week."

At 9:02, Emily proves how well she knows me with another text: I'm serious, Em. ASK. HIM.

I bite my lip, debating the words to use. "Graham, um, Emily sent me a link to some photos…" I hope he knows about them already, that he can explain them away.

"What photos?"

"Of you and Brooke?" I hate the inflection of my voice—like this is a harmless question.

"Brooke? I don't understand." He doesn't know. *Damn.*

"I'm sending you the link." My heart is pounding as I watch him pull up a browser and click on the link, no sound but the tapping of his laptop keys.

It's obvious when the link is loaded—his brows knit and he looks pissed. "What the *hell*. This was last night." He examines the three photos closely, and then his eyes scan side-to-side as he reads the accompanying story. I wait silently for his response.

Finally he pulls up the Skype screen, and my first instinct is to hide my face. "Emma, you know none of this is true, right?"

This is what I want him to say. Exactly what I want him to say. The last thing I want to be is a clingy girl who's so insecure that she can't handle her boyfriend talking to another girl, but I can't brush aside the uneasiness. "But the pictures—the way she's touching you…" A knock sounds on my door, and I'm glad for the escape. "Just a minute."

When I pull it open, Reid stands there with the room service menu in his hand. "Hey, did you want some—what's the matter, Emma?"

I shake my head, feeling like an idiot and trying not to cry. "I'm fine."

He tosses the menu in a chair and his hands go to my shoulders. "What's wrong?"

"I'm fine," I repeat, stepping back and grabbing the menu. I hand it back to him. "I'm not hungry, but thanks."

He spots the open laptop on my bed and arches a brow. His voice lowers to a whisper. "Talking to Graham?"

I nod.

He takes my chin in his hand, looks into my eyes, and in the same low tone tells me, "Come talk to me when you're done, if you need to." Fantastic—he's definitely seen the photos.

I nod again, so he'll leave, and I shut the door behind him once he does.

Graham's expression is shuttered when I return. "Was that Reid?"

"Yes."

"Why is he coming to your room?"

My answer slips out before I consider the implications of it. "We're in a suite."

He gazes at me silently, sitting back slowly from the webcam, becoming blurry. His hand lays curved across his mouth as though he's literally preventing himself from speaking. His fingers shift and two words escape. "A suite?"

"There are *two* bedrooms." My tone is defensive. He's questioning Reid sharing a living room with me for one night, while the *whole world* is viewing photos of him with Brooke pressed to his chest as she gazes up at him, her fingertips grazing his forehead in an intimate caress.

"Awesome."

"What are you implying, Graham?"

He takes a deep breath. "I'm not implying anything. I just don't trust him." He stares away from the screen, silent after this pronouncement, and my screen's image of him is still too distant for me to guesstimate his theories. His physical withdrawal is easy enough to read, though, even from thousands of miles away.

The constricted sensation that keeps me from swallowing

prevents me from replying as well. Not trusting Reid shouldn't affect Graham's confidence in *me*.

Finally, he looks at the screen and leans closer, and I gulp at the lump in my throat, sliding down like a grapefruit in my windpipe.

"I have a research paper to finish and turn in tonight, so we'll talk tomorrow, all right?" he says, and I nod and whisper goodnight.

GRAHAM

What did I tell Emma before—that I'm not possessive? Screw *that*.

During the past three weeks, we've spent an hour or more on Skype every night that we weren't together. She's relayed stories about her stepmother, childhood acting gigs and Emily, and I've strummed my guitar and sung her lines of songs that I might or might not have written, which might or might not be about her.

Tonight we were off in fifteen minutes. Her naiveté about Reid Alexander was pissing me off and I was about to unleash a whole string of assertions that can't be unsaid.

I've watched my parents when they argue. Their disagreements seldom become elevated enough to include raised voices, but whenever my father's jaw is so clenched that he could grind diamonds between his teeth, he goes for a walk around the block. It doesn't matter what kind of weather it is, either—I've seen him take off in tempest conditions and come back soaked to the bone with an inside-out umbrella. The point is to never say words you can't take back.

"I thought you were supposed to *communicate* with each other?" Cassie asked Mom once, years ago, after Dad stomped rigidly out the front door. "Isn't that what your whole, like, *career* is based on telling people to do?"

Brynn and I eavesdropped from around the corner. We stared at each other in mute acknowledgement of Cassie's direct hit. Cassie was often Dad's advocate, though Mom usually told her to stay out of it. This time she merely sighed. "Yes, but there are exceptions. When you find yourself about to say something that crosses a line, something that could cause irreparable harm, sometimes the best you can do is just not say that thing."

"Dad would never say something like that," Cassie huffed.

Mom laughed once, no amusement in the sound. "Exactly."

I do have a paper due tomorrow, but the body of the paper is done; only the citations page remains. Inadvertently, I've instituted my own version of walking around the block, because there are a load of words threading through my skull right now and *none* of them are easygoing or objective.

I don't fault Reid for his multitude of casual hookups. I'm a guy—I've had plenty of my own and I'm not that big of a hypocrite. What I fault him for are the two times I know of that he actively encouraged a girl to fall ass over elbows for him—as Brooke would say—when he had no intention of sticking around. I could excuse what he did to Brooke as immaturity, if he hadn't done the same thing to Emma *recently*. As soon as he doesn't get what he wants, he's out screwing as many girls as he can run through.

Emma seems to think that because he's playing nice at the moment, he's above suspicion. Like he took no for an answer where she was concerned. But I watched him that night everyone went out—the calculating gaze he leveled on her. If this was two hundred years ago, I'd have contemplated taking him outside and beating the shit out of him for looking at her like that—and that *pinky swear* thing he did with her would have guaranteed it.

My paper submitted, I'm unofficially finished with college. At one time, I considered pursuing graduate degrees and becoming a professor like my parents, but that was a year or so ago, before I began getting more steady work as an actor. Standing in front of a class droning on about analytical symbolism and rhetorical theory while striving for tenure and churning out research? Strangely, some of that *is* appealing. But I enjoy acting more, and I don't need to reach Reid Alexander status to feel successful doing it.

It's almost 11:00 p.m. in San Diego, but Emma has to be up early to get to the studio. As sure as I am of her, as sure as I want to be, I don't want to think about the fact that I left her hurt and angry tonight, with no one to talk to but Reid Alexander. Not my brightest move.

Damn.

I didn't ask her about her interview in San Bernardino. I didn't find out if the drive to San Diego in Reid's bright yellow Matchbox car was as uneventful as he'd predicted. I didn't tell her the end of the story where I'm the TA in her literature class, and she's the student who forgot to turn in her paper on time...

I hadn't batted an eye at the photo and story of Reid kissing her at the airport. She told me it was on the cheek (the photo angle made it impossible to tell), and over so quickly that she didn't even feel it.

I know how the paparazzi play their games.

And I do trust her.

So she should trust *me* when I tell her there's nothing between me and Brooke but a strong, committed friendship.

I pull up the photos again, and read the short blurb.

Is another undercover romance blooming inside the *School Pride* cast? Brooke Cameron (of *Life's a Beach* fame) was spotted cozying up to costar Graham Douglas late Wednesday in the doorway of his Manhattan brownstone. They spent a long evening catching up, we presume, as Ms. Cameron left the home alone and none the worse for wear after a visit lasting a bit over three hours. Cameron and Douglas play Caroline Bingley and Bill Collins, respectively, in one of the most highly anticipated teen hits of the summer.

Me: I'm sorry for bailing on you so early. Skype tomorrow at 9?
Emma: Okay
Me: Miss you
Emma: Miss you too

Chapter 22

Brooke

Reid: Bullseye. She was pretty much in tears.
Me: Goooooal!
Reid: You are completely deficient in empathy, aren't you?
Me: When required, yes. So did you comfort her?
Reid: Offered. She stayed in her room.
Me: Losing your touch?
Reid: My touch is as intact as ever, thx.

Growing up in the suburbs of Austin meant playing soccer. I got stuck in the goal far too often during the first couple of seasons, and since my team sucked ass, I was repeatedly scored on. I often left the field crying and wiping snot onto my sleeve. My coach—another player's father—took my tears as typical feminine weakness, patting my shoulder and telling me not to cry—all *we'll show 'em what-for next time*.

Coach Will missed the point. I wasn't dejected; I was pissed as hell that my team didn't have a single player who deserved to call herself a *defender*, including his incompetent, stuck-up daughter. What my coach failed to understand was that as much of a *girl* as I appeared to be—fat blonde curls tumbling from my ponytail, the ribbons in my hair and threaded through my shoes perfectly matching my uniform—I was in actuality a carnivorous monster

154

who wanted to chew up the field with my custom-ordered pink cleats.

I was six.

By age seven, my father had me enrolled in summer soccer camps run by actual adult soccer players, and my natural abilities began to shape into skilled aggression. When fall rolled around, Dad demanded that they put me on a better team with a coach who wasn't "an inept dumbshit who couldn't tell his ass from a hole in the ground." The first game of the season was against my old team. I scored three goals and fouled my ex-coach's daughter with a perfect ankle-hooking trip that left her face-planted in the middle of the recently muddy field.

I had to sit out the rest of the game, which we won because of my pre-halftime scores. I was the star forward from that point on, and the only time I played dirty was when it was called for. People would be surprised how frequently playing dirty is called for when you're the prettiest, fastest player on a competitive first-place team, especially when that team is named the Butterflies.

Dad stopped coming to my games once he had a new wife, a new family, and new-and-improved soccer players to half-raise and discard. I don't know why I gave a shit whether or not he came, but I did. Maybe because the soccer field was the only place I ever felt like he *got* me, so it was like I didn't exist for him anymore. When I started high school I quit cold turkey, which was fine with Mom. She never understood Sporty Girl-Power Brooke anyway.

She submitted my picture to a modeling agency and I got a print ad, and then I got a commercial, to be shot in LA. Mom had always staunchly refused to be a soccer mom; stage mom was more her speed. The rest, as they say, is history.

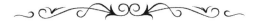

REID

"Déjà vu, eh?" I hand Emma the pull-handle to her carry-on, and she holds it, and her laptop bag, firmly between us. Her tense smile tells me she expects me to respect the not-so-subtle barrier she's erected. Unless I'm willing to breach a wall of luggage, there won't be a repeat of the kiss on her cheek that showed up all over the Internet a week ago, giving the impression of more than it was. Much more.

"I guess I'll see you in a couple of days?" she says, holding out her hand.

I've kissed this girl. Made out with this girl. Still remember her breathless, "Yes," from that afternoon when I told her I wanted her in my bed, before everything fell apart. Somehow, though, none of those memories feel connected to *her*—this girl standing in front of me, extending a hand for me to shake like we're respectable business colleagues and I've never had my tongue in her mouth or my hands up her shirt.

I've gotten way too good at my own ability to disengage.

I take her hand, but instead of merely shaking it, I lean forward and pull it up to my lips, kissing her just behind the middle knuckle. "I guess you'll be meeting me in San Fran after all, huh?"

She inclines her head and smirks, pulling her hand from mine and readjusting the laptop strap. "I guess. But I get the feeling that meeting Monday and Tuesday mornings at 5:00 a.m. for more morning show interviews isn't what you had in mind."

Correct. "Come on, Emma. We *have* to go somewhere cool Monday night." I turn to walk back around to the driver's side, because we're getting some attention from other departing passengers who've begun to figure out who we are. She's flying home to Sacramento while I'm driving back to LA alone. "San Francisco is a culinary heaven. And I'll have you back to your room in time for your Skype appointment." I wink at her and she rolls her eyes.

"Oh-*kay*," she says, as though she's exasperated and I've worn her down.

I feel as though she just moved a game piece that puts her that much closer to check mate, and I can't help thinking what a bastard I've turned into.

All's fair in love and war. A fine sentiment—if this was either.

"John. Please tell me you have something stimulating on tap for tonight."

The I-5 is two hours of spotty cell service with occasional ocean views, until it veers away from the Pacific and loses all aesthetic appeal, becoming frequently punctuated with snarls of traffic in heavily populated areas. I'm already bored out of my mind and I still have at least another hour to go, probably two, because of traffic anywhere near LA this time of day.

"That depends what you mean by *stimulating*, man. On a scale of one to porn, where do you wanna be?"

There's a car full of girls next to me, all of them trying to see through the nearly opaque window tint. Right before the light turns, I roll the windows down and glance over, watch their mouths all turn into "O" as the signal switches to green and I'm gone. "One to porn. Hmm. I'd say a solid eight or nine would do."

John yawns into my ear. "Eight isn't out of the question. This girl who was on my econ project team is having a dinner party tonight—"

"*Dinner party*? What the hell man—we're not thirty-five."

"Yeah that's what I thought, until she dragged me to one last week that her sorority sister was hosting. Basically everyone sits around being all pseudo-intellectual and getting stoned. All I had to do to seem like the smartest guy there was shut the fuck up."

"So pretty much your natural state when stoned."

"Yeah."

Less than two weeks until the premiere—at which point one of two things will happen. Most likely: Brooke will succeed with Operation Graham, and Emma, in her emotionally defenseless state, will fall into my arms with one good pull. Less likely: Brooke will fail, Graham and Emma will run off into the sunset holding hands and making everyone within a ten-mile radius vomit, and I'll be free to go back to the openly hedonistic life that other nineteen-year-old guys would kill to have. It's win-win, if I can just get to it.

When we arrive, John's girl answers the door, pressing herself into him. "You're late. I thought you weren't coming," she chides. She's one of those squeaky-voiced girls, which fits her tiny size. Standing behind him, I can't actually see her. I only know she's on the other side of him because I can hear her.

He hitches a thumb over his shoulder. "I had to pick Reid up. You *said* you needed another guy for the boy-girl balance, so I delivered."

Her eyes peek over his shoulder then, and immediately widen. "You brought—*Reid Alexander*?" she squeaks. "That's who you meant when you said you were bringing *Reid*?"

John isn't usually one to keep our friendship secret, our relationship being a major part of his social resume. Then again, he sometimes savors other people's shock when he introduces me as a friend in person. I don't mind. I actually sorta like it.

"Didn't I tell you that already?" His voice is all blasé and it's an effort for me not to laugh. He glances back at me with the same laugh-evading expression I'm wearing. "I'm almost sure I did."

"Uh, *no*. I'd have remembered that. Ohmigod."

I step up to stand next to John, handing over a bottle of wine I took from Dad's collection right before we left. Hopefully it's something old and expensive, but not old enough to taste like shit.

John makes the introductions, epitomizing the perception of no big deal. "Reid, Bianca. Bianca, Reid."

She takes the bottle with a strangled, "Nice to meet you." John chuckles when she tosses a small glare at him, mixed with newfound appreciation, before turning and walking into the open room and announcing, "Hey guys, this is John, and, uh, Reid..."

Five people—three girls and two guys—sit mashed around a table that looks thrift-store shabby but upon closer inspection was just made to look that way. The chairs and dishes are mismatched, too, as though this in itself coordinates with the cinderblock walls and exposed pipes. Pretend grunge annoys the shit out of me for some reason, but I'm not here to pass judgment on the décor.

Four people stare at me, open-mouthed. The other guy looks at me, then John, then the others, and back around full-circle, confusion etched on his face. He says something to the girl near him, who says something back. "Ohhh," he says, and then his expression catches up with everyone else's: slack-jawed awe at a celebrity, in the flesh, at their intimate little dinner party. I glance at John. He eats this shit up.

Bianca and one of the other girls share the open-loft apartment. Everyone attends USC, where John is, shockingly, still on track to complete the business degree his CFO father expects.

We're lingering over the barely-edible pasta the girls made and John is opening our fourth or fifth bottle of wine, and the talk has strayed to classic hipster topics—philosophy and music—neither of which will ever have a definitive answer. Animated conversation ensues, and John and I follow his earlier edict for dealing with this kind of bullshit: shut up and stay that way.

Bianca's roommate, Jo, has turned narrowed eyes on me several times. So far, I've been ignoring her. Finally, while the others all talk over each other, I lean up, catching her pointed stare and hold it. "Do I know you?" I ask, and she laughs without a trace of humor.

"Really? I thought you celebrity types were above *lines*, especially something so passé." Her voice is a direct contrast to her roommate's—husky and almost masculine.

"You think that was a pick-up line?" I laugh once and shake my head. "Sorry, sweetheart, but *no*. I was just wondering what I'd done to earn the death-stare. I figure either I screwed you at some point and I don't remember—and you're pissed… or I didn't bother—and you're pissed. So which is it?"

Her mouth drops open and her eyes blaze. Grabbing two of the empty wine bottles, she stomps into the kitchen. I think about following her, but decide against making the effort. At least now she has a *reason* to hate me.

A couple of hours later we're like a heap of puppies on the floor, heads on thighs, feet in laps, arms draped over abdomens. People get a lot friendlier when they're high, though not necessarily more interesting. Bianca's reclining halfway on one of the guys, who's delivering an address about what constitutes a lie, philosophically speaking, and quoting Kant and Augustine. John is caressing Bianca's calf, making her moan and then giggle once he gets to her ankle. She sits up and swats his hand, and then they're kissing. Easy enough to see where this party is going.

When I look away from them, I catch Jo giving me that same glare from the other side of the circle. Hell, even being high doesn't calm her inner bitch. She would incinerate me on the spot if she could, and I have *no* idea why. I give her a hooded smile.

When Bianca takes John's hand and pulls him down the hall, one of the other couples breaks off into a recliner in the corner, leaving Jo, me and two other people who look like they'd rather mess around with us than each other. We ignore them and they eventually take the hint, twisting around each other on the sofa, and then Jo gets up and walks to her room down the hall. I get up and follow.

I wonder if she'll bite my tongue if I go for it, if she'll draw blood. She's standing in the middle of her room and I walk up to her, leaning down to kiss her, nothing touching but our mouths. I trace her lips with my tongue. When she opens and I thrust my tongue in her mouth, pulling her closer, it's good for a few seconds… and then she's shoving her tongue in my mouth, pulling my hands down to my sides and taking charge.

I don't mind aggressive girls—hell, Brooke had no problem telling me what she wanted and how she wanted it, and some of my older partners have been the same way. Telling me what to do, where to go? No problem. Sticking a tongue down my throat? No thanks. What's arousing and what isn't is individual, and there's no changing it.

This will require as little kissing as I can manage.

I close the door and pop the lock as she's unbuttoning her blouse, and I'm still curious about the earlier animosity. Especially now. "You have to tell me."

She shrugs off her shirt. "I don't have to do anything. Just shut up and get undressed."

For half a second, I consider. It's no-strings sex, and she *is* attractive. Most guys don't generally turn down sex in these circumstances.

I'm not most guys.

I turn and unlock the door, pulling my phone from my pocket to call a taxi. This situation is close enough to humorous that I'm smiling. Before I get the door open, she's pushing it closed, taking a deep breath. "Okay, wait. Yes."

My hand is still on the doorknob. "Yes what?"

"It was the second one. We were at a party, making out, and some blonde *whore* walked up and grabbed your hand and you just went off with her." She says all of this in such a rush that the words run together. "It was years ago. Before anyone knew who you were. I remembered, though, because no guy had ever humiliated me like that. No one's done it since, either."

The blonde was undoubtedly Brooke. This was one of her favorite little games—she'd pick some random girl at a party or a club, and tell me to go get her mindless. And then she'd just walk up and take me away. I was so hot for Brooke that I never really thought of how the other girls felt, being deserted like that.

"I'm not sure what you want from me now, to make it up to you. Send me packing tonight? The only guy in the house not getting any?" I give her half a smile, hoping for that outcome. I'm *so* not in the mood right now.

"No. Make it up to me there." She points to her bed and lays her hand on mine—the one on the doorknob.

Shit. I'm trapped. I guess I've been stuck in worse encounters than having sex when I'm not really motivated to. "As long as you know it's just tonight."

She laughs. "Yeah, I know all about your little romance—is it real, or publicity?"

It takes me a second to realize she's talking about Emma. "Yeah, *not* discussing that."

She nods. "Sure. Okay. I get it."

I drop my hand from the doorknob. "Okay then."

She takes my hand, pulls me back across the room. "Okay then."

Chapter 23

Emma

I called the hotel this morning to make sure Reid and I were booked into separate rooms for our two nights in San Francisco. Not because I don't trust Reid, but because Graham doesn't.

Which bothers me, but I understand it. The relationships we've had with Reid and Brooke trigger that small voice of *what if* in each of us. He thinks *what if she's not over Reid*, and I think *what if he's really in love with Brooke*.

Thursday night, after Graham texted and said he missed me, I answered that I missed him, too. And then I lay in bed, scrolling through our old messages to each other, all the way back to the one where I asked him to meet me that morning before Dad and I left New York. He hadn't answered, but he'd come. That morning, I wanted him in my life so much that I was willing to accept friendship-only terms, willing to swallow my desire, even if the thought of him with someone else induced a soul-deep ache.

I wouldn't be able to do that now. I'm in too far. I want too much.

I think, too, about Reid's request. I ignored it, because of course Graham's not going to screw this up. And then I picture Brooke, pressed against him, touching him, and I tell myself for the hundredth time that he isn't lying to me. But I'm worried that he's lying to himself.

I wish I'd never seen that paparazzi photo. The thing I fear most would be so much easier to dismiss if it hadn't been burned it into my eyeballs in living color. While I'm at it, I wish *Emily* had never seen it. She won't drop the fact that he was secretive about Cara, even when I tell her that he isn't secretive, he's *guarded*, and yes, there's a difference. "Emily, *I trust him*," I say, and she harumphs. Maybe she hears the fear in my voice. Because that's what it is—this isn't distrust. It's fear.

When I sign into Skype, Graham is waiting for me.

"Ten more days," I say, and he smiles.

We talk about our days. He took Cara to the park. I got my first slightly traumatic, very awkward airport pat-down.

"Strangely enough, the fact that she snapped on latex gloves beforehand *didn't* make me feel any better. She kept stopping and saying, '*Sensitive area*,' when she was about to go somewhere I don't let anyone touch me." I blush when I realize that isn't quite true, and even if my webcam doesn't reveal redder toned skin, I must be giving something away, because Graham arches a brow.

"Hmm."

"What?"

He shakes his head slowly. "I think maybe you've been a very naughty traveler, Emma."

I fall over onto the mattress laughing, embarrassed and turned on. "No more blue gloves! Please!" I say from my prone position. At most, he can see the edge of my hip.

"You know the rules," he says. "No glove, no love."

I sit up. "I cannot *believe* you just said that after what I went through today."

He laughs again while I pout. "I couldn't resist. I'm sorry." He tells me he's been through the pat-down and a couple of body scans while traveling, and whenever he wears one particular band T-shirt to fly, it seems to provoke a random luggage search. "It's bizarre. Radiohead T-shirt equals luggage search. *Every. Time.* I'm a little worried they'll go for body cavities at some point."

We talk a few minutes more, and then he clears his throat and says, "Um, I need to tell you about something."

His tone tells me this isn't a good something. For a couple of seconds, I can't breathe. My heart is thudding in my chest. "Okay."

He takes a deep breath. "You know I'm graduating on

163

Wednesday."

I nod. "Yes." I sense he's not going for congratulations.

"Brooke is coming to the ceremony." He runs a hand through his hair. "I would have told you before, but I honestly forgot about her plans to come whenever we were talking, and I didn't want to just text it to you."

Brooke is attending Graham's graduation. I frown. "When did you invite her?"

"I didn't, really, she just offered, last week. We met right before I started at Columbia, and I guess she just wants to show her support—"

"I get it." I stop him before he offers more details about their years-long, dedicated friendship. "You're really close and you have been for years before you met me, so there's nothing for me to be *concerned* about." *Jealous* about. *Jealous* is what I want to say. But I *am* concerned. I *am* jealous. I am Emma the green-eyed monster.

"Emma, I don't want to upset you…"

Too late.

"There's nothing going on between Brooke and me—any more than there's something going on between you and Reid."

I gasp. "That's not the same at all."

"You're right, it's not. You've actually been intimate… with him." He realizes mid-sentence what he's stepped into, but it's too late to extricate himself from it.

"What exactly do you mean?"

He's not looking at my face on his screen. His eyes are turned away. So I wait. Finally, they blink back at me, dark and unreadable. "I guess I don't know what I mean. And I know it's none of my business, and I have no right to ask."

"Ask *what?* Ask if I've slept with him?"

A muscle clenches at his temple. "I'm not asking you, Emma. It's none of my business."

"So you don't care?"

Sighing, he sits back against his pillows. I hate it when he does that, because I can't see his face clearly at all. "Of course I care." His voice is so soft, and I don't know if it's because he's speaking softly or if it's just because he's moved away from the laptop microphone.

"Okay. So it's not your business. But I didn't." I don't tell him how very close we came. He doesn't need to know that. His eyes close and he breathes another sigh. "Your turn," I say.

A crease appears between his brows. "My turn for what?"

I tilt my head. "You. And Brooke."

"No." There's no hesitation. "I've never slept with Brooke. I thought I told you, the morning we first talked about all of this—"

"You told me you didn't love her. You never said you hadn't slept with her."

We fall silent after this exchange, and the huge space between us feels electrically charged. My throat closes up and even though I'm relieved, I feel like crying.

"Emma, what's wrong, baby?" He's never called me that before. Close to the webcam now, his eyes are worried. "I'm sorry. I don't want you to feel..."

"Insecure?" A tear winds down my cheek and I thumb it away.

He shakes his head. "You aren't insecure. This is new for both of us—this relationship. And we're trying to build it from a distance, after months of separation..." He runs a hand through his hair again and makes a frustrated sound. "It's difficult. But not impossible. I'm sorry about Brooke, and for asking you about Reid—"

"I'm not. I want you to know." My voice lowers. "You need to know, right? That it will be the first time for me..."

"I suppose so, yeah. I hadn't... really thought of it that way. I've never, um..." He chews his lip, eyes shifting down and then back up to watch my face on his screen. "I've never been with a virgin."

My mind is racing, but coming to no conclusions at all. "Oh."

His hand rubs over his face. "God," he mumbles. "I'm going to make you want nothing to do with me."

"Graham," I say, and he moves his hand down to his mouth, uncovering his eyes, watching me. "Trust me. That's not possible."

REID

Emma and I are meeting in the lobby at 5:00 a.m. for the first local station interview. We have a second one Tuesday, followed by a live radio interview in the afternoon. Thursday, we're taping *Ellen*.

When I tell Brooke what I said to Emma—that I wanted another shot if Graham fucked up—she freaks. "Oh my *God*, Reid. *Shit*. That was a huge risk… but maybe she'll automatically turn to you when she realizes he's with me."

"That was my thought." I'm clicking through muted television channels, reclining against a mound of pillows on the hotel bed. Emma is just down the hall. I texted her earlier, told her I was here, and suggested that we meet in the lobby tomorrow morning. I've made plans for us tomorrow night, so I'm giving her unpressured space tonight.

"But she didn't answer you?"

"I told her I didn't want one. That I just wanted her to know where I stood." Leaving the television tuned to music videos, I set the volume on low, like white noise. Emma plays videos in the background in her hotel room like some sort of soundtrack to her life, and I've wondered but forgotten to ask her if she does this at home, too. "So what makes you think you love him?"

"What?" Her voice is confused.

I don't know if I inherited the capacity for debate or I just picked it up as a result of growing up with an attorney, like self-preservation. I'm already imagining what Brooke might say, and what I'll counter with. "You've said a couple of times now that you're 'right' for Graham. Do you think you love him?"

She's silent for a long moment and I think she's about to tell me that how she feels about him isn't my business and by the way go to hell. "I do."

"Why?"

"Why what, Reid?" Exasperation saturates her words. "I don't understand what you want to know, not that it's your business anyway. But I'm in the mood to humor you. So why *what*?"

"Why do you think you love him?" Accent on *think*. Which she catches.

"That's a weird way to put that," she muses. "*Why do you think you love him* rather than *why do you love him*."

"You know I don't believe in love." Whoa—that came out a little bitter. Wounded, even. Shit.

She's quiet again. And then, "You used to."

"Yeah, well. You know how *that* ended." *Dammit.* Why am I saying this to *her* of all people? She grows quiet again and I wish I'd never asked the question.

"Kathryn told me once that loving someone means you want what's best for them. And I'm what's best for him." Kathryn is Brooke's stepmother—one of them. She's the one Brooke is closest to. Ironically, they didn't have to have any relationship at all, because Kathryn was her father's *first* wife—but for some reason, they've always been close. Which is good, because Brooke's mother is one crazy bitch.

"That sounds like convoluted logic to me. My father would say it's a conflict of interest for *you* to decide that *you're* what's best for him." And there's my alter-ego again.

"Are you trying to talk me out of this? Because you'll never get Emma away from him if I don't succeed."

Wow—complete avoidance of my argument *and* a below-the-belt insult. "No, I'm not. Ever heard of devil's advocate? And what the hell, Brooke? I mean shit, I *know* you think he's better than me. I get it. You don't have to fucking underscore it every time we talk."

She huffs a sigh. "This conversation has gotten way out of hand. Look, we're allies on this little venture, but we aren't *friends*. When this is over, I don't care if I ever talk to you again and I'm sure you feel the same."

"Damn right."

"Then let's stop pretending we're BFFs and focus on what we're doing. This week is all about me winning his family over—God, what a pain in the ass that'll be—and you continuing to be emotionally available for Emma. While keeping your dick in your pants."

"You really have a way with words. You know?"

"So I'm blunt. Sue me."

I knew Emma would love the seafood place in Union Square, with its century-old architecture and an interior resembling an underwater fantasy. One look at her face as we entered confirmed my assumption. We're escorted to the glass-walled semi-private room I reserved, where we can observe the rest of the place while the bodyguard who accompanied us blocks the door and any possible intrusions.

"I feel like we're inside an aquarium," she says, leaning closer. "I keep expecting someone to tap on the glass or make fish faces at us."

We've had caviar and oysters on the half shell and tomato bisque soup, with the main course and dessert still to go. Emma has vowed to be on her stair-stepper from the moment she gets home tomorrow afternoon until Thursday morning, when we meet in Burbank to tape *Ellen*.

I lean up on my elbows after the waiter clears the second course dishes. "So when did this thing with Graham begin?" I expected to startle her with this question, but I didn't foresee the full-on blush that floods her face. My eyes narrow. "Wait... was it *before* that night in the club?" The night Graham threatened to kick my ass if I hurt Emma. Which I'm *not* telling her, because girls love that shit.

"What?" The blush surges until she looks sunburned.

I had no idea she had such an overactive conscience. Of course, I didn't know she was capable of what that blush entails, either. She and Graham were screwing around while I was pursuing her? Holy *shit*. She's staring into her lap and I'm torn between amused as hell and seriously ticked off. "So you guys were messing around before you broke it off with me?"

On second thought, I'm not all that amused. Controlling my expression is abnormally challenging, and the aquarium-like walls are suddenly the worst idea *ever*.

"No. It wasn't like that." She looks up, straight into my eyes. Still tomato-red from her hairline to the neckline of her sweater, she seems sincere, though I'm probably the last person qualified to judge honesty or lack thereof in anyone. "We kissed once, before you kissed me. I mean, before *you* kissed *me*, outside of our Will and Lizbeth roles. Nothing else."

Like a slideshow through my head, I recall those photos of the two of them in Austin, running together or preparing to. And then the looks they shared that Brooke and I both noticed, and the protective way he sometimes acted around her. I all but missed that because he seemed even more so with Brooke. Now it all looks like evidence, and I'm not sure I believe her.

"Here's the unavoidable question—especially given the fact

that you two are a thing *now*—why did you begin a relationship with me, instead of him?"

Eyes dropping to her lap, her voice is low. "It was that photo of you and me at the concert. He thought we were already involved." She shrugs. "After that went viral, he decided not to intrude."

So he just backed off and let me have a shot at her with no competition. Interesting. "Hmm. That seems a little… sacrificial."

The anticipated crease appears in her forehead. "What do you mean?"

I lean closer, staring into her eyes in the muted light, my voice restrained, but with an underlying edge I know she'll detect. "There's no way in hell I would have given him the same consideration, if our positions had been reversed." I watch my words sink in and then I back up a bit, reducing the physical tension just enough to convince her that I'm speaking in past tense. Probably.

She clears her throat. "I guess he's just not that, um, competitive."

Spoken like a true hetero-feminist—the girl who *says* she admires guys lacking that aggressive alpha gene, while dreaming of a guy who'll push her up against a wall and kiss her breathless before telling her to shut up and hold on.

"So you and he got together—when—after you and I broke it off last fall?"

If that's true, they were together when I voiced that groveling apology and asked for another chance. I'm not sure which would be worse—if I said those things with no chance at all, or if I said them when she was free and clear, but got shot down anyway.

"No. I ran into him in a coffee shop in New York when I was there a month ago, visiting colleges." She leaves out the Graham-has-a-kid part, predictably better at keeping other people's secrets than Brooke, though I suspect Brooke lets slip only what she means to disclose.

We're silent while the third course is laid out and our glasses are refilled. "Would you like anything else now?" the waiter asks, and we look at each other and shake our heads.

"No thanks, man, we're good."

I picture Emma spotting Graham in some overcrowded

Manhattan coffee shop, with his kid next to him, and I itch to ask her what she thought when she found out. Like, how is that *not* an instant deal-breaker? What eighteen-year-old girl wants her boyfriend to have a secret kid? And how the hell did he end up saddled with it? I can't imagine my parents' reaction if they'd have found out Brooke was pregnant (they didn't) and then I said *Oh and by the way, I want to keep it.* I'd have been under psychiatric observation before I could whimper one more word.

"That's a bizarre coincidence—running into someone in New York," I prompt.

"Mmm-hmm," she says.

"So when are you planning to move there? In the fall?"

"Yeah... maybe before that."

"Oh?"

She takes a bite of her pan-seared Alaskan halibut, as much to stall as anything else, I think. I take a bite of maitake mushroom and wait her out.

Chapter 24

Emma

I'm never sure how Reid gets me to reveal information that might not be hush-hush, but is still personal. He has this way of posing questions—like he's just curious and we're old friends, no big deal, and then *boom*, I'm blurting out stuff about Graham and our relationship. Then I catch myself and I think *crap, how did that happen?*

I haven't even broached the subject of moving to New York early with *Graham*, and I just mentioned it to *Reid*, who's forking bites of grilled ahi tuna while waiting for me to make another unbridled announcement about my private life. The silence stretches taut between us, and finally I glance at him. His dark blue eyes regard me closely, and his compressed lips tell me he's amused.

"What's funny?"

"You, realizing you've said more than you meant to."

I sigh, and laugh, and he laughs, too. "How do you *do* that?"

He shrugs, unashamed, as always. "I was raised by a master cross-examiner. Plus, I'm sneaky."

"*Yeah*, you are. I have an idea. Can we talk about *you*?"

He smiles. "All right. What do you want to know?"

I prop my chin on my fist, *Thinker* style. "Hmm. Okay—you said a few days ago that you and Brooke had reached an understanding." Last fall, I'd have never thought the two of them could coexist in the same room for long. Now they're exchanging pleasantries and acting normal. It's freaky. "What did you mean by that?"

His eyebrows quirk up. "I wouldn't call us friends." I stare at him and he knows I'm waiting for more of an answer. "But like I said, we decided to call a truce of sorts. What happened between us was a long time ago. We were kids."

I'm not as good at this as Reid, because when he stops there, I don't know how to press him further. More than that, I'm face to face with the knowledge that my true reason for prying has everything to do with Graham. He's tangled up in their history, and I've felt left out. Until this moment, that feeling of being excluded was unconscious. As if I'd have wanted to be any part of that train wreck.

"What, no other questions, counselor?"

My thoughts are full of Graham, and I fight clicking my phone to check the time. Reid did promise to have me back in time. His smirk is too superior to ignore, even if he *is* playing at condescension.

"I do have one more critical inquiry," I say, and he leans up, all ears. Suppressing the urge to laugh, I fix a puzzled expression on my face. "So… is yellow your favorite color, or what?"

He growls good-naturedly. "I swear, I'm getting rid of that car next week—right after the premiere. I'd tell you what I'm considering to take its place, but you probably aren't interested in talking makes and specs. Suffice it to say, it won't be *yellow*."

I arch a brow. "Is that a nice way of saying I wouldn't have the faintest idea what you're talking about?"

He laughs, turns one palm up. "Well… unless you've become a closet car aficionada in the past few months…"

It took Stan, the on-set mechanic for *School Pride*, half a day to teach me to unlatch the hood of that car for a scene. "Er, no, I wouldn't say that. But I can drive, as long as it's an automatic—um—motor?"

"*Transmission*." He's chuckling again. "Yeah, Emma the car enthusiast—not-so-much."

"I guess it's a good thing I'm moving to New York, where I won't need a car."

His smile falters, but he recovers quickly. "If you object so strongly to yellow, how will you put up with taking taxis everywhere?"

I smile. "I was thinking I might actually learn to use the *Metro*."

"There's one of those normal, everyday things I'll never be able to do—use public transportation," he says.

"Definitely not, especially with your I-heart-Reid-Alexander stalkers."

"My what?"

Crap. I forgot he wasn't aware of Jenna's term for his fans. "Er, nothing. You seem to like being recognized everywhere you go, though."

He shrugs. "It has its benefits. And it's part of the job. Anyone who doesn't understand that going in is unrealistic."

"Maybe. But not everyone gets as famous and well-recognized as you are—*most* actors aren't. Graham and I didn't have much of an issue, jogging in the mornings, but you couldn't even step outside the hotel without being mauled by fans."

He toys with his spoon, rotating it through his fingers, over and under. "People love what I do, and I love doing it. Those are the most important parts of the equation. And I'm rich enough to *buy* more seclusion, if I feel the need for privacy, so I can't really complain." He tilts his head, watching me closely. "You'll have a surge of recognition once *School Pride* is out. But if you don't do any more movies, it'll probably die down. Is that why you wanted out?"

"No. I'm not *afraid* of fame, though I'd never be as comfortable with it as you are. But I do crave some normalcy. I'm excited about going to college. Scared, but excited. And I love the idea of acting on a stage instead of in front of a camera. After college, I guess I'll do what everyone else does. Weigh my options and make the best choice I can at the time."

He nods his head. "Fair enough."

173

GRAHAM

My family couldn't be less thrilled that Brooke will be attending my graduation ceremony with them, *and* staying over two nights. I've already endured and ignored Cassie's and Brynn's opinions on the matter; I finally had to bite the bullet and tell Mom. Her reaction: "Well, *shit*."

Luckily, Cara's in bed. She's at that age where she mimics *everything*. Brynn can't get through a conversation without at least one inappropriate word, even when she bleeps herself... which Cara has also picked up. A couple of days ago I got all sorts of looks when our line at Dean & Deluca stalled and Cara demanded loudly, "What the *bleep* is going on up there?"

"I can't exactly ask her go to commencement by herself," I say. Behind my mother's eyes the gears turn furiously, trying to figure out how to make that exact thing happen.

Dad recognizes the distracted look on her face for what it is— plotting. "*Audrey.*"

"Hmm?" Pulled from her reverie (where she is no doubt personally loading Brooke on a flight to Uzbekistan or somewhere equally distant), Mom blinks innocently. Dad and I know better than to fall for her angelic expression.

"Audrey, Graham's *friend* is coming to watch him graduate. He's invited her; we aren't going to uninvite her."

This probably isn't an ideal time to admit that Brooke invited herself.

"Can't we at least put her up in a nice hotel, where she'll be more comfortable?" Mom's voice is sugary with a veiled edge of *for-the-love-of-God-please*.

Brooke was a demanding guest two years ago—questioning the thread count of the guest bed sheets, asking where we kept the new toothbrushes and razors for visitors, and even putting in an order for a specific brand of bottled water. Mom spent the duration of Brooke's visit seething, and she hasn't forgiven or forgotten.

"Between Columbia and NYU commencement ceremonies, the hotels are all booked and have been for months." Dad's voice of reason falls on deaf ears.

"She could stay nearby. In Jersey, say."

"Mom!" Torn between amusement and exasperation, I'm not

sure what to add to the exclamation.

Dad sighs. "She's staying here, Audrey. We'd better get the guest room set up."

"And alert the servants," she mumbles. "Oh wait. That's *me*."

I slide an arm around her shoulders as she rinses dishes and I prepare to load the dishwasher. "Mom, Brooke has matured over the past two years. I doubt you'll have the same issues you had with her as before." I should be crossing my fingers behind my back.

"I won't be holding my breath, Graham."

Emma is a few minutes late signing in, and I assure her it's no big deal, even though she was out to dinner with Reid. In San Francisco. One of the most romantic cities in the US. When she can't help but gush about the renovated 1920s building, the glass jellyfish chandeliers and the amazing food, I listen patiently. Thank God for the fuzziness of webcam technology, which allows my tight smile to feign rapt appreciation.

I've never in my life had this kind of issue with jealousy. Watching Zoe with other guys after we broke up (and a few heavy flirtations *before* we broke up, because I think she liked to keep me off balance) was frustrating and unpleasant, but that was nothing compared to this slow, deep burn. Even what I felt during filming last fall, when I watched Reid with Emma, wasn't like this. I feel like I've swallowed a meteor.

I can't talk to Mom, or Brynn, or Cassie about it.

Possessiveness is nothing more than insecurity, Mom would say.

That macho protective bullshit is just some asshat man *pissing on his territory so the other dogs will stay away*, Brynn would say.

Graham, you aren't that chauvinistic type of guy. You're better than that, Cassie would say.

They're all right… and they're all wrong. In this moment, if I could physically keep Reid away from Emma, I would do it. And if that makes me *that type of guy*, I don't give a goddamn.

"Sounds like you had a perfect night," I tell Emma. Tightly.

She shakes her head, giving me that subtle smile of hers—her mouth turned up on one side like she's trying to contain it, while it steals out on one side. "If it had been perfect, you'd have been there with me," she says, and the meteor in my gut melts to a more manageable size.

When I mention Brooke arriving in New York tomorrow, I do so unmindful that I hadn't told Emma where she would be staying. "I've warned her that I'll be holed up in my room with you by nine p.m."

"She's staying with you?"

Oh, God, I forgot to tell her. "With my family, yes." As though that makes it better. "The hotels are always booked during the week of NYU and Columbia commencements." I never intended to send Brooke to a hotel, but I'm keeping *that* to myself. "And several smaller colleges have their ceremonies the same week."

"Oh."

I wish there was some way to assure her that Brooke is no threat to her. I hate seeing that look on her face, the uncertainty that I know all too well. I was going to tell her that Brooke said, *TMI on the cybersex details!* when I told her about our nightly Skype ritual, but suddenly that isn't so funny, and I'm scrambling for something to say.

"So *Ellen* on Thursday, huh?"

"Yeah." Her voice is strained. Damn this distance. If I could kiss her she'd know exactly how I feel about her.

"I miss you, Emma."

I'm not sure, but it looks like her eyes tear up. "I was fine for months without you," she says, the words hushed and forlorn. "Why does it hurt now?"

I'm sighing and shoving a hand through my hair, which I know from experience leaves strands of it stabbing out in numerous directions, defiant and crazy-looking. Maybe crazy is exactly how I feel. "Because now we have hope of something more."

She takes a shaky breath and sighs. I've said the right words, for now.

Chapter 25

Brooke

I remembered to pack a toothbrush and a razor this time. I thought Graham's mother would blow a gasket the last time I visited, when I asked if they had those things. I admit I was being a bitch, because I'm used to mothers hating me. Or at least not trusting me to leave their baby boys uncorrupted. I couldn't stand another failed attempt at being sweet, only to be treated like an STD-carrying skank. So I just bitched up right off the bat.

Probably not the smartest move on my part, given that now I have to backtrack and make her like me, when I've already shot myself in the foot.

Dr. Douglas is a licensed therapist as well as a professor of psychology. She analyzed me the whole time I was there two years ago—I could tell. I don't want to know her conclusions. I just have to make her believe they're no longer valid. No big deal, right? As my plane touches down at La Guardia, I'm trying to forget how her eyes looked like they might shoot lava when I questioned the thread count of the guest bed sheets.

Kathryn, my father's first wife, taught me this saying: *When you find yourself in a hole, the first thing to do is stop digging.* Unfortunately, I've never been good at following that bit of common sense. I blame that on my parental role model—my mother—who's never met a hole that can't be just a little deeper.

When I first arrived in LA, not only was I all knees and elbows awkward, but I had that vile drawl. It marked me wherever I went, and there was nothing I could do about it short of keeping mute. If I walked into an upscale boutique with Mom, the salesgirls were courteous and attentive until one of us opened our mouths, and then the sidelong glances would start. I knew what they were thinking. *Hicks.* There was no way to combat their prejudice.

Just before Mom and Rick got married, he took us out to dinner. Trying to butter me up to get on her good side. He didn't know that she couldn't have cared less if I was happy with her matrimonial choices. We went to a trendy place that served burgers for fifteen bucks and boasted hundreds of domestic and imported beers from all over the world. The beer was the attraction—if some remote brewery made it, they had it. That sort of thing.

Rick (who thought Mom sounded like Scarlett O'Hara—like that's a compliment?) got up mid-meal to fetch a side of pickles for Mom and get himself another imported beer. When he was a dozen or so feet away, my mother called to him. She was just loud enough for our entire half of the restaurant to hear her: "Hey, Rick, *git* me another *Currs Light!*"

There was a long beat of silence, because the request for a cheap domestic beer in her trailer park twang paused all conversation. And then laughter erupted. My face flamed. I wanted to dive under the booth rather than sit across from my uncouth hillbilly of a mother. I was positive that this was the Most Embarrassing Moment of my life.

But Mom wasn't finished digging her hole, with me right there, praying for invisibility. As she glanced around at all the pretentious, sniggering patrons, her face twisted into a haughty demeanor. "Well, *fuck all y'all!*" she declared. The wave of laughter crashed over me, and invisibility wasn't good enough. I think I prayed for death.

A few months later, my new manager strongly suggested speech therapy to rid me of my accent. I jumped at the chance. The most puzzling thing was Reid's objection. "I like the way you talk," he said, running his fingers through my hair as I lay with my head on his lap while we watched a movie. "It's different. It's *hot.*"

"Pshh! No it's not. I sound like a redneck with a fifth grade education."

"But you're not."

"It's what I *sound* like, so it's what everyone thinks."

"Who gives a shit what everyone thinks?" he said. I see now that this has long been some sort of mantra for him. I've never been that free. I want to be, and sometimes I pretend to be, but I'm not. I'm forever chained to giving a shit about what *someone* thinks.

"Is she your girlfriend now?" Cara's idea of whispering is anything but.

I've made it a habit to avoid my younger half-siblings when possible—all too simple, living in another state, especially after passing the age of mandatory visitation. So I don't spend much time in the company of small children. I'm not used to the way a kid Cara's age just blurts out indelicate questions. In the middle of dinner, no less.

Every eye at the table shifts to Graham, who chuckles at his daughter. "No, Brooke is a really good friend—like Daniel or Rob." These two are classmates of Graham's. We're going to a party tomorrow night that one of them is hosting. I'm not so sure I want to be grouped with a couple of *guys* in Graham's head. Talk about the friend zone.

Audible exhalations of relief come from his mother and his sister, Brynn, who came over for dinner tonight because she can't take off work for the ceremony tomorrow morning. I plaster a rigid smile on my face at their oh-thank-God sighs. What the *hell*.

The kid taps her fork against her plate, her head angled like a puppy hearing an unfamiliar noise. "So Emma is your girlfriend?"

Graham sighs. "Cara, it's time for dinner, not twenty questions."

She gives him a cheeky look. "That was two questions, Daddy. *Two*."

"Yeah, well, just because you ask a question—or *two*—doesn't mean you get an answer." He winks at her and she rolls her eyes like she's heard *that* before and digs into her lasagna. Then Graham turns to his family and says, "Brooke is going to be filming a romantic comedy here in New York, starting—when is it, Brooke, mid-August?"

"Yes." He's letting his family know I'll be around in the

future. This is good. I'm closer to being able to tell him that I've sublet an apartment with a lease running from the beginning of August through December.

"Are they still talking to Efron about the male lead?"

"No. I think he's had some other contract he can't get out of. I'm not sure who they're considering now."

"Congratulations, Brooke," his father says as his mother and Brynn mumble vague acknowledgements.

On the outside, I thank them graciously and smile obliviously, like the vacant little bimbo they seem to think I am—totally unaware of their disdain.

On the inside, I'm snarling *fuck all y'all.*

GRAHAM

Cara gets a case of the giggles when she sees me in my graduation garb, and I haven't even donned the cap yet. I shake my head as she collapses onto the bottom stair, sliding into a prone position and laughing like she does when Brynn tickles her. Finally, she pauses long enough to tell me that I look like Cinderella, before she dissolves into another round of unreserved laughter.

"She has a point, Graham," Cassie says, juggling Caleb. "You are *rockin'* the baby blue satin in that commencement dress."

Cara slaps the wooden step with her small hand, howling with laughter. I'm afraid to put on the cap and tassel in front of her, because she might lose the ability to breathe. Mom insists, though, because the ceremony is outdoors and unless she pins it beforehand, one gust of wind could send it flying. Once the cap is affixed to my head, Cara is beside herself for another five minutes, and I wonder how she'll react when confronted with several thousand graduates in light blue caps and *dresses.*

Brooke's eyes are sparkling, and for a split second I realize how rare it is to see them free of her guarded cynicism. She seems like she'd be the last person on earth to censor herself, when in actuality, that's *all* she does.

A few hours and a long, strangely exhilarating ceremony later, I text Emma to tell her I'm an official college graduate. We arrange an early Skype time because of the graduation party tonight and her flight from Sacramento to Burbank tomorrow morning. Neither of us mentions the fact that Brooke will be tagging along to the party, meeting my school friends and possibly inciting more photos and stories for the rumor mill.

"So... do I look smarter as a college grad? Or at least hotter?" I smooth my hands over the light blue Columbia T-shirt before shrugging into a plaid shirt, leaving it open over the T-shirt and dropping into the desk chair. I angle the monitor so that Emma's face is clear.

She laughs and looks me over. "Definitely both. I like the baby blue on you. I don't think I've ever seen you in that color."

"I do tend to prefer black."

"You should meet Emily. Black is ninety percent of her wardrobe." She gnaws her lip for a moment. She's been a bit pensive the past few of days when we talk, and I find myself wishing I knew her better, so I'd know if she's worried or upset, or if she's just got something on her mind.

"I definitely need to meet Emily," I say. Wanting me to meet the childhood friend, the best friend, the like-a-sister friend is the equivalent of me taking her to meet Cassie. "Maybe after the premiere—"

"I was thinking—"

We both stop. "Go ahead," I urge, hoping she'll tell me. "What were you thinking?"

She sighs and looks down, probably picking at her fingernails—something she does when she's nervous. "I was thinking I could... maybe..." She sighs, and I wait.

Out with it, Emma. Just tell me.

"How would you feel if I move to New York early? Like, before the end of summer?"

My answer comes in a rush, uncontainable. "I would love that." I try to remain calm, as though we're discussing some mundane order of business. "How early are we talking about?" I'm envisioning her here, in my city, in all the places that—five minutes ago—were just familiar landmarks of my life.

She shrugs. "I don't know. Maybe next month? I don't know how long it would take to find an apartment..."

I almost tell her I can start looking tomorrow. *Tonight.* Screw the party.

But then I recall scraps of our conversations about her desire to do the normal-girl thing, and I wonder if getting an apartment has too much to do with *me*. I don't want her to give up a single thing she wants or needs, because she's had to do that for far too long. I swallow my selfish excitement and say, "I thought you were determined to live the whole dorm experience?"

A slight crease mars her forehead. "Since NYU doesn't really have a campus, the dorms are all over Manhattan anyway. I thought having my own apartment would be more private…" This *is* because of me. Because of us. "You don't agree?"

My inner Graham is roaring *just say 'yes, I agree,' you dumbass*, but I shove what I want aside. What I want doesn't matter. This is *her* college experience. She'll only do it once, and then it will be over. Having graduated today, I know this. Cara was born two months before I began college, so I never even considered leaving home. I was lucky that *home* was New York City, and my academic record got me into the Ivy League school I wanted to attend.

"I don't know, Emma." I force a contemplative expression onto my face. "You should definitely think this over. Even if the dorms aren't clustered on a traditional campus, there are all-night study sessions, pillow fights in the hall, roommate quarrels, someone sneaking in a keg for a floor party… essential components of the full college experience." I smile, but her eyes are downcast again and she doesn't see it.

"Oh."

There's a tap at my door and when I look up, Brooke is standing in the doorway holding two tops on hangers. I could have sworn I'd closed the door all the way, but I must have left it ajar.

"Hey, I need your assistance in choosing what you want me to wear tonight." She glances at the screen in front of me. "Oh, Emma! Oh shit, I'm totally interrupting—so sorry!" Emma blinks, looking at Brooke, who is no doubt appearing behind me now on her screen. "You might as well give me your opinion, since you're almost like right here. What do you think—this one?" She holds up short-sleeved, dark purple, cleavage-baring cashmere sweater. "Or this?" She switches to a silky baby blue top that matches her eyes and the T-shirt I'm wearing.

Emma clears her throat. "It's a Columbia graduation party, so the blue, I guess."

"Oh, you're so right!" She turns to me, her fingers grazing my chest. "And it coordinates with what you're wearing, Graham." The sparkle in her eyes from earlier today gone. Her shields are back up. She couldn't have known I'd be Skyping with Emma now, or I'd think she planned this interruption.

"I'll be ready in like, half an hour." She turns to go and I see that she's wearing a tiny bathrobe that just barely covers her butt.

I turn back to Emma, whose eyes are on Brooke's retreating, scarcely-clad backside. "I'm getting ready to go out with Emily, so I should probably get ready, too," she says.

We'd planned to talk for another half an hour, until it was time for me to leave. She's clearly upset, and Brooke's untimely appearance in my bedroom wearing a skimpy robe has to be the reason. I clench my jaw. Tomorrow, Brooke will be back in LA, and Emma will return home from her last interaction with Reid for the week. Everything will work itself out.

"Have fun with Emily," I offer, and she nods.

"Enjoy the party. Talk to you tomorrow." Her smile appears forced, and before I can say a proper goodbye, she signs off.

"So you guys are a couple, huh?" Daniel hands me a beer and clinks his bottle to mine. Half the eyes in the room follow Brooke as she winds through the crowd on her way to the bathroom.

I glance in her direction and back at him. "No, we're not."

He arches a brow. "Dude. Have you told *her* that?"

Wouldn't *that* be awkward. "Unnecessary. We've been good friends for several years. It's never been like that."

Daniel's roommate confers with him about a beer run while I think about Emma, wishing she was here with me instead of Brooke. That line of thinking leaves me feeling guilty. Brooke is taking time from her life to be supportive to me, and I should be more appreciative. I watch the mouth of the hallway where she disappeared. She's had a couple of beers, but she seems fine.

When she reappears, several girls stop her, and within seconds she's wearing her genial talking-to-fans face.

"*Never?*" Daniel is staring again, not that I blame him. Brooke is a beautiful girl. Her eyes find me then, and she smiles an apology before turning back to her fans. "Are you sure about that?" he adds. Brooke hasn't left my side for long all evening, which I attribute to the fact that she knows no one else here.

I don't answer, because Daniel's not really listening. He's wearing the same bewitched expression I've seen on guys a hundred times. Some she'll play with, some she won't, but none of them have ever mattered to her for long.

I try, unsuccessfully, to suppress a smirk as Daniel separates from me and meanders closer. He's a good guy, but not for her. Brooke needs someone larger than life. Larger than her life, certainly. She needs a guy who can see through that spellbinding façade of hers, see her for what she is, and accept it.

Chapter 26

Brooke

Graham has kept tabs on me all night, but whenever some guy hits on me and I send him a telepathic *oh brother* look, he seems amused. Amusement is not my preferred reaction—not since watching him nearly lose his shit while observing the photo shoot with Reid and Emma. *That's* the reaction I want.

When his friend Daniel joins the girls who recognized me from *Life's a Beach*, I welcome the interruption. I've spent ten minutes listening to the three of them discuss my alter ego, Kristen Wells, like she's a real person, going so far as to apologize to me when one of them refers to her as a bitch. People *always* think Kristen was a bitch—because she was scheming, manipulative, and willing to do whatever it took to get the guy or the job she wanted. So yeah, a bit like me.

I'd love to say, "You do realize she's a *fictional character*, right? I'm not actually *her*." But no. My career is comprised of striving to bring fictional characters to life, so I shrug and laugh it off.

"Hi. I'm Graham's friend, Daniel." Charming and confident, he sticks his hand out. "And you must be Graham's friend, Brooke."

I give him my hand with a smile. "I am."

His hazel eyes are glued to mine, which tells me he's already taken the time to examine me head to toe before coming over. His strawberry blond hair is perfectly styled bed-head, and when he leans closer I catch the masculine scent of his cologne.

"Well, Brooke, you look like you could use another beer."

My five-second assessment: this boy has spent four years tearing through girls like finish line ribbons.

"Daniel, *rude*. We're talking to her!" One of the girls punches him in the arm, lightly. She gazes up at him, far more earnestly than she should. She would give anything for him to look at her like he's looking at me.

Aww, honey. It's not going to happen. Guys don't suddenly wake up one day and get interested in girls they've never noticed before. Unless you're watching a sitcom or a movie of the week.

"Yeah, Daniel, do you even know who this *is*?" one of the others huffs. "This is *Brooke Cameron*. She was Kristen on *Life's a Beach*. You probably don't even know what that is."

"Sure I do. She made me jealous of every drowning victim on that show."

Game point to Daniel. Almost.

"Including the ones Xavier gave mouth-to-mouth to?" I ask, arching a brow. (Xavier: my gorgeous costar, who, sadly, proved to me that the large hands correlation doesn't necessarily hold true.)

Daniel mirrors my smartass grin. "No. As hot as Xavier was, his mouth-to-mouth technique was lacking in some crucial way I can't quite put my finger on." His eyes flick to my mouth and back. "Let's get you that beer." Taking my hand, he heads for the kitchen. I glance across the room where Graham stands surrounded by a fresh group of friends. He's watching. I roll my eyes, and he smiles and rolls his in response. Not a hint of jealousy crosses his face.

Dammit.

When the taxi drops Graham and me at his front door, it's almost 3:00 a.m. Inside, Cara's cat is the only one awake, and it begins meowing like a small siren the minute we get the door open. "Noodles, shhh!" Graham says, which it ignores. To shut it up and stop it from winding around his legs, Graham gives it a snack before we tiptoe up the stairs.

I pull him into the guest room with me. "I'm totally wired. Come sit and talk."

He kicks off his shoes and collapses on the bed, leaning back on the pillows. I slip out of my heels, remove my earrings and slide the bracelets off my arms.

"So. Daniel?" he asks.

"Total player." Lifting and dropping one shoulder, I dismiss any thought of Daniel.

Graham chuckles. "Yeah. But I thought you liked that, sometimes."

I turn towards at him. "I'm growing out of that phase." When I start unbuttoning my blouse, he cuts his eyes away.

"I should go to bed, I guess." He starts off the bed.

This is *not* a problem I would have had with Daniel.

"No, stay. I'm just taking this uncomfortable stuff off. I trust you."

"Um. Okay." He shuts his eyes, leans his head back again and folds his hands over his perfectly flat abdomen.

I remove the shirt, unhurried and facing him, slipping buttons out of buttonholes as though he's watching me like I wish he was. Willing him to open his eyes, I let the silky fabric whisper over my shoulders, leaving them bare, and drop the shirt to the floor. A moment later, the ice blue bra follows. Standing a scant ten feet from him, I'm wearing nothing but a miniskirt. There's no response, no movement, *nothing*. Obviously, he's not even peeking.

I strip all the way down, cloth rustling as I shimmy out of the skirt. Deliberating, I'm immobile. And then, inexplicably, I'm not sure enough of what his reaction will be if he opens his eyes. Shit. I'm *never* apprehensive about *this*. Seduction is a strategic maneuver at which I excel. Except with Graham.

I pull a nighty short set out of my suitcase and put it on. "All clear," I say, but he doesn't stir. Stepping closer, I see that he's fallen asleep. As carefully as I can, I curl up next to him. His arm curves around me, but he doesn't wake.

"Emma," he breathes. *Fantastic.* He thinks I'm her. And I'm just pathetic enough to lie here and accept that.

For the first time in the past month, it occurs to me that I may not succeed. Once the premiere is over, the need for a pretend romance between Reid and Emma will go away. Nothing will stand in the way of Graham and Emma establishing a relationship that threatens everything I want. I've known Graham for four freaking years. He belongs to me—and I don't give a shit how that sounds. I can't lose him now, and I'll do whatever I have to do to make sure I don't.

The light from the corner streetlamp just outside is bright, blocked by the dark blinds except for tiny pinstripes that lay across our bodies. I trace them with my fingers, coming to the end of me, tracing onto Graham. Up. Over. Back again. And then I slither to the end of the bed and find my bag in the dark, digging through it for my phone. After angling the blinds so that they cast wider bands of light on the bed and across Graham, I climb back in beside him and lay my head on his shoulder, our faces turned slightly towards each other.

"Mmm," he murmurs, his arms pulling me closer. Before I can change my mind, I click the phone to camera mode. I have to take three pictures to get one that's clear enough. It's fuzzy, but it will do.

Me: DON'T transfer this to her, just show her, then delete it. That way she has no evidence.
Reid: Finally bagged him, did ya?
Me: I told you it's not about that.
Reid: Yet you didn't send me a photo of you two immersed in conversation
Me: Shut up.

REID

Thursdays are long for the crew at *Ellen* because they tape Friday's *and* Monday's shows that day. Emma and I are lucky, because we're on Friday's show, so we go first and get the host and the audience fresh.

Waiting backstage, we have some time before our segment. Emma is sipping chai tea and attempting every stress-relieving, deep-breathing technique she can think of. She's in the middle of some sort of yoga pose, eyes closed, and I'm considering whether showing her the photo now would freak her out too much. But I'm probably not going to see her again until next week—the day of the premiere.

With a final, slow inhale/exhale, she opens her eyes, unfolds her leg and lowers her arms. Her cheeks glow pink when she realizes I've been watching her. "What?"

I shake my head slowly. "I'm just weighing whether or not to show you something that might upset you."

She glances at the phone in my hand. "An unflattering paparazzi photo or another baby bump watch? Uh, no thanks."

"Mmm, no. I don't think this one will make it to the tabloids." Now that I think of it, I'm not sure about that. I wouldn't put it past Brooke to leak it to the tabloids, if she was so inclined.

Emma's features fall and she sighs. "Let me see." She sits next to me on the sofa.

"Brooke is probably just trying to yank my chain. This kind of thing goes back a long way between us." There. That's as much softening of the blow as I can do. Some circumstances can't ever be made soft. Like: *Your boyfriend is hooking up with someone else.*

I pull up the picture, full screen, and hand it to her. She sucks in a breath, her opposite hand pressed to the center of her chest. "When? When was that taken?"

She's asking, but she knows. I see it in her eyes.

"Last night, I guess." I take the phone back, glance at the photo again, hit delete.

"Wait—"

"Oh, sorry—too late. I don't want to keep that crap on my phone. Seriously, I'm sure she staged that for my benefit. Brooke has a warped sense of humor. Maybe it's nothing."

She slumps next to me, wearing that Lost Girl look, not buying my attempt at tempering the shock of seeing a close-up of her boyfriend sleeping with Brooke's head on his shoulder. I turn the phone off and stow it in my pocket, take her hand. "I knew I shouldn't have shown you."

She stares at her hand, intertwined with mine, but makes no move to withdraw it. When her eyes meet mine, I squeeze her hand. "Don't worry about it right now. Brooke is all about these little games. I should know. I've known her even longer than he has."

There's a rap at the door before it cracks open. "You guys are on in five," says a guy with a headset. His eyes immediately fall to our close positions and clasped hands. He smiles and pops back out, shutting the door behind him.

Emma is slightly distracted during the taping, giving an impression of shyness. She's too professional to let anything personal throw her completely off. She does, however, allow me to be more suggestive of a hidden relationship when it comes to the inevitable questions about our possible involvement. Where for months we've only smiled and denied, today I'm giving silly but full-of-insinuation answers, and she's laughing bashfully. The audience *loves* it.

Before we go our separate ways, we have a moment alone offstage. Now that the cameras are off her, she's unfocused and preoccupied. "Emma." Tipping her chin up, I lean quickly and kiss her, just a whisper of my lips on hers, and pretend not to notice that she's already withdrawing when I pull away. "I'll see you next week."

Premiere night, I'll likely have Emma where I want her— where I've wanted her since I first laid eyes on her. But I can't assume she'll come to *me* when she breaks it off with Graham. She's just self-sufficient enough to slam the door on us both—she proved that well enough last fall. On the other hand, she'll be more receptive if for no other reason than to thumb her nose at Graham over what he's doing with Brooke.

Am I okay with being exploited like that and then tossed aside?

Hell. Yeah.

Chapter 27

Emma

When Reid showed me that image of Graham and Brooke, everything came to a stop. I asked him when, *when*, but I knew, because Graham was wearing the Columbia T-shirt and the unbuttoned plaid shirt he had on when we Skyped last night. Right before the party.

I couldn't breathe. I couldn't think. My life didn't feel real.

Perfect time to appear on a hugely popular Emmy-winning talk show for the first time, huh? Reid was charming and flirty with me, with her, with the audience—and they ate it up. When Ellen suggested we use her show to clear up any *rumors* floating around, he grabbed my hand and kissed it (the audience screamed, "Woooo!" while my face overheated).

And then he looked at me and said, "We might as well come clean." I wondered what we were coming clean about and the whole audience shifted forward in anticipation. He assumed a very serious look. "Emma's pregnant with triplets." The audience gasped. My mouth gaped. I don't know what Ellen did, because I was staring at Reid and thinking that maybe I had just dreamed this entire day, and there was no photo of Graham sleeping next to Brooke. For one heartbeat I was so relieved.

And then Reid said, "After the premiere next week, we're getting married in a hot air balloon, and then we'll honeymoon on our private island until the babies come. Oh, and we've decided to name all of them Reid, with numbers for middle names. But in French—un, deux, trois—so it'll be classy." Everyone laughed. Ha, ha, so funny.

We showed clips of *School Pride* and discussed the Jane Austen novel that inspired it. I smiled tightly and kept my opinion on the script's inane dialogue to myself for the hundredth time. Reid plugged the movie he'll be filming next fall in Vancouver, I talked about my college plans, and then it was over and Reid and I were backstage. He kissed me goodbye, sort of, but I didn't really respond, and I couldn't feel it. I don't think I realized until that moment that I'd spent the whole hour and a half taping numb.

I was supposed to text Graham after the show, before my flight. I didn't. Just before I powered it down, my phone buzzed with a new text. I didn't look at the message.

Now I'm in the air between Burbank and Sacramento, and the anger has made a tornado of the rest of my emotions, tossing and twisting them until all I can feel is the destructive point where the indignation touches the landscape. I haven't felt this angry since I confronted my dad about wanting to make my own decisions. Does that mean I should confront Graham now? Just because I've learned to stand up for myself doesn't mean it's appropriate in every situation. Or easy. I stare out the window and consider possible scenarios of truth-telling.

Emily and Derek pick me up when I land. Her hair is newly hot pink and pixie-cut. "Like it?" she asks, and I tell her I love it.

Derek is Abercrombie-boy gorgeous from the top of his head to just above his ankles—he's wearing high-top Chucks in the same shade of neon fuchsia as Em's hair. I point at the shoes and smile. He shrugs. "I'm a supportive guy."

In the Jeep, I power up my phone and read the messages—all from Graham. He goes from asking if I was at the airport yet to wondering why I wasn't calling. He left one voicemail: "Emma, I know you're upset over Brooke staying at my house the past two days. She's gone, and I've already told her she can't stay here again. Please call me when you land… Okay. Talk to you soon."

I message Dad to tell him I've landed and I'm on my way to Emily's. Tomorrow is Senior Skip Day, so I'm staying over at her place. When the phone rings, my heart stops, but the photo smiling up from the display is my agent.

"Hey, Dan."

"How was *Ellen*? So exciting!" Dan has a habit of answering his own questions.

"It was awesome. Reid told everyone we were having triplets and getting married next week. I think there was something about a balloon. Anyway. It went well."

Emily twists in her seat, staring back at me open-mouthed, and Dan is either speechless or we've been cut off.

"Dan?"

"Emma, there's no need to be snarky. I'm still trying to manage what's left of your film career, in case you ever want to come back... You haven't changed your mind, by any chance? Because I got a call today from Paramount—"

"No, I'm still going to college. And I wasn't being snarky— Reid actually said that stuff."

He was quiet for two seconds. "I never thought I'd say this, but I think I'm glad I'm not that boy's agent."

I laugh, and the phone beeps in my ear. Graham. "Um, I've got another call. I'm sure I'll talk to you tomorrow after *Ellen* airs."

"Sure thing. Talk tomorrow. Ciao!"

I take a deep breath before hitting talk. "Hello."

"Emma. Are you okay? Why didn't you call?" His voice is guarded.

I tell myself that confrontation is good when it means standing up for what I need. When it means getting everything out in the open. "Is there something you want to tell me?" Crap. *Vague*, Emma. So much for *confrontation*.

He's quiet. "Emma, just tell me what you want to know. I've told you, I'm not good with games or ambiguous questions."

"This isn't a *game*, Graham." Emily and Derek exchange a look in the front seat. I swear I can feel the adrenaline shooting through my bloodstream. Heart hammering, hands shaking. "I saw a photo of her and you. In bed."

Emily turns all the way around in her seat, her eyes shooting flames. Derek lays a hand on her leg and they have a fierce, low-level conversation. I think he's telling her to stay out of it and she's telling him where to stick that recommendation.

"*What?*" Graham says, but I don't answer or elaborate. He's cursing, but not at me—he's holding the receiver away from his mouth. "Where did you see this photo?"

"On Reid's phone."

There's a long pause. "On Reid's phone," he says.

"Yes."

"Send it to me."

"I can't."

"Why not?"

"He deleted it."

"Well isn't *that* convenient." When I don't reply, he sighs. "Emma, this wasn't something I wanted to talk about over the phone."

Oh God. I hang up. I can't do this. Waiting for the phone to power down, I bite my lip and fight useless tears. Emily reaches back with her left hand, which I take and hold in a cemented grip all the way to her house.

Emily and Derek try their best to take my mind off my disastrous love life, but my brain has a sort of three-strikes-and-you're-out mentality about the whole thing, and Graham is strike three.

With Reid, I was too mesmerized by his super-celebrity to embark on any equal sort of relationship—if he even wanted a relationship. Reid Alexander was that guy on the magazine covers and movie posters. The guy with pages and pages of images on the web.

Marcus was a rebound, pure and simple. An attempt at something "normal." I thought he was someone I could be friends with first. A theatre person, like me. The only thing good about that relationship was that I wasn't all that into him, so he was easy to get over.

Graham is simply threaded through everything. I trusted him. I still want to.

After pizza and mini-golf, Derek drops us off at Em's house. I go inside and help Mrs. Watson make cookies while Em and Derek say goodbye for half an hour in the Jeep until her dad flicks the driveway lights on and off a couple dozen times.

She breezes in a few minutes later. "Thanks, Dad—we felt like we were at a rave! I'm getting glow sticks for next weekend."

He growls and stomps upstairs.

Emily and I watch our favorite movie, *The Philadelphia Story*, which is always good for short-term distraction because Kathryn Hepburn and Cary Grant can take my mind off *anything*, even if we've seen it fifty times. Emily is vehemently Team Jimmy Stewart, so we have a long history of good-natured arguments during and after.

Tonight, I decide that what Tracy Lord (Hepburn) really needed was some time alone.

"Not a traditionally admired concept in romantic comedies, or, let's face it, in real life," Em says, gesturing with a Twizzler.

"True that," I answer in the voice of Em's dad, who attempts to relate to his kids by picking up their lingo. The fact that he's always five years behind the curve (and that he uses the word *lingo*) pretty much ruins the effect. We bump fists before dissolving into muffled laughter.

After the movie is over, we lie in the dark as we have hundreds of times before. "Why did you hang up on him, if he was about to tell you the truth about her?" Between us, Emily links her hand with mine.

"I guess I just wasn't ready to hear him confess it."

"So you're expecting a confession."

I turn my head and look at her. "What else follows those words? *I didn't want to talk about this on the phone.*" My voice breaks.

Hector jumps on the bed then, walking over our clasped hands and flopping between our shoulders, purring and kneading my bicep with his cotton-ball paws.

"And Wednesday, when I talked to him about moving to New York early and getting an apartment? He didn't seem to think that was a good idea."

I hear the frown in her voice. "Why not?"

"He said something about me having a *normal college experience...* and then Brooke walked into his room wearing a bathrobe sized for a small child, wanting help picking which sex-kitten top to wear to the party they were going to together!" I bite my lip. I'm pissed. I *will not* cry. "It all looks connected now. And I feel like an idiot."

Emily raises herself on her elbow so I can see her face over Hector's mound of white fur. "There's *no reason* for you to feel like an idiot."

"Yeah, there is." I'm *not* going to start bawling, but that doesn't keep tears from trickling out. They seep into my hair as I stare up into her concerned eyes. "I'm an idiot because I still want to trust him. My instincts are all screaming at me to trust him."

Emily purses her lips and lies back down, still holding my hand like we've been doing since we were five. "Wow. That sucks ass."

"Yeah."

GRAHAM

Yesterday morning, I woke up in bed with Brooke. Dressed and on top of the covers, but still. Not exactly the sort of thing I'd want my mother, my daughter or my girlfriend to walk in on, no matter how innocuous it was.

She woke when I was starting to move out from under her leg (imprisoning my thigh) and her hand (on my chest, gripping my T-shirt). Smiling up at me, she said, "Morning."

I froze. "I'm sorry. I guess I was pretty wiped last night."

"Me, too. It's no problem. I liked sleeping with you."

What the hell could I say to that?

And then she shifted up and kissed my jaw. I was fully awake by the second kiss, which landed just under my ear. She made a disappointed noise when I sat up, while I scrambled for something to say. Sitting up behind me, she pressed her chest to my back, her fingers trailing down my arm, and I stood and spun around to face her.

"Brooke, I hope falling asleep next to you didn't give you the wrong impression, but nothing's changed between us. You're one of my oldest friends—but that's what we are. Friends. You understand that, right?"

She smiled with those shuttered eyes. "Yes, I know, Graham. And I'm fine with that."

I know Brooke has different relationship parameters than I do, but she's going to have to defer to mine. Kissing? Sleeping together? Not things I do with friends. "Um. Okay."

She swung her legs to the ground and took my hands in hers. "That doesn't mean I'm blind to how great you are, or that I don't sometimes, you know, think about you in other ways…"

Shit. "Brooke—"

"Hey, shh, I'm just talking. No danger, see?" She dropped my hands, still smiling. "Emma better take good care of you, though, or she'll have to answer to me!" Her tone was so lighthearted that I felt almost silly for the warning I sensed under the words.

"It would probably be better if you don't stay here anymore—I know you'll be in New York while you're filming this fall— "

She waved a hand. "I'm getting my own place. No worries."

"You are?"

"Yeah, I figured I was going to be here three or four months, and I've recently considered moving to New York, so I thought I'd sublet a place, see how I like it."

While I was trying to imagine Brooke—every inch a California girl—living in Manhattan instead of Hollywood, she tossed her empty suitcase on the bed and gave me a gentle push. "Now scoot. I have to get packed and ready to go back to LA."

Emma's phone has been off since late yesterday, right after she hung up on me. She never signed in to Skype last night, I don't know her home number, and it's unlisted. I don't have Emily's number, either. My choices were limited to watching her on *Ellen* or getting on a plane.

I opted to do both.

I'm not a guy who makes rash decisions. Yet, I boarded a cross-country flight five hours ago with no thought in mind but *see Emma.*

I still don't understand the whole photo-in-bed thing, and Brooke never answered my text asking her about it. If such a photo exists, Brooke must have taken it… and texted it to Reid? In what universe does that make *any* sense?

Watching Emma and Reid on *Ellen* supplied my final incentive to do something, *anything*. When he took her hand and kissed it, I had to stand and pace the room to keep from destroying the TV. And when he said, "We might as well come clean," I think my heart actually stopped beating. He then proceeded to take every bit of tabloid gossip ever written about them and weave it into one insane story, but the way he looked at her said more than his words.

I know he wants her still. Why wouldn't he? Even if I doubt his capacity to comprehend what a loving, compassionate person she is. He's shallow and he has access to beautiful girls everywhere he goes, but it's rare when one turns him down. He may want her for no other reason than to clear up that misstep in his perfect record, and that rouses the protective, possessive *thing* in me like nothing ever has.

I get a taxi straight to the hotel I booked, since even gaining three hours between New York and California didn't get me here early enough to casually stop by her house. It's almost 11:00 p.m. When I'm checked in, I try calling her again. Her phone is still off. That, or she's blocked my number. My *God*, she's stubborn. I can't help smiling at that, because her obstinacy is what kept her from sleeping with Reid last fall.

I hit Brooke's speed-dial number. If she's not answering texts, maybe she'll answer a call.

"Graham! Hi, baby." Great. She's more than a little trashed.

"Hey, Brooke. Quick question—I texted you last night about a photo you may have taken of the two of us…?"

The blaring pop music and voices yelling back and forth in the background tell me she's at a club. "A photo? What? I can barely hear you." She giggles and says something about another round to someone. "*Oh*, do you mean the one I took of us sleeping? Oh shit—I deleted that! How did you get it?" Well, that answers one question.

"Who did you send it to, Brooke?"

"What? Oh. I think just Reid."

"You *think*—" I stand and pace. Inhale. Exhale. "Why in hell would you send him that? In fact, why in hell did you *take* it?"

"Don't be mad, Graham. I'm really sorry. I was still a little hammered when I did it. It was stupid. I'm really, *really* sorry!" My teeth grit and I almost hang up, because I've got the information I need and she's so out of it she probably won't even remember this conversation.

"Fine. I'll see you next week, Brooke."

"Wait. Graham, please don't be mad, okay? I'll tell him to delete it. I'll threaten him. I'm *soooo* sorry."

"S'okay. Later." I hang up and sit on the hotel bed, staring out at the Sacramento skyline, the sprawling suburban neighborhoods so unlike New York.

This situation is far from *okay*. Brooke wasn't drunk when we got home from Daniel's party. A little buzzed—maybe. But drunk? No. I can't fathom what gave her the idea to stage that photo, and even more confusing—why she sent it to Reid Alexander. I don't know what the hell is going on between the two of them, but I'm quickly progressing to not giving a shit.

Emma's feelings are all that matter. I don't really have a plan. I feel like I just leapt from a plane without checking to see if there's a parachute strapped to my back. I've always been the guy who analyzes and evaluates everything. I consider pros and cons. I weigh options. I make informed decisions. These precautions don't eliminate mistakes, but they certainly reduce the likelihood of them.

And then I met Emma, and as logical as she is, she makes me feel reckless. I'm heedless of consequences. My plans and targets and goals and common *sense* go out the window in the face of what she makes me want. She scares the hell out of me and calms my soul at the same time. Maybe that's what love is—a total contradiction that somehow balances out.

Chapter 28

Emma

Emily is dropping me off at home just before noon. She has a twelve-to-six shift at the mall, so she's decked out in Hot Topic gear. Today's version is oddly similar to Chloe's *Madonna circa Like-a-Virgin* costume from last Halloween.

I'm so *not* going to mention that thought to Em.

"We'll pick you up at 7:00. Be ready, and be hot. Because Joe is *tssss*."

"Emily, I really don't feel—"

"Eh-eh-eh!" She holds up a hand and closes her eyes, like these things will keep her from hearing my objections to being set up with another of Derek's friends.

I try a different approach. "I've intruded on the last two nights with you guys... Don't you want some time to yourselves?"

She lowers her chin and levels a look at me over her purple-lensed sunglasses. "*Yes*. That's why we're pawning you off on Joe for the night. Now be a good girl and play nice. I'll see you at 7:00."

I pull my overnight bag onto my shoulder in defeat. I know she and Derek are only trying to dissuade me from wallowing in depression over Graham, but it took me months to get over him last time, and there wasn't even a significant relationship to get over. I'll probably be twenty-five before I get over this. I can't divulge such a pathetic outlook to my best friend, though, because she'd likely answer, "Challenge. Accepted." And then I'd be subjected to a parade of boys all summer long... Although it appears that strategy has already begun. Ugh.

She cranks her stereo and pulls away as I trudge up to the house, where I'll no doubt be assaulted by the smell of Pine Sol and bleach. Saturday is housecleaning day, and Chloe *loves* Pine Sol. When I was eight or nine, I asked her why, and she said, "It smells so clean!"

"It smells like a hundred car air fresheners hanging in a hospital," I retorted before Dad said my name in his *stop-taunting-your-stepmother* voice. I've been cleaning my own bathroom since then, using the same non-toxic, environmentally safe stuff Mom used. I've heard that the sense of smell is more powerful where love is concerned. I don't remember if my mother wore perfume or if her shampoo was scented like flowers or fruit, but I remember the minty smell of the kitchen after she'd wiped down the countertops.

I unlock the front door, and surprise, *Pine Sol*. Blech. "Dad, Chloe, I'm home!" I call, closing the door and heading for the stairs and the sanctity of my room, inside which no Pine Sol is allowed.

"Emma?" Dad calls from the living room. "Come in here, sweetheart. You've got a visitor."

I still smile when Dad calls me sweetheart.

And then I register the other part, and turn back from the staircase. I have a visitor? Dan, maybe? He's only been here a handful of times, but Reid and I are doing *Conan* on Monday, so maybe—

Graham is sitting on the sofa.

Graham. Is sitting. On the sofa.

I'm frozen on the opposite side of the room. Staring at him. Speechless.

"Well, come on, Chloe, we've got cleaning to do." Dad hustles her from the room.

His eyes never leaving mine, Graham stands, smoothing his hands down his thighs in a nervous gesture. He seems taller, standing here in my living room. He's wearing his thick-soled boots, barely laced, jeans haphazardly rolled at the bottom, T-shirt inscribed with (of course) the name of the band Emily was just introducing me to in her car.

Graham runs a hand through his hair and takes a deep breath. Finally, with a determined scowl, he crosses the room. My flip-flops leave me more than a head shorter and craning my neck to look at him, because he doesn't stop a safe distance away. His hands grip my shoulders. "We are not," his voice is a gentle tremor, "breaking up."

"Oh?" I say, still stunned. Graham is standing in my living room.

"I fell asleep next to her. That's all. I don't know why she took that picture. I don't know why she sent it to him. But it's nothing. And I will *not* lose you over it."

I take a huge, shuddering breath, as though I haven't been able to breathe fully in two days. Maybe I haven't. He's getting blurry from my tears. I blink them away.

"I'm sorry," he says, one hand sliding to the small of my back while the other moves to cradle my face. He kisses me, lightly. "I'm sorry." The second kiss is deeper, longer. I lean into him, on my toes as he pulls me closer. "I'm sorry," he whispers, and I shake my head, my arms knotting behind his neck, pulling him to me. His tongue sweeps through my mouth as I hum my surrender.

"Oh!" my stepmother exclaims from the kitchen door.

Chloe. Ruins. Everything.

"So sorry! Um. Coffee in the kitchen. If you want it." She scurries away. I'm not sure I've ever seen her scurry before. I laugh, muffling the sound by leaning into Graham's chest. He's laughing quietly, too.

"That must have been a pretty good kiss," he says. I look up into his dark eyes. One eyebrow angled up, he's every inch a very self-satisfied boy.

"You don't know if it was?"

He leans closer, his breath in my ear. "Oh, I know it was, all right. Let me prove it to you."

"Huh," I say.

He chuckles, the tip of his tongue touching the skin behind my ear. When I shiver and melt into him, his arms surround me, pulling me in tight before he claims my mouth again.

Me: Change in plans...graham is here.
Em: Brooke—>bed—>photo—>not speaking to him???
Me: Misunderstanding
Em: What about joe? ARGH. Calling you when I get off.

With a sigh, I cram the phone into my front pocket and reach for Graham's hand as we stroll the last half-block to the park.

"She's not happy, huh? If you want to go without me—"

"*No*, I'm not going without you." I stop walking and pull my hand from his, crossing my arms over my chest and scowling at him.

He turns back, his eyes that rich caramel they become in the sunlight. God, he's beautiful. But I wish he'd stop being so... *complacent*. Taking in my posture, he grins towards his feet and releases a pent-up breath. His expression is hypnotic when he raises his eyes to mine. "Emma." He steps close, tracing his fingers from my shoulders to my elbows. "Are you upset that I'm not more... possessive?"

"What? No—that's the last thing I'd want." My arms loosen. The memory of Meredith and Robby last fall makes me shudder. When I talked to her a couple of weeks ago, things weren't going well. The enraged phone calls and accusations had started up again, and her emotions were a mess. I can only hope that Robby's angry verbal outbursts never become physical.

"Really?"

I roll my eyes a little—Graham's notion of possessive would probably consist of a sharp glare and terse answers. "Well. Maybe not the *last* thing..."

He laughs. "Oh yeah? What would be last?"

I chew my lip, not meeting his eyes, until he tips my chin up. He's wearing a cocky grin that I'm about to make cockier. "Disinterest. Goodbye." I shrug. "Those would be last."

Instead of a smug look, he shakes his head and slides his arms around me, resting his forehead against mine. My hands come to rest on his chest. "Never, Emma."

GRAHAM

"I forgot to ask—when did you get here, and how long can you stay, and are you staying with me?" Her questions are rapid-fire, shading her cheeks a little pink.

We've been sitting on a park bench, people-watching. Emma's neighborhood park boasts a man-made pond with a fountain in the center. It's about half the size of Turtle Pond in Central Park, and it contains a collection of fat, lazy ducks. When small children toss bits of bread on the water, the ducks only gobble it up if it's within a close enough range. Anything thrown outside of a four-foot sphere surrounding any duck just gets soggy and sinks.

"I landed in Sacramento late last night. I leave tomorrow at noon—which gets me to JFK around eight New York time. And I'm staying in a hotel downtown."

Her eyes follow an elderly couple who amble by on the paved sidewalk, holding hands. "Why didn't you call when you got in town last night?" I give her a hooded look and wait for her to remember her powered-down phone. "Oh. Right. But you can't stay later tomorrow, or another night?"

Chuckling at a small boy whose goal appears to be nailing the ducks in the head with hunks of bagel, I allow myself a private smile at the barely-discernible sulk in her tone.

"Cassie has to take Caleb for a checkup, and everyone else is working Monday, so I'll have Cara. And I promised her a trip to the zoo since I've been gone or studying so much lately."

"Oh, of course." I watch her face as she pretends to watch the ducks and roller-bladers while she contemplates my responsibility to my daughter. I sense, too, the other question she isn't asking.

"I'd love for you to stay with me tonight," I say, and her eyes shift up to mine. "But I'd rather have your dad like me."

"He does."

"I'd rather him to *continue* to like me."

Emma stares at the ducks again, which have all paddled just out of bagel-hurling range. "I talked to him about getting an apartment instead of a dorm." The wind kicks up and sends a strand of hair across her face, and I automatically reach to tuck it back behind her ear. She turns to me, her forehead creased, her eyes searching mine. "I know you think living in a dorm would be more normal-girl or whatever, but I want an apartment. I've wanted a cat ever since Chloe made me give Hector up, and no dorm will allow that. And I want the plants Chloe said would suck up all the oxygen."

I narrow my eyes, sure she's making that up. "She did not."

She nods, laughing. "She *did*. She also said they would ruin the floor, which might be true, but I don't care. I want to try to grow things. I want to cook. And make non-flavored coffee. And leave my shoes in the living room, and bowls in the sink. And never, ever, ever use Pine Sol."

I pull another strand of hair from her face. Her skin is soft, and she's so beautiful. My fingers are restless, pushing into her hair, stroking behind her ear. "And Graham, I told him I wanted more privacy than I'd get in a dorm... because of you."

My hand freezes. Her father hadn't punched me in the face or tried to kill me this morning when I showed up at his door, unannounced. He hadn't even been rude. My thumb strokes across her lower lip. "What I said before about moving into a dorm, I said because I don't want to be one more person who hinders you living your life as it should be. I want you to be free to make the choices that are best for you, without regard to me."

Her small hands close over my forearm, and she leans her face into my palm. "Then you have to trust me to make those decisions. Even if some of them have *everything* to do with you." When she speaks, the vibrations of her voice travel through my hand. "Just because I consider you when I'm deciding doesn't make it any less *my* choice."

I close my eyes. I don't deserve this, I don't deserve her, and yet here she is.

She kisses me once—a swift, shy brush of her lips. "I'd like to come have breakfast with you tomorrow, before you fly home, if that's okay."

"Yes."

"And tonight, you'll meet my best friend, and she will love you, or she will rue the day."

I laugh softly and she does, too. "I guess I'd better make sure she loves me, then. I don't want to be responsible for you losing your best friend."

When Emily calls, Emma walks into the hall with her cell, leaving me sitting on her bed perusing old photo albums her mom put together before she died. Emma's side of the hallway conversation is still perfectly audible, even if executed almost completely in coarsely hissed tones.

"No, you can't bring Joe *for comparison*."

"I know, and I'm sorry."

"Emily, I turned my phone off. He had no other choice—"

"*No*, you don't get a vote."

"He's nothing like him at all."

"Okay. See you in an hour."

She walks back into the room, her mouth screwed into a grimace. "You could probably hear all of that, huh?"

I subdue a grin and pat the space next to me. "Come here."

Her eyes shadowed with worry, she tosses her phone on the bedside table and comes to stand next to me. I pull her onto the bed and kiss her until she relaxes into me. "Stop worrying. It will all work out."

A slight pucker remains on her forehead. "How?"

"To be determined. But it will." Picking up the photo album, I point to a series of photos she'd told me about—the ones taken in Griffith Park. "You look like your mom."

"Except for her eyes." She leans her head back against my shoulder. "Mom's eyes were very dark brown, like yours. Mine are like my dad's."

I use this excuse to examine her eyes again. If I was painting them, I would use a base of stormy gray, with flecks of green layered on top, and miniscule slivers of gold. "I remember thinking that when we met in the café—how you look nothing like him, except for your eyes. I've never met anyone with eyes like yours, and they're the exact likeness of his—the beautiful color, the slightly tilted shape. Based on eyes alone, anyone would know you're his."

"Cara has your eyes."

I nod. "She does."

"And her mother's hair?" I nod again, watching her confusion build. "But she's never met Cara, or called, or requested a picture, anything?"

I shake my head.

"Is Cara okay with that? Does she ask about her mother?"

"She's fine. She's great, in fact. Mom, Cassie and Brynn more than fill that vacancy."

Emma stares at the photos of the mother she lost at six. "That's good. I'm glad." I watch her face from above, the way her cheeks raise a fraction with her smile. "My grandma and Emily's mom did an okay job filling in, I think. Teaching me how to be a girl."

My fingers trail down the side of her face. "They did an incredible job." I tilt her chin up and bend my face to hers, silently praising every woman who's had a hand in making her who she is. Even Chloe... though I'll never tell Emma that. A truth learned from four years of literary study: nothing beats an antagonist for character-building.

Emily is so directly opposite of Emma in looks that I have to give myself a mental shake. Pink hair. Combat boots. Darkly-lined eyes. Emo girl with an anime bent. And a preppy boyfriend?

Of course this girl is her best friend.

When we're all seated in a booth at Chili's, Emily gestures to my T-shirt. "So, you, uh, like them?" Sneaking into her offhand tone is a note of fangirl enthusiasm.

I glance down at my chest and back up. "Oh, yeah. They're brilliant. Have you seen them perform live?"

She shrugs. "Not yet, but I definitely will. You?"

I nod. "A couple times."

"What? Really?" So much for indifference. She clamps her lips together to try to rein in her interest while Derek and Emma exchange suppressed smiles.

"Yeah, I know the bassist and the drummer—they were classmates of mine at Columbia. Cool guys."

Her mouth drops. "Get *out*."

"Yeah. They're supposed to do *Unplugged* later in the summer, I think. I could probably get you into the taping, if you're going to be in New York." Emma's hand slips into mine and she pulls it onto her lap. I squeeze her hand and she squeezes back.

Emily blinks, stunned. I would guess she doesn't stun easily. Or often. "Uh, yeah, that would be great."

Derek clears his throat to hide a laugh. "So you went to Columbia, man?" he asks. I nod. "Theatre, right?"

"No. Literature." I expect him to react like Reid: *Ah,* and nothing else to say. But no, he plans to study English at CSU Long Beach, where Emily plans to major in anthropology. When we start to discuss literary theory and writing programs the way some guys discuss sports stats, the girls mock our academic jargon, but they grin at each other, covertly.

And just like that, I'm in.

Chapter 29

REID

The last expression I expect to see on Emma's face Monday afternoon is joy.

After makeup does their damage, we wait backstage to be called onto the *Conan* set. At first, I think she's faking happy to get through the interview. Then I realize it's legit. Four days ago, I showed Emma a photo that should have devastated her, and wrecked any would-be relationship she'd begun with Graham. Instead, she looks like *sunshine*.

"This is an unexpected transformation." I smile tightly into her glowing face. The green room sofa is small and our knees touch, lightly. She doesn't seem to notice. There's no doubt in my mind that her current state of mind has nothing to do with *me*.

"You were right about that picture."

"Oh?"

"They fell asleep next to each other, but nothing else happened. You must have been correct about her playing mind games with you or whatever, because it looks like you're the only one she sent it to."

So Graham didn't own up, even after that photo—and he managed to convince her that *nothing happened*? I'm in awe. The guy has bigger *cojones* than I thought. I consider the two possibilities: either he intends to string them both along... or he considers Brooke a one-time hookup—a mistake that he doesn't intend to repeat.

"I know what you're thinking," Emma says.

Doubtful. "What am I thinking?"

"That he's lying to me. But I know he's not."

Unbelievable. Practically everything I did last fall earned Emma's distrust, but *this* she's willing to overlook? "So even after a compromising—some might say incriminating—photo of him *in bed* with Brooke, you aren't worried that he *might* be cheating. I gotta hand it to the guy—he's a god, if he can get away with that one."

She sighs. "Not every guy is a player, Reid."

"Ouch."

"I didn't mean it like that."

I look steadily back at her, and don't ask what other way she could possibly mean it. The possible responses are a jumble of pithy and serious and harsh and flirtatious, and in the end nothing works so I say nothing. After a few seconds, she looks away.

A set assistant pops in to tell us we have five minutes. We can't go out there like this—awkward and avoiding eye contact. Intending to make small talk and bring us back to center, I ask what she did over the weekend.

"I hung out with Emily. And, um, Graham was in Sacramento Saturday and Sunday."

"Ah." The hell? My brain is whirring with the reasons why Graham would travel cross-country to make sure of her. I suspect Brooke is unaware of this little development.

"We saw a movie Saturday night, and they played the trailer for *School Pride*. I know it's routine for *you*, but watching myself on that huge screen felt so strange. The movie looks pretty good, though."

"You sound surprised."

She laughs. "I guess I am, a little. The last time a Jane Austen novel was modernized well on film was *Clueless*."

I smirk at her. "Book snob."

She smirks back. "Guilty as charged."

Before I can wrap my brain any further around *Graham in Sacramento*, the door opens and the set assistant reappears. "You guys are on."

Conan goes well—the combination of the comedic venue and the fact that it's our last interview help make it the best one we've done. When asked about the stories I ad-libbed on *Ellen*, I embellish them with help from Emma, who offers to let Conan feel the babies kick. The audience thinks we're hilarious. I introduce a couple of clips from the movie—one of which includes a scorching kiss between Emma and me that gets everyone hot and bothered, and we're out.

Before we part, I give Emma a swift hug and brush a kiss on her cheek—because the side of her face is what she offers when I lean towards her. Then she's in a limo to the airport and I'm in my car, dialing Brooke's cell.

"Are you aware that Graham was in Sacramento this weekend?"

"*What?*"

"I'll take that as a no. He's obviously playing both of you. Emma showed up to the *Conan* taping happy as shit. She was blissed *out*, and completely convinced that nothing happened between you guys. He's more like me than I gave him credit for."

"He's *nothing* like you." Her tone lashes me.

"Jesus, Brooke, seriously? He's got you snowed, too? Or is he planning to screw you on the side—with your blessing—while he keeps Emma for a *public* relationship—"

"We didn't have sex, okay?" Her words are angry, like she's spitting them at me. "What he told her was true. He fell asleep, and I fell asleep next to him."

I'm driving in a state of shock. I actually have to snap my mouth closed. "Okay, wait. Are you telling me he hasn't nailed *either* of you? You're right. Forget the *like me* comment."

"No shit."

My hands tighten on the wheel. "Now what?" A more pointless question has never been asked. There is no *now what*. This is done. We've lost. On the other hand, neither of us has actually *lost* anything. We just managed to land right back where we started, like that damned board game with the ladders and slides that Mom played with me when I was a kid, before she decided to become a full-time drunk.

"Premiere night," she says.

"Premiere night *what*? Are you planning to drape yourself over

211

the buffet table naked and hope that gets his attention? Sounds like he's made his choice to me."

"What happens between Graham and me is *my* business, not yours," she shoots back. I imagine her frothing at the mouth, because frankly, that's how she sounds. "Yours is to be there to console Emma when she needs it, because she's going to need it."

I shake my head, incredulous at how confident she is in the face of failure. "Right."

Ignoring me, she strategizes out loud, and I listen in spite of my misgivings. "Go to her room before we all leave for the premiere. Discuss walking the red carpet together, the seating arrangements at the theater, hanging out at the party, whatever. While you're there, leave something in her room, somewhere not very visible—like your phone. Turn it to silent and lock it, of course. And delete all the messages, just in case."

Brooke has gone off the double agent deep end.

"I don't think Emma's the sort to break into my phone and read the messages—"

"Shut up and let me think." God*damn* I'll be glad when this is over. I'd love to tell her to go to hell, but she's still dangling Emma as a possibility, so I bite my tongue. "As soon as we're all in our rooms after the party, call her from your room phone. Tell her you left your cell in her room, and ask her if she can bring it down the hall to your room, because you aren't feeling well. When you hang up with her, call my cell. Be ready to come out and handle her. Think you can do that?"

"Yeah, sure, I can *handle* her. What exactly am I going to be handling?"

"I don't know. I have to think. Just be ready. When I hang up, give it a few seconds and then come into the hallway and find her."

GRAHAM

I fly into LA with Tim Warner—Mr. Bennet in *School Pride*—who also lives in New York. We discuss future projects and chat about Reid—specifically, Reid and Emma's fake relationship. I find myself drumming the arm of the seat and not making eye contact when he mentions that they're cute together.

"Is something wrong?" Tim says with a small tilt of his head.

"Um, no." I try to appear confused by the question, shaking my head and giving a small shrug.

"Humph." He's not falling for it. "Graham, I was a gay boy in Alabama in the early eighties. In the interest of saving my own ass, I learned how to be enigmatic, and how to outright fib, so I know it when I see it. You have the mysterious part down, but son, you can't lie worth a crap. Confession is good for the soul, I hear. So, what's got you coming out of your skin?"

Like Brooke, he has no accent. "You don't sound like you're from Alabama," I hedge.

He shrugs. "I shot off to New York when I was seventeen, determined to separate myself from my past in every possible way. A good thing overall, but also a little tragic. But we're not talking about *me*. We're talking about *you*. Since we have a five-hour flight ahead of us, you might as well start talking." He raises an eyebrow. "I'll wear you down eventually."

I sigh, conceding defeat. "Have you ever had to pretend to be in a relationship with a costar, because production wanted you to?"

He gives me a pointed look. "No, but I've certainly had to pretend *not* to be in a relationship with a costar because production didn't want me to."

I stare at my hands. "Yeah? Well, me too. Though production doesn't actually *know* about it. It's more an unspoken clause, under the edict that Emma and Reid look *involved*."

"I thought they were? They had a tiff or something—"

"No, they broke up last fall."

We both accept coffee service and a warm cookie from the flight attendant. Say what you will—flying first class is a shocking illustration of dissimilarity between the privileged and the non-privileged. While Tim and I will enjoy a catered meal, several snacks, hot towels and all the attention we could want, hundreds of people in the back of the plane are lucky to get a bag of pretzels and a can of soda.

"Ah... Well, as my gaydar is going *pbbbt* where you're concerned, I'm guessing your secret lover is Emma, not Reid. For how long is this edict in place?"

I chuckle at the mere thought of Reid and me in a relationship, but my blood runs molten at the notion of Emma as my lover. "Uh, yes, Emma. And until after the release."

"The premiere is tonight, and the release is Friday—that's only two days away! What's with the mopey puppy face?"

I run a hand through my hair. Gay or not, Tim is a *guy*. "I can't stand watching the two of them *pretend*. Maybe because they *did* have a thing going last fall—I keep imagining them together, which is senseless and asinine. But it's driving me nuts. I've never felt like this."

He nods, lips compressed. "The caveman," he says finally.

"The who?"

"Every man has an inner caveman. Unless he's a flaming queen, in which case he has an inner wild-eyed, jealous bitch—as in the case of an ex of mine. But I digress." He starts to eat his cookie and I think maybe that's the extent of his reflections on Neanderthal impulses, until he looks me in the eye. "Imagine you and Emma are alone. She looks deep into your eyes and declares: *you're mine*. How does that make you feel?"

It's freaking obvious how that makes me feel—my fingers curl into my palms, my pulse hammers, my breathing speeds and I wouldn't be surprised if my eyes just dilated.

He chuckles. "In private, between the two of you, there's nothing wrong with a little… caveman sentiment. Or cavewoman, as the case may be. It's natural."

I'd practically driven Emma across her hotel room and onto her bed the first time I saw her after we decided to be together. The chance that will happen again, as soon as I get to the hotel this afternoon, is high. I want to touch her so badly that my skin tightens at the thought of her, nerve endings sensitive and raw. These reactions are visceral—primitive, and I've been trying to repress them ever since the first moment I saw her. What a waste of energy *that* has been.

"Thanks, Tim."

"Glad to be of service." He waggles his brows once, pulling Bose headphones on and leaning his seat all the way back.

Chapter 30

Emma

I'm about to text Graham to see if he's checked in yet when there's a knock at the door. Glancing in the mirror as I pass it and wishing I'd had two minutes to check my hair and brush my teeth, I take a deep breath and make myself walk to the door. I want to run to it.

I pull the door open and feel my smile falter and resume half-heartedly. "Reid."

He sighs. "God, woman, at least *try* to look like I'm not the last person on earth you'd like to see at your door. My self-image might never recover. You don't want to be responsible for destroying my career, do you?"

Rolling my eyes at Reid's exaggeration—as if I could deliver any kind of blow to his sense of self—I ignore his silly speech, backing up to let him in. "What's up?" I shouldn't have expected Graham. I don't even know if he's arrived at LAX yet.

Reid drops onto the small sofa. "We should talk about tonight's logistics. The red carpet, the seating during the showing, whether or not you'll need a paper bag to breathe into while you watch an *entire film* full of Emma Pierce on the huge screen…"

"Ha, ha," I say with a nervous flutter in my stomach at the thought of that. Discomfort at watching yourself onscreen isn't unheard of—some big-name actors even refuse to do it, which keeps me from feeling like a complete weirdo. I won't need the paper bag if Graham is sitting next to me. He can unwind me with a look, or the smallest touch.

Rather than joining Reid on the sofa, I go back to unpacking, calling the concierge to have my dress for the premiere steamed for tonight. "I guess we'll be walking in together, sitting next to each other during the showing. But... I'd like to have Graham on the other side of me."

His mouth tightens a fraction with a smile that doesn't quite meet his eyes. "Should be fine. If anything, it will just add to the drama. I take it production doesn't have any clue about you and Graham?"

I shake my head, pulling out the pretty silver stilettoes I'm sure to hate by the end of the night. Chloe helped me shop for the shoes, and the dress. She was ecstatic when I agreed to let her assist, and she would have earned the Emily stamp of approval for the withering rebuke she sneered at a clerk at the boutique who wasn't accommodating enough:

"This is *Emma Pierce*, and we're choosing a gown for the worldwide premiere of the film *School Pride*, in which she stars alongside *Reid Alexander*! Fetch someone who can figure out what that requires, or we will take our business elsewhere!"

The snooty clerk, wide-eyed with panic by the time she heard Reid's name, sprinted to the back. Minutes later, we were shown to a private dressing room and offered champagne while dozens of dresses were presented for our inspection. After narrowing these as though she was choosing weapons for battle, Chloe had me try on the few that made the cut. The green and silver dress we chose— our agreement my second shock of the day—is backless and flows to mid-calf.

I can hardly wait for Graham to see me in it.

Reid watches me remove the dress from my suitcase and hang it on the door. "That's going to be *stunning* on you, with your beautiful green eyes."

I clear my throat and murmur, "Thank you," recalling what he said a couple of weeks ago—that if Graham screwed up he wanted another chance. And that kiss on Monday—what was *that*? Even if I didn't feel it or respond to it, the fact that he did it was disconcerting.

When I turn away from the door, he's standing close enough to startle me, my heart galloping under my hand. "God, Reid." Instantly recognizing his heated expression, I brace my hands against his chest. *"Don't."*

He presses no closer, but he doesn't step back, either. "Do you think you're in love with him, too?" His voice is very soft, his eyes almost navy blue in the entry alcove of my room, away from the windows and light.

"Too?"

A knock at the door sends me stumbling into him. He steadies my shoulders under his firm grasp as my heart races from the hard, unexpected knock.

"That must be laundry pickup, for the dress." My voice is breathless, and he smiles.

Reaching behind me, he retrieves the dress from the hook and hands it down, and then he opens the door. On the other side is not a hotel employee. The forceful knocker is Graham, his smile fading when he sees Reid standing right behind me, in my room. I'm still holding the dress. I turn and shove it into Reid's hands, and he rehangs it without comment.

"Hi." I push the door further open, to let Graham in. To let Reid out.

Moving into the doorway, Reid turns back to me. "The concierge will call when the limos get here. I suggest you and I share one of them on the ride to Grauman's, so the exit will be simple. There will be too many flashes to be able to see. You'll never locate anyone who isn't already right next to you."

"Okay."

Reid turns to Graham. They're standing two feet apart—the tension rocking between them like punches thrown. And then suddenly Reid is completely at ease. "Graham," he says.

Graham's jaw remains rigid. "Reid."

Boys.

REID

I learned years ago that the most defenseless you can ever be is when you believe yourself to be in love. I say I don't believe in love, but that's not really true—*love* is just the name of an emotion. It's *like* on steroids. It's *lust* with ethics. And emotions— fear, hate, whatever—come and go.

What I don't believe in is the notion of being *in* love.

People talk about falling in love as though it's accidental. As though it surprises the hell out of them. I understand those impressions, because that's how I felt with Brooke. Unlike most people, though, once it was over and I got some emotional distance, I saw it for what it was—an obsession.

Consequently, believing myself to be in love isn't a high I crave—it was a total loss of control that I hope to never experience again. I'm attracted to Emma. I'm amused and distracted by her. I can even say I care about her. But I'm not *in love* with her. There's no need to sacrifice my metaphorical heart on a platter when all I want is a temporary diversion.

With the whole cast assembled along the red carpet en masse, the paparazzi are like barracudas in a feeding frenzy. Between their usual catcalls and the screaming fans, the noise level is insane. The bodyguards have their hands full keeping people from jumping the velvet cords. I take Emma's hand as we exit the limo, and she accepts the support, clutching my hand so tightly I'm worried she's about to freak out. Every time I glance down at her face, though, she's smiling and seems perfectly calm.

The dress, as I predicted, is stunning on her—the green of her eyes more potent next to the silky emerald fabric, the silver threads shimmering with every flash. I can't resist the thought of trailing my fingers down her bare back, or slipping the straps from her shoulders. She looks like a goddess, and I'd be content to worship at her feet. She eclipses everyone here, even Brooke in her predictable little black dress.

My ex-lover is jealous. Posing for photos between Graham and Tadd, she smiles charmingly, but when she directs one unguarded look in Emma's direction, the resentment is palpable. When her gaze shifts to me, my deliberate grin makes her eyes blaze.

Yeah. She'd still definitely kill me if she could.

None of us can see for five minutes after we finally complete the extended fifteen-minute walk from the limo to the theater doors, and we're half-deaf as well. I take the seat next to Emma,

No

and Graham takes her opposite side. Her body language is clear. When he leans closer to make a comment or observation, she sways towards him like gravity is involved. Brooke takes the seat on the opposite side of Graham.

The movie isn't perfect, but none of them ever are. It's a little sugary, trying too hard to be like the classic novel on which it was based. That will carry box office sales, though, and girls will gobble it up like candy. Sorry, boyfriends everywhere—you're doomed to sit through an hour and forty-seven minutes of syrupy drivel. The payoff? Between my face, Tadd's abs and Quinton's biceps, your girl will be ready for takeoff as soon as the credits roll. You're welcome.

The official after-party is being held on the third-floor terrace of the hotel. Some of us take the opportunity to change outfits, some don't. I'm glad to see Emma doesn't. All the guys remain in dark suits and ties, though jackets are ditched, ties loosened, buttons undone and sleeves rolled. Tadd's wearing the bolo tie and cowboy hat he bought in Austin, and next to him is MiShaun in the silky white and gold number she wore to the theater. Meredith and Jenna switched to jeans, and Brooke swapped her black gown for a powder blue micro-dress that matches the frosty blue of her eyes and shows off her runway-smooth legs. Her effort yields striking results, but not enough to surpass Emma.

"Nice dress," I say when Brooke joins me at the table. No one else is sitting there at the moment, everyone either admiring the buffet with its ice sculptures and chocolate fondue setup, or rubbing elbows with other Hollywood elite. "Matches your eyes."

I laugh when she narrows those eyes at me.

She glances around to make sure no one's near. "You know where the rooms are located, right? Graham's is in that alcove area on the other side of the elevators, and Emma's and mine are in between yours and his."

I nod. I'd checked out the locations she'd given me before leaving. "Did you have something to do with where our rooms are, Brooke?"

She shrugs, and I wonder if she didn't miss her calling as a CIA operative.

"You left your phone in her room?"

I smile. "Ingeniously wedged between sofa cushions."

"We'll leave when they do. As soon as you get to your room, call and convince her to bring your phone to your room. When you hang up with her, call me. I'll be in the hallway between your rooms, and she'll overhear my *conversation*. When we hang up, come out of your room and find her. Keep her faced towards you—that's *really important*. Are you listening?"

Something about her superior way of giving instructions just makes me want to pay no attention. "Yeah. Ask her to bring my phone. Then call you. Then come into the hallway. Real complicated."

Her jaw sets. "Reid, I swear to God, if you screw this up—"

"Reid Alexander!" A woman appears next to our table with a girl of twelve or thirteen, who's staring at me with a dumbfounded expression.

"Uh, yes?"

"I'm Johanna and this is Christina Noel and may I say that we are such *huge* fans of yours!" She sticks out a clammy hand for me to shake, barking, "*Christina Noel*, shake his *hand*!" The girl complies, her hand trembling. "We won tickets to the premiere and this after-party shindig and traveled 1421 miles to be here!" The woman says, leaning closer to stage whisper, "This hotel costs a *fortune*!" Straightening, she adds, "Worth every penny—but it's a *lot* of pennies!" She hoots with laughter while the girl turns bright red. "Anyhoo, we are just *speechless* with delight to be here!"

Speechless is not the word I would have chosen for her, though it appears fitting for her unfortunate kid.

"Oh, and look!" Staring at Brooke, she elbows the girl. "It's *Caroline*." I feel Brooke stiffen beside me at the condescending tone. "You were in that little cable series—what was it called— *Life's a Beach?* We don't let Christina Noel watch trashy stuff— no offense—so we haven't seen it. But I'm sure it's just *peachy*, for what it is."

Oh shit. Cleanup at Table One in three, two…

"Do you have a camera?" I ask. "How about a photo of me and Christina, er, Noel." I gesture to the girl to stand next to me, since we're about the same height if I remain seated. She inches closer, visibly shaking. Her mother tears through her bag hunting for her camera, tossing tissues, celebrity maps, and bottles of lotion and hand sanitizer on the table, oblivious to the fact that Brooke is giving her a marked-for-death stare.

"Ah-ha!" She produces a cheap camera and turns it on, but instead of lining up the shot, she thrusts it into Brooke's hands. "Be a dear and take our picture, will you?" She squeezes herself on the opposite side of me from her daughter, all but knocking Brooke off her chair.

Brooke snaps one photo before giving me a piercing glare as though I had anything to do with the insulting speech. "Call me. *Later*." Shoving the camera back into Johanna's hands, she spins and strides towards MiShaun and Tadd, disaster somewhat averted.

"Well, gracious me, what bee got into her bonnet?" Johanna mutters.

Chapter 31

Brooke

My phone buzzes. When I answer, Reid says, "You're on."

Emma is in the corridor, about to turn the corner. My heart is thumping so hard I can barely hear her footsteps. I face the window, like it's normal to be taking in the 3 a.m. courtyard view while talking on the phone, no big deal. Here we go.

"Graham's supposed to call me soon, but I wanted to let you know the soon-to-be-news," I say, listening for Emma's footfalls. She hears Graham's name and stops at the corner, just as I knew she would.

"So am I going to get the dirty details?" Reid says, determined to make this artificial conversation miserable, just because he can.

I concentrate on saying what I want *her* to hear. "You know how impatient I am. I'll be happy when he's taken care of this so we can be together openly. All we have are stolen moments when she's not around."

"Your cruelty knows no bounds, does it?" Reid says. I want to tell him to shut the hell up. He's only on the line to know when to exit his room, the jackass.

"He doesn't want to hurt her, but we're meant to be." I try to sound casual, but Reid's comments are making my teeth grind. "My *God*, that night we spent—I mean, I've been with a lot of guys—" Reid laughs softly in my ear, the bastard "—but he was *mind-blowingly hot.* Better than anyone, *ever.*"

"If only it were true..." Reid says. I'm going to kill him.

"We should have given in to this thing between us *years ago* instead of putting so much effort into remaining friends only."

"So he's never, in *four years*, made a move?" Reid laughs. "Man, what that must have done to your colossal sexual ego."

Son of a—*ignore, ignore, ignore.*

"I'm sure he'll tell her soon. He knows I'm better for him— I'm even ready to be a step-mommy to Cara, and he *knows* Emma's too young for that. Hey, he's calling in—gotta go."

I pretend to flash over. I imagine Emma around the corner, pressed to the wall, listening to every word I say. Time to step it up.

"Hey gorgeous." My voice is a purr. "When are you going to tell her?" She's probably leaning against that wall, stunned. I shove the guilt away. *I'm right for him.* "Graham, I know it seems brutal, but you've got to rip the bandage off. I want to be with you, out in the open."

Reid murmurs, "Brutal indeed."

"Yes, I can come down there now." I start to turn in Emma's direction. "I want you, too. You'll see just how much when I get to your door."

Reid starts to make another comment and I hang up on him.

Emma scrambles into the alcove labeled *Ice and Vending* just before I round the corner. Hearing one small, audible sob, I hesitate, but I force myself to glide towards Graham's room without looking back. *I'm right for him.* I turn into the short hallway where his room is located and wait. I would say now comes the tricky part, but this whole damned thing is tricky. I don't think she'll come to his room to confront us. I gambled on the fact that she wouldn't confront *me*, ten seconds ago, but who knows. Which is why Reid is about to *inadvertently* intercept her.

"Emma?" I hear his voice around the corner, on cue. "What's the matter?"

I creep quietly towards the corner, not daring to peer around yet. I hear her gasping and hope she doesn't start hyperventilating or something, because that would screw up our plans right quick. "I can't—I can't—" she says, the sob in her throat breaking free.

I edge around the corner, carefully. Reid is facing me, Emma facing him. Perfect. There's no betraying glance from him, though I know he's aware of me. He takes her face in his hands and stares down into her eyes with the most compassionate look I've ever seen on his face. My God, he's good.

"Come with me," he says. "We can't talk out here in the hall." She sobs again as he pulls her close, one hand gentle on the back of her neck, the other flat at the small of her back. Bending his head to hers, he murmurs something I can't decipher, and she nods. They turn, his arm around her, and walk to his door. They go inside.

I pull back around the corner and walk to Graham's room, scrolling through the photos I've just taken, making sure each one is clear.

This may be the most underhanded thing I've ever done, and the guilt is a bit crushing. I console myself with the knowledge that Reid really does seem to care about her. He'll take care of her well enough. For a little while.

Pushing Emma's tears from my mind, I focus on the goal at hand. My mother used to be fond of archaic sayings like: *Don't put all your eggs in one basket* and *You can't make an omelet without breaking a few eggs* and *I'm always walking on eggshells around you.* The last time she declared one of these I said, "What's with all the damned *egg* wisdom? Is this all *You can take the girl off the farm...*" reminding her of her hog-slopping, chicken-chasing, Neiman Marcus-free past. She never said anything about eggs again.

Now, for some unfathomable reason, those clichés are pouring into my head—because my eggs are all in one basket. And I just broke them all to make one giant-ass omelet. And every step to Graham's room is on eggshells, because this has to work. This has to work.

I'm right for him.

I knock on his door and he opens it with a smile, which fades a bit when he sees me. My heart falters. He was hoping for Emma. I drink in the jealousy because it obliterates any feeling of remorse. His head angles the tiniest bit. "Brooke?" he says. I push myself to stand taller and look him in the eye with an expression of pity.

"Graham. I have... something to show you."

He doesn't move from the doorway. "What?"

I indicate his room. "Can we go inside, please? I need to show you in private."

He frowns, noting that I'm holding nothing but my phone, and stands back so I can enter.

I perch on the edge of his bed and pat the space next to me. "Sit."

He sits, still frowning. "What's this about?"

It's about damned time, I think. "It's about Emma. And... Reid." His frown deepens and I pull up the photos on my phone. "I was going to get some ice, so I could chill a little Patron. I overheard them in the hall, whispering. And when I looked around the corner..." I hand him my phone, with the first photo pulled up.

He scrolls through them, slowly. One. Two. Three. Four. And again. And again. He hands my phone back to me, silent. A wild pulse vibrates at the base of his throat, and he's so quiet I'm afraid to breathe.

"Graham—"

"I'd like to be alone, Brooke." He doesn't look at me.

I swallow. The key to this working is no confrontation, no communication between them, just like last fall. "I can't leave you alone, Graham." I place my hand on his arm, carefully. "You don't have to talk. But I'm not leaving you alone with this."

Covering his eyes with both hands, he lies back on the bed, knees still bent at the end, feet on the floor. I lean next to him without touching him, prop myself beside him on my elbow as he inhales, exhales, inhales, exhales. Finally, his hands drop and stares at the ceiling. He's not crying. He doesn't look angry. His face is nearly devoid of expression, as though someone took an eraser to it. Except his eyes. In his eyes, thoughts are rolling like a searchlight, scanning dark corners.

I reach and lightly turn his face towards me. "Graham," I say, and then I lean down and kiss him.

REID

I take her to the loveseat, not the bed. We sink into it, and she's boneless and crying, easy to pull into my arms, onto my lap.

Sobbing, she curls into the smallest possible Emma, her face turned to my chest as I hold her. She's still wearing the goddess dress, barefoot and so undeniably lovely. My fingertips whisper over her back, her skin warm and soft.

At the outset, I thought this was simple. Not necessarily simple in execution, but simple in potential conclusions. Brooke would seduce Graham, and I would reap the benefit when Emma needed comfort and a shoulder to cry on. And here, literally in my lap, sits my hoped-for conclusion.

It's the execution I'm having issue with.

I fully assumed Brooke would succeed in seducing Graham, but that has not been the case. The fake phone call was, for some reason, a deception I can't slip past as easily as I'd like. Thanks to Brooke's clever scam, Emma and Graham each believe the other is cheating. And having exclusive knowledge of the entire scheme makes me an accessory to purposefully breaking Emma's heart. As my father would say in closing arguments—there is no other verdict to be reached.

I know how this feels—to think you love someone, to think you're loved in return, only to be slammed breathless by betrayal. Brooke did that to me.

Absently stroking her, I notice that she's grown quieter, still dragging in shuddering breaths. I grab a tissue box off the side table, pull a few tissues out and hand them to her. She blows her nose and dabs at her eyes, which somehow starts the whole process over again. It's a full ten minutes before she's calm.

"Emma," I say, the sound of my voice like the crack of a rifle. An alarm is going off in my head, telling me not to say what I'm about to say. I ignore it. "Last fall, you never asked me about Brooke, or the pregnancy. You never asked if there were extenuating circumstances, or how I felt at the time, or if I wished I'd made a better decision."

Her tears start to flow again, but she says nothing.

I close my eyes, inhale the familiar herbal scent of her shampoo, memorize the feel of her in my arms. I can't say I love this girl. But I know someone who might. "You need to ask the questions this time, Emma." My voice is soft and low.

She looks up at me, silent, and I'm staring back. Amazingly, her eyes are trusting, and I don't know why. I don't deserve her trust. I can't and won't tell her everything.

"What are you saying?" Her voice is raw, her face streaked with tears, and she has never, in my presence, been more vulnerable.

I press my lips to her temple, her cheek, the corner of her mouth, and her eyes close. She doesn't protest. Fucking hell, it would be so easy. So easy. It's been ten, maybe fifteen minutes. Graham may or may not have succumbed to Brooke's lies and misleading photos. I'm positive she's pulled out all the stops. As much animosity as there is between us, *I'd* have a difficult time refusing her under those circumstances—and Graham has naively trusted her for years.

"Go. Ask him the questions you need to ask. *Now*. Before I change my mind." Cupping her face in my palm and pressing another tissue into her hand, I add, "And if you need to come back, come back. I'll be here."

Chapter 32

GRAHAM

Brooke hasn't kissed me in two years—not since the one drunken endeavor that went nowhere, which we both pretend never happened. I'm not counting the kisses along my jaw a week ago. Maybe I should.

I am numb. Lying motionless under her practiced hands and mouth, there's nothing but the memory of kissing Emma, just a few hours ago. Before she entered Reid's room, with his arm around her. It's like last fall all over again except much, much worse. My heart squeezes so tight I think it might stop beating. For the barest second, I don't care if it does.

And then the shock begins to fade. When my brain begins to power up, it does so sluggishly, like a cold engine that might or might not catch and turn over. I register the fact that Brooke is kissing me, and that I'm sort of responding, on autopilot. Taking her by the shoulders, I push her away, gently, and sit up.

She clutches my arms, moving onto my lap, and the sensation is like having a tub of ice water dumped over me. Clarity rushes in.

Brooke sent the photo of Reid and Emma kissing last fall, taken with her phone. She sent a photo of me, asleep with my arms around her, to Reid. Now, the current batch. Again, on her phone. Something more nags at the edge of my consciousness. I shove her away and stand.

"There's no need to confront them." Brooke holds onto my wrist as though she can anchor me here, in this room. "Maybe the studio edicts just made it too difficult. All of that onscreen chemistry they have—it just translated too easily into real life."

I close my eyes because all I see with them open is *red*. Everything, everything awash with red, like a fine spray of blood across a window pane. "*No*," I say, my eyes flashing open. She blinks, hard.

She moves in front of me, grabbing and holding both of my hands, which still feel numb. "Graham, stay here with me. I'll make you forget her. I'm right for—"

"*No*," I say again, louder, and then I look down and see the naked hunger on her dazed, upturned face and the needling detail clicks into place in my brain. "Where's your ice bucket?"

She frowns, shakes her head. "What?"

"You said you were getting ice. Where's your ice bucket?"

Her eyes widen, shift away and come back to mine in the space of two seconds. "I—I forgot it… Graham—"

Brooke pleads that she doesn't want me to get hurt any further. Ignoring her, I focus on a building resolve: I have no idea how long Emma has been with Reid, or what they're doing, but by God, if she's disregarding every murmured longing of my heart and soul, she's going to do it to my goddamned face. I leave my room and head for Reid's, Brooke following. I don't know if she's still talking. I can't hear anything over the monster roaring in my head.

At the intersection of the hallways, I collide with Emma, grabbing her shoulders, hard, unable to slow quickly enough to avoid plowing into her. I've lifted her and propelled her forward a yard by the time we come to a stop. My first thought: her face is a wreck.

I've seen her cry. I've witnessed her grief over memories of losing her mother, and her misery over a spat with Emily last fall—tears I'd thought were over losing Reid. But nothing did *this* to her. She's lost and hollowed out.

Her eyes dart over my shoulder, where, I assume, Brooke has come up behind me.

"Did you… did you sleep with her?" Emma says, voice hoarse and breaking, tears streaming down her face.

I feel as though she's slapped me. "No. No! Why would you

think that?"

The anguish in her eyes is unbearable. "I heard her talking on the phone to someone… about it…"

"What about *him*? You went into his room, Emma—"

"When?" she cries.

"Just *now*. Ten, fifteen minutes ago—"

"After I heard her say…" She closes her eyes, unable to look at me. "I heard her say you were the best she's ever…" Releasing one sob, her hands fly up to cover her face.

I tug her to me as everything begins to fall into place and fit, like footage of something breaking into hundreds of pieces, played in reverse. "Emma." I pull her hands from her eyes and hold them. "You went into his room because you thought I'd betrayed you?" I feel sick. I can't look at Brooke or even think about her proximity, because I have never and will never in my life be physically violent with a woman, but right now *I want to hurt her.* "Did you—ah, God, I don't want to know—"

"Nothing happened. He told me to come ask you about… about her."

"Son of a *bitch!*" Brooke says, storming around us. My eyes narrow on her as she charges around the corner and bangs on Reid's door. And then I just don't give a shit about her or what she's doing.

Emma starts to tremble, biting her lip so hard to keep from crying that I'm worried she'll split it. A door across the hall creaks open an inch. No telling how many people are glued to their peepholes. Screw this.

"Come on." I take her under my arm and lead her to my room.

Once inside, the rest of the world locked out, I hold her close and murmur the words I could have blurted out the first time I saw her, because I fell in love with her in those few seconds, months ago. I just didn't know it yet.

Her arms loop around my neck. "I love you, too," she answers, her voice raw from the battle we've just waged, and won.

I sweep her up and we fall onto the bed, and I kiss her so hard that I know I must be bruising her mouth, but she's responding in kind, our teeth tapping against each other, our fingers digging into flesh and scraping skin and pulling at the maddening layers of clothing between us. I'm trying to slow down, to savor her and this moment, but I need this, need her, need *us*, too much. I rise above her. "Look at me, Emma."

Her eyes are full, the lids heavy. "Graham," she breathes.

"I need you to hear me." Cradling her head in my hands, thumbs sweeping her tears away, I stare into her eyes. "I belong to you. There is *no one* else. All I want is to be where you are."

Emma

"I'm right here," I say, touching his face.

"Yes." His voice is husky and strums some deep new chord—the kind you feel more than you hear.

"I'm right here," I repeat, whispering into his mouth. "And I belong to you, too."

He kisses me, restraint evident in the tremor along his arms, under my palms. He closes his eyes and rests his forehead against mine. "I want to read this right, Emma. I don't want you to feel pressured by the emotion of this night—"

"Graham." I wait until his dark eyes open, his body motionless and pressing mine into the mattress with very little between us. "I know what I want. And I'm not nearly as principled as you are. Because if I have to pressure you right now, I *will*." I run my hands down his back, sliding my fingertips lower, skimming under the minimal fabric remaining between us. Arching into him, I watch his resolve travel from control to something altogether opposite.

When his mouth crashes down on mine again, I know I won't have to say another word. His decision made, he begins to slow everything down—every kiss, every movement tender and careful—but his apprehension is gone. The pace he sets is excruciating and perfect, allowing me time to realize, over and over, exactly what I want him to do seconds before he does it.

Sometime later, our hands are intertwined just above my head and he's kissing me gently. At my sigh, he whispers, "Did I hurt you?" His lips are soft against my neck, and I tilt my head towards my shoulder.

Smiling, my eyes close as he ignites my desire for him all over again. "It's supposed to hurt a little, you know," I whisper back. "This time."

He props himself on one elbow, releasing my hands to stroke his fingers over the side of my face. "So I've heard, but that doesn't mean I can be cavalier about it. I can't stand the thought of hurting you."

I mimic his caress, my fingers cataloguing the contrasts between us—the short hair at his temple, the closely cropped sideburns, the faintly rough expanse of stubble across his jaw. His concern is unwarranted. I don't know that I've ever felt this whole. "It will never hurt again. Or so *I've* heard."

He chuckles softly and shakes his head.

I clear my throat. "So... do you have another... erm..." My face warms, but timidity is silly at this point. "Because Emily made sure I came to LA with a ginormous box of them stuffed into my luggage, which I didn't know about until I unpacked..."

I was so, so grateful that I hadn't been selected for a random luggage search at the airport on this trip when I unearthed the box of condoms that had stowed away in my suitcase. A sticky note was attached, reading: *Happy "PREMIERE"!!! luv, em.*

He cocks an eyebrow up and locks his lips together, trying not to laugh at my pointless embarrassment. "Are you suggesting we take this celebration to your room?"

At his words, I imagine confetti falling all around the bed. "Is it a celebration?"

His fingers journey down my side, keeping me close as he lifts his weight from me and lies on his side, positioning us face to face. "Hell *yes* it is."

My hands curl against his chest. "What are we celebrating?"

Closing his eyes, he presses his face to mine and hums a warm breath past my ear. "That we will be doing this—" he skims my face with his and then kisses me until I'm breathless with want "—for the rest of the night, and most of tomorrow, and however long you'll consent to be mine."

When I can breathe again, I ask how long he's got.

"Hmm. Sixty, seventy years?"

"I guess that will have to do," I laugh, pushing him onto his back.

Chapter 33

Brooke

The sun's not quite up when I check out. No one comments on the fact that I'm wearing my sunglasses. Not the bellhop, not the front desk, not the valet. They all assume I'm masking the hangover I would welcome in place of this aching emptiness.

It didn't take long to get Reid to open the door last night. He had the gall to appear utterly indifferent, standing back to allow me into his room as though I'd rapped politely rather than cursing and banging on it with both fists. As though I was expected. Which I guess I was.

"What the *goddamned hell*, Reid? You lying bastard!"

His mouth twisted with amusement and my hands became hard fists at my side. The door shut behind me and he followed as I stormed into his suite. "Are you sure you want to fling that particular insult, Brooke?"

I hit him. Or I would have, if he hadn't dodged so that it barely glanced off his shoulder, harmless. I tried again. Grabbing my wrist, he just shook his head like he was sort of sorry for me, but not really. I swung my other fist at him and he caught that one, too.

"It was a house of cards, Brooke. You had to know it."

"You *told* her. You *told her* to go talk to him!"

He peered at me, still holding my wrists. "I know you think I've got no morals, but I seem to have at least *one* you don't."

I tried to yank my arms free but he held them fast. I knew what he was going to say. I didn't want to hear him say it.

"I've never lied to get a girl into bed with me."

"I know," I sneered, "because you're the almighty Reid fucking Alexander and you don't have to lie to get whatever girl you want. How well did that work with *her*, though? *She* didn't want you."

There. He still had my hands imprisoned but he looked like I'd slapped him. Eyes widened. Mouth slightly ajar. He recovered too quickly for my liking.

"You're right." His expression transformed from shock to contempt right in front of me. He didn't just release my wrists, he threw them down. Turned and walked to the minibar. "She didn't want me." He grabbed a bottle and twisted the cap, leaning a hip against the bar. "Just like *he* didn't want *you*. The difference is, I'm not willing to lie to get her, or I'd have told her last September that I was falling in love with her. How fast would she have fallen for that? How persuasive do you think I could have been?" His mouth lifted on one side. So charming. So beautiful. Damn him. She'd have melted on the spot, and don't I know it.

My body was on fire. I hated him, standing there like he was better than me. *Again.* "You say you've never lied to get a girl? You lied to *me*. You said you loved *me*."

He looked at me a long minute. Drank the contents of the bottle down, his eyes never leaving mine. "I did."

Did *what?* Did lie to me? Did love me? Does it even matter now? I will never ask him.

"I hate you, Reid."

He laughed—no amusement, just insolence. "I know."

That was when the reality of what had just occurred hit me. What I'd done. What I'd lost. I'd made an all-out play for Graham, and it had failed. Crash-and-burn failed. But it was more than that. After years of friendship between us, I'd betrayed that relationship. Completely. Betrayed him. And now, he knew it.

"Oh my God." My legs collapsed under me and I sank to the floor, my nails anchoring into the carpet. "Oh my God." I'd lied to him. Tricked him. The full impact of what I'd just lost crushed me. Our friendship was over. I'd been so sure I was prepared to gamble it away on the prospect of getting more. Such an absurd, senseless risk. I started sobbing and couldn't stop.

"Shit." Reid heaved a sigh and came closer. Squatted down in front of me. "Give him some time. Maybe he'll forgive and forget."

I shook my head. "He'll never speak to me again."

Reid had no answer to this. I struggled to stand, ignoring the offer of his hand. "Brooke, I just couldn't—"

"I get it. Please stop talking."

I wanted to blame Reid, but I couldn't. Graham had already figured something out when he left his room. The conclusion might have been different had Emma not been on her way to him at the same time. If they hadn't met in the hallway. If Graham had been the one to slam his fist against Reid's door instead of me. If Reid had taken her to his bed instead of obeying the one sliver of ethical principle in his body. But no, Graham would have forgiven *her*, no matter what, because the deceit was all me.

My friendship with Graham was over the moment he trusted Emma over every bit of circumstantial evidence I could throw in front of him. The moment he left his room. The moment he saw her tear-streaked face.

Reid's lips flattened and he didn't say another word. I was grateful for that. But he could afford to be generous, couldn't he? He was no worse off than he was when we started, while I'd just lost the best friend I've ever had.

REID

Jesus, what a night. I'm a bit hungover this morning. Or this afternoon. Whatever the hell it is now. Drinking myself into a stupor alone isn't generally my thing, but the confrontation with Brooke called for a certain level of private oblivion.

The valet will deliver my car to the back exit. The paparazzi are aware of that alternative way out, of course, but it's a tighter squeeze, with more vegetation providing cover, making the fine art of hounding people for photos more challenging. With my personal bodyguards and the hotel security standing watch, it's an easier escape. I'm not in the mood to be hassled or adored—which often feel like the same thing.

The door to Brooke's room is propped open, a housekeeping cart in the doorway. I'm not surprised she checked out early, maybe even right after she left my room. There was no reason for her to hang around. I thought she was prepared to deal with the consequences if her play for Graham didn't work. After last night, I'm not sure she even considered the consequences.

A *Do Not Disturb* tag hangs on Emma's door latch.

Pulling into the driveway, I scroll the window down and punch in the security code. Wait for the heavy wrought iron gate to open. Pull in and park the car that bores me. Walk into the house, so familiar that I could jog through it blindfolded without running into anything.

The hum of a vacuum comes from Mom's room, along with the maid's voice—singing along with her iPod. Her vocals are bookended by the drone of lawn service equipment out back. The rest of the place is quiet. I'm sure Dad's at work, given that he practically lives there, and Mom must be out.

Just as I toss my bag on the bed, my cell starts playing *Just the Way You Are*. Fishing it from the deep front pocket of my jeans, I check the display needlessly; I knew it was Emma by the second note. She asked me a couple of weeks ago why I'd kept that song as her ringtone all these months. I just shrugged and said it fits her.

"Hey. What's up?" I clear my throat, wondering at her calling me, in view of the tag on her door this morning.

"I stopped by your room to talk to you, but you'd already checked out." Through the raspy evidence of last night's tears, she sounds content. Happy.

"Do you need something from me, Emma?" My careful tone doesn't match the terse words. I shove my opposite hand into my pocket to keep from punching a wall or throwing something.

"No… but I want to thank you. And tell you that I was wrong. There *is* more to you, Reid. You just never let me see it." She sighs. "Not like you did last night."

I shake my head. It figures that in giving her up, I earned her approval. "Emma, last night was just a confirmation of your effect on me."

Tonight, I'll go out and get wasted with John, and tomorrow

night, Quinton. Sometime during the next week, I'll ditch the Lotus, buy a new Porsche and squeeze a meeting with my PR guy and manager between hangovers and social obligations. And before filming starts this fall, Tadd and I will engage in an exhaustive tour of Chicago nightclubs.

"No. I don't believe that. Evidently, there's more to you than *you* know, too."

I drop onto the end of my bed, rub my palm back and forth on my thigh, like I'm scrubbing away a stain. "Well. Don't tell anyone. I've got a rep to maintain, you know."

She laughs softly and I picture the roll of her eyes, her lingering smile. "This is where I jokingly say *you're hopeless*. But you're not." Her voice catches, and my hand curls into a fist atop my leg.

"I hope you'll be happy, Emma. That he'll be good to you." My voice is gruff with conflicting emotions, but I don't care if she hears it.

"I am." She sighs. "And he is." Ah, there's that trace of satisfaction in her voice again—a jagged bit of torture she's unaware of inflicting.

"Good," I murmur, caught somewhere between meaning it and not. "What I said about coming back, if you need to—that didn't expire last night." As certain as Brooke was that she was right for Graham, I'm more sure that I'm *not* right for Emma. But that awareness wouldn't keep me from taking her if she showed up at my door. I'm not as noble as she thinks I am. "Goodbye, Emma."

"Goodbye, Reid."

"So?" John answers when I ring his cell.

"Not happening. And I don't want to talk about it." It's not even 5:00 p.m. and I've just downed a Jack and Coke. Maybe there's a luxury rehab place with a mother-son option. But rehab would never work; I'd have to actually quit drinking while I was there.

"That's cool, man. No problemo. What about the Porsche? You still trading up?"

"Definitely. Soon as possible." Dad already cashed out one of my investments; the money is sitting in my account. All I have to do is choose a car.

"Rest up, bro. We're going out tonight. Time to get you back to your pointless, pleasure-driven life." That sums it up. Back to the clubs, the parties, the hookups. New car. New project to train for this summer and film next fall.

"Is that all it is—a pointless, pleasure-driven life?"

He sighs. "Shit, Reid. I don't know. If you're *lucky*. It's either that or aspire to be some Dark Lord asshole like my father, with a boring-as-shit trophy wife like Elise, who has nothing to do but work out, get plastic surgery and have sex with my dad. I'd fucking kill myself if I was her."

My parents: Dad works, Mom drinks. Besides that, what? I think I'm nothing like them—as though my career and celebrity will make my existence more significant, but that's bullshit and I know it. "Guess I'm feeling introspective."

John makes a sound of dismissal. "Dude, forget that shit. Talk about pointless."

I'm not sure what it will take to forget Emma Pierce's belief that there's more to me.

Maybe I don't want to forget.

ACKNOWLEDGMENTS

Thanks to my lovely critique partners Carrie Sullivan and Elizabeth Reyes. I appreciate your support, encouragement, and willingness to be tough on what I write, even if I whine. As one of my writing professors (Patrick Murphy) said: "You can't explain to your reader what you *meant* by that line." You guys help me stick to that bit of wisdom as closely as I'm able.

To my beta-readers—Ami Keller, Robin Deeslie and Hannah Webber—thank you for quick turnarounds on manuscript bits and the tons of suggestions, beneficial comments, and WTF-is-this observations. As always, thanks to Kim Nguyen-Hart for reading and *trying* to be objective (I love that you sorta can't), and for being the best BFF ever.

To my new copy editor, Stephanie Lott (aka Bibliophile), it was wonderful to put this manuscript in your capable hands and have you find the errors missed by my brain as I was reading through it for the hundredth time.

Thanks Mom and Dad for the supportive phone calls, asking how the book is doing and how the writing is going. Your cheerful encouragement means so much. Still sorry about the cursing. I love you!

Zach, your dream was the inspiration for this entire series. Thank you for taking time to share info on the technical aspects of your craft, as well as the gossipy bits. I'm so proud of you.

Keith, thank you for liking and understanding Reid. You've helped me flesh him out better than I ever could have without your input.

Thank you Paul, for taking care of me—making sure I'm fully stocked on coffee, doing laundry, grocery shopping, cooking, and being the inspiration for every guy I will ever write—yes, even the really naughty ones. I love you even more than I did at seventeen, though I couldn't have imagined this life, or this love, at the time.

Finally, thank you to every reader who took a chance on *Between the Lines*, and enjoyed it enough to come back for more. Without your support, doing what I love would be a lot less fun.

ABOUT THE AUTHOR

Reading was one of my first and earliest loves, and writing soon followed. My first book was about a lost bear, but my lack of ability as an illustrator convinced me to abandon that effort and concentrate on passing 3rd grade. I wrote sad romantic poetry in high school and penned my first half-novel when I was 19, for which I did lots of research on Vikings (the marauders, not the football team), and which was accidentally destroyed when I stuffed it into the shredder at work.

Addictions: coffee and Cherry Garcia frozen yogurt. Also carrots, but not with coffee or frozen yogurt, because that would be disgusting. I also love shopping for earrings, because they always fit - even if I occasionally "forget" to work out. I'm a hopeful romantic who adores novels with happy endings, because there are enough sad endings in real life.

Facebook.com/TammaraWebberAuthor
TammaraWebber.com
Twitter.com/tammarawebber

18041191R00133

Made in the USA
Lexington, KY
14 October 2012